# Free Trader on the High Seas

## Free Trader Series
## Book 6

### By Craig Martelle

# Other Books by Craig Martelle

## Free Trader Series

- ➤ Book 1 – The Free Trader of Warren Deep (February 2016)
- ➤ Book 2 – The Free Trader of Planet Vii (March 2016)
- ➤ Book 3 – Adventures on RV Traveler (April 2016)
- ➤ Book 4 – Battle for the Amazon (August 2016)
- ➤ Book 5 – Free the North! (September 2016)
- ➤ Book 6 – Free Trader on the High Seas (October 2016)
- ➤ Book 7 – Southern Discontent (January 2017)
- ➤ Book 8 – The Great 'Cat Rebellion (2017)
- ➤ Book 9 – Return to the Traveler (2017)

## Cygnus Space Opera – set in the Free Trader Universe

- ➤ Book 1 – Cygnus Rising (Sep 2016)
- ➤ Book 2 – Cygnus Expanding (Nov 2016)
- ➤ Book 3 – Cygnus Arrives (2017)

## End Times Alaska Trilogy, a Winlock Press publication

- ➤ Book 1: Endure (June 2016)
- ➤ Book 2: Run (July 2016)
- ➤ Book 3: Return (August 2016)
- ➤ Book 4: Fury (December 2016)

## Rick Banik Thrillers

- ➤ People Raged and the Sky Was on Fire (May 2016)
- ➤ The Heart Raged (2017)

## Short Story Contributions to Anthologies

- ➤ Earth Prime Anthology, Volume 1 (Stephen Lee & James M. Ward)
- ➤ Apocalyptic Space Short Story Collection (Stephen Lee & James M. Ward)
- ➤ Lunar Resorts Anthology, Volume 2 (Stephen Lee & James M. Ward)
- ➤ Inanna's Circle Game, Volume 2 (edited by Kat Lind)
- ➤ The Expanding Universe, Volume 1 (edited by Craig Martelle)
- ➤ The Misadventures of Jacob Wild McKilljoy (with Michael-Scott Earle)

The beauty of the sea

The freedom of the open ocean

Serenity of waves lapping

The fury of unconquered waters

# Table of Contents

# Acknowledgments

James M. Ward helped me with an element of Free Trader Six's plot that was bothering me. Just talking with Jim over a casual lunch cleared everything up in short order. Jim is a master at figuring things out and he is a superb mentor to those of us finding our way in this business. Thank you, Jim, and in your honor, the ship in this story is called the Warden.

The ship is inspired by the Sea Orbiter, an incredible design that I hope someone builds someday, just so we can see it and know that humanity won't be denied. Learn to live as one with the sea, for it cannot be dominated by brute force.

In this book you'll see the influence of H.G. Wells and Jules Verne. I love the science fiction classics and tried to give some of their ideas life with the Free Trader. Of course, there's always inspiration from David Weber and Anne McCaffrey. I think it all came together in a story with more action than we're used to seeing, but there's always something going on, and you get to see this world through all kinds of different eyes.

As we are bombarded by the media with the worst the world has to offer, I bring to you the character Bronwyn, who is all about the freshness of youth and finding the good in people, no matter who those people are or what they look like.

Thank you to Stephen Lee for all of his work with the 77 Worlds concept. I've been honored to include some short stories in his anthologies, and hope that I can do the game credit at Gary Con IX! We are talking about some other things, too, and I hope we have good news to share some time soon.

I want to thank some readers by name as they are the ones who we look to when we're feeling a little down. Diane Velasquez and her sister Dorene Johnson are incredible advocates and very supportive. Norman Meredith has thrown out a number of ideas that keep the creative juices flowing. The following people have also been very kind with their comments. Bill and Linda Rough, J.L. Hendricks, E.E. Isherwood, Heath Felps, Chris Rolfe, Barry Hutchison, Joe Jackson, Angela Hill, and so many more. It makes a day spent writing so much easier and more fulfilling when people appreciate the stories.

## Humans and the Intelligent Creatures

### The Hillcats ('cat)

The Golden Warrior – also called G, G-War, and Prince Axial De'atesh, can share his mindlink with others

Fealona – from G-War's home village and his mate

Treetis – A young 'cat, very much like G-War

### The Humans

Braden – The Free Trader

Micah – The Warrior, Partnered with Braden

Axial & De'atesh – Braden and Micah's twin children

Bronwyn – Gifted child, able to speak with all creatures

Dr. Johns – a clone, leader of the survivors from Cygnus VI

Zeller – a Free Trader, from Trent, the same village as Micah

Young Tom – a blacksmith from Whitehorse, Zeller's partner

Mattie & Caleb – Micah's parents

The Professor – an ancient

### The Hawkoids

Skirill – also called Ess

Zyena – Skirill's mate, born on the RV Traveler, also called Zee

Zeeka – Skirill and Zyena's daughter, first Hawkoid born in the south

### The Tortoid

Aadi – First Master of the Tortoise Consortium

### The Aurochs

Brandt Earthshaker – King of the Aurochs

Arnie – Zeller's partner in trade, pulls her wagon

The Queen – Brandt's queen that he rescued from Toromont's Run

### The Lizard Men (Amazonians)

Pik Ha'ar – Lizard Man from the ship RV Traveler and friend

### The Rabbits

Ferrer & Brigitte – a Rabbit couple moved from the Traveler to Vii

### The Dolphins

Chlora & Rhodi – genetically engineered creatures of the sea

### The Whale

Rexalita – engineered from a Sperm Whale, the largest creature on Vii

# Raiders!

Zeller's wagon bounced lightly as it crossed the stream, until Arnie stopped to drink. The Aurochs was barely winded, even after the long day's pull. The Old Tech wagon used the power of the sun to assist in turning the wheels, aiding the great beast as he trotted across the countryside.

Caleb rode in the back, sleeping, watching, and sleeping some more. The wagon's padding made for an embarrassingly comfortable trip. They also carried fishing gear that Caleb intended to give to the new residents of White Beach, the village on the shore of the Western Ocean where the old inhabitants had been taken into the sea by vehicles of the ancients, operated by the Bots.

The new residents saw the potential in fishing, and the Bots had not been seen for cycles. Fear disappeared over time and the people migrated, looking to make their own mark in the world. They moved to the empty homes, finding serenity in sleeping near the beach, in eating the crabs and clams they easily found on the shore. They could see fish and other sea life, but they had no luck in catching them. They tried using gear that they found in the huts and homes, but nothing seemed to work.

The Free Traders carried word to the west, and Micah asked her father if he could help. He was powerless to resist, since Mattie wouldn't let him turn their daughter down.

That was how he found himself on the long journey west, traveling across the south, from one ocean to the other.

He liked the padding of Zeller's wagon, but he was also cramped among Amazonian rope, bags of mushrooms, sweetened pork that made him perpetually hungry, and special metal tools carried all the way from Old Tom's forge. Zeller's mate, Young Tom they called him, was building his blacksmith business outside River Crook. Old Tom's tools would be put to good use as Young Tom started churning out the implements that farmers, hunters, shepherds, fisherman, and everyday people needed.

Caleb noticed a marked increase in the wagon's speed the closer they got to River Crook and Zeller's mate, usually a three to four turn effort from Bliss. Caleb wondered if she was trying to cut the time to two turns.

Arnie bugled his dismay at something unseen and bolted forward, only to slide to a sideways stop a few heartbeats later to avoid a barricade of logs blocking their way. Caleb was thrown about within the wagon, pummeled as the cargo dislodged.

"To arms!" Zeller yelled as she jumped from the wagon's buckboard to the ground and with her sword, hacked through the harness to quickly free the Aurochs. He danced out of the fallen straps and ran to the right, to the north.

Caleb jumped out the back, brandishing a spare sword that Zeller kept in the wagon, just in case. He hadn't practiced with it, but if nothing else, he was confident that he had a strong arm and a keen eye.

Neither the sword nor his fisherman's vision protected him from the flight of arrows. He dodged, trying to get behind the wagon, but one arrow caught him in the calf and another, the thigh. Both thudded deeply, and he fell. Caleb crawled, furiously, seeking the wagon's shelter to protect him from the onslaught. A hand reached out and grabbed him, dragging him onward, while the other hand whirled a sword, knocking two more arrows away.

"What the..?" Caleb stammered, sitting awkwardly against the wagon's wheel to keep the arrows embedded in his leg from wedging into the ground. Four men with bows crouched behind a series of rocks, not far from the trail.

"Give us what's in the wagon and no one has to get hurt!" a gruff voice called.

"Come and take it," Zeller bellowed in reply. Caleb looked up at her, shaking his head.

"There's not much we can do if they come for us. Sorry about getting myself shot," Caleb told her, grimacing as she gripped the first arrow and yanked it out. The world spun before his eyes, then darkened to a pinpoint, before slowly coming back. She watched him and the wound, then quickly glanced under the wagon. The men had left cover and were spreading out, walking cautiously toward Caleb and Zeller.

She tugged the other arrow out with one mighty heave. Caleb howled in agony and gripped his leg. Zeller expected him to pass out, but he didn't.

He writhed in agony as she haphazardly shoved numbweed into the wounds.

"I need you up and ready to fight!" she pleaded, shaking him. Caleb was not a small man and wasn't intimidated by other human beings, but he saw in Zeller a battle partner, fierce, not to be denied. The fisherman gritted his teeth and tightened his grip on the sword. He used the weapon as a crutch to help him stand. There was no time for bandages, but the numbweed had slowed the bleeding.

Caleb and Zeller stood back to back, swords ready to fend off arrows, at least as much as they could. The men positioned themselves in a semi-circle around the wagon, keeping their distance from the armed Free Trader and her companion.

"We could kill you where you stand. Walk away and live," the man attempted to negotiate. Zeller was furious. She'd heard stories about raiders on the trade routes, but chalked that up to desperate people and bad traders. She never believed such highwaymen existed, because she hoped she wouldn't have to fight. On the journey she'd taken with Braden and Micah to Warren Deep, she'd seen ambushers and men who freely took from others. It grated on her soul, but killing them was even worse. She wasn't Micah and didn't find it easy to end another's life, even if they asked for it, or maybe even demanded it by the evil of their actions.

She realized that she had no choice. Those men could not be allowed to interfere with trade. She hadn't asked for the violence, but it came anyway. She wrapped her mind around the thought and became one with Micah and why she did what she did.

There and then, Zeller couldn't allow thievery, not in the south, where her friends had fought a war to make sure that trade flowed from east to west and north to south.

"No," Zeller said icily, barely above a whisper, flexing her knees as she prepared to fight. Caleb hopped on one leg, keeping weight off his injured leg, even though it no longer hurt. It felt like a dead stump.

The men seemed confused. It was a big step from raider to killer. They watched the Free Trader, understanding from the look in her eyes that she had already taken lives and was capable of taking more. The leader of the band loosed an arrow at her.

With a flick of her wrist, she deflected it, then lunged forward a step.

The leader flinched and fell backwards. She laughed at him.

*'I'm coming,'* Arnie told her in his thought voice.

"Shoot her, you idiots!" the raider yelled while sitting on the ground. The others drew their bowstrings more tightly as their leader scrambled to his feet. "SHOOT!" he screamed maniacally, the sound of his voice disappearing in the approach of pounding Aurochs hooves. One man inadvertently let go, sending his arrow arcing high overhead and into the distance. Another turned and released an arrow toward the charging bull. He was amazed that he missed, but turned to run, too late as Arnie bowled him over.

The Aurochs angled sharply toward the second man, who stood dumbfounded. He held up his hands weakly as Arnie ran him down and continued running in a tight circle around the wagon.

When the men noticed the approaching bull, Zeller sprinted forward, observed only by the leader whose attention was pulled in two directions. He didn't have an arrow nocked for a second shot, so he futilely swung his bow at Zeller. She cleaved the man nearly in two as his bow slapped harmlessly against her outstretched arm. She turned to face the remaining raider, checking her balance as she arced her blade through the air before her.

The man was aiming and then released. The arrow flew past her and into Arnie's shoulder as he completed his turn. He snorted through the pain and thundered past her as the man threw down his bow and put his hands up. The Aurochs didn't recognize the gesture. Even if he had, he probably couldn't have slowed his stampede. The man tried to dodge at the last heartbeat, but Arnie was a big animal and ran him down, finally slowing.

Zeller ran after the bull, begging him to stop so she could tend his wound.

Caleb limped to the last man that Arnie had knocked down. The man was alive, but playing dead. The fisherman used the tip of his sword to send the bow a few strides away. Caleb kept his distance, in case the man tried something. With the tip of his sword, Caleb probed the man's back.

"Turn over now. Let's have a look at you," Caleb told the face-down, would-be raider. The man groaned as he rolled over, holding a clearly broken arm. "Where are you from and how many more of you are there?"

"River Crook," the man panted. Zeller made a fist, and her lips were white from clenching her jaw. She walked, with the Aurochs close behind, toward Caleb and the other. The arrow in Arnie's shoulder had already been removed, and numbweed had been packed into the small hole.

"There are good people in River Crook," she exclaimed, barely controlling her fury. "All these people come from there?" She didn't recognize them as she looked from one to the next. She'd never seen their leader before.

"No. They came through nearly a moon ago, with promises of a better life. I was tired of digging in the fields," the man gasped, struggling with the pain of his broken arm. It didn't help that Caleb kept prodding the raider with his sword point.

"You shot Arnie," Zeller said when she returned from checking the men, taking their weapons and pouches. She took the injured man's items, too, without any concern for his injury. "I should kill you right here."

Caleb looked harshly at her, and she bowed her head, then walked away to repair the straps on the wagon. She was also upset that the repairs would take  product that was destined for trade. Caleb watched her go about her business, readying the wagon so they could continue their journey.

Zeller said they could still reach River Crook by nightfall off-handedly while she worked.

"Let me help you into the wagon," Caleb offered, waiting for the man to agree, before offering an arm. "If you try anything, I will simply kill you and leave your body for the vultures with the rest of these vermin."

The man nodded. "Darius. They call me Darius, and I surrender. I'll take my punishment." Darius looked at Caleb's arm, but didn't climb into the wagon.

Caleb knew Darius wasn't going to attempt an escape. He'd made a mistake by joining the others. At least he'd survived to see another day, but his fear grew with each heartbeat. His arm was useless, and he needed River Crook to take him back if he was to heal. He started apologizing to Caleb and Zeller, even Arnie, sobbing as he did so.

Zeller was unconvinced by his remorse. She joined Caleb and Darius at the back of the wagon. She stopped them both and told Caleb to hold the man. He started flailing, thinking she was going to kill him, even though she dismissed his fear with a shake of her head.

"I'm not going to kill you," she said calmly. He wasn't reassured as Caleb wrapped two strong hands around the man's elbows as Zeller seized Darius's wrist in hers. He howled at the pain from his broken arm.

"Wait! Do you hear that?" Zeller waited for the man to stop screaming, then nodded over his shoulder. When he turned to look, she yanked his wrist straight out, using her body weight to stretch the arm's muscles and tendons, pulling the bones past each other before letting them snap back into place. The man collapsed, taking the one-legged Caleb with him as he went to the ground.

Caleb pushed the man from him and glared at the Free Trader. "Sorry," she mumbled as she helped him to his feet. The arrow wounds on his leg continued to leak. She packed numbweed in, then gathered more of her precious cargo, the Amazonian rope, to tie a bandage around Caleb's leg and a splint around the young raider's arm.

"We can't leave them because other traders come through here. It just wouldn't do to have dead bodies lying around." She reluctantly agreed and methodically dragged them one by one to a dip away from the road. The leader was messy, so she dragged him by his feet, leaving a trail of blood and guts behind her. She tumbled the remainder of his body into the depression. She threw a few rocks on top of the men, declared it good, and returned to the wagon.

Caleb was leaning heavily against it, drinking water from a flask. Arnie had pulled the wagon around the blockade and forward until he was standing knee deep in the stream, also drinking his fill. Caleb limped around the wagon and stood upstream of Arnie to refill the flask before offering it to the injured young man.

Zeller wanted to kick the raider. Arnie was injured and so was Caleb, Micah's father. It wasn't her fault that it happened, but there was a certain fire in that family that gave her pause. "You know, this wasn't my fault?" she probed.

Caleb started to laugh, understanding the full reasoning behind Zeller's question. "I'll tell Micah and Mattie that it was my own fault for being old and slow and that you saved me!" The young man saw no humor in any of it. As the pain in his arm ebbed, he was more solemn and even angry, maybe with himself, but the Free Trader didn't know and didn't care.

"Get in the wagon," she ordered the raider. Caleb helped the young man in and pointed to where he should sit. The older man climbed in after him.

"This could go easier on you if you cast aside your evil ways and return to the fold of the righteous," Caleb intoned, feigning the speech of a preacher, although he'd only ever seen one of those in his life and that was a long time ago. The reference was lost on the young man and fear gripped him anew. "We're not going to hurt you. Do you know of any other people like that, raiding the trade route?"

The young man shook his head.

"Well, Darius, I'm pleased to meet you," the fisherman said more gently, seeing the other's demeanor lighten as he submitted to his fate.

"I think I'm pleased to meet you, but not sure what my future holds," he said resignedly.

"Your future is much brighter now than it was just a little while ago. You know that Braden and Micah wouldn't allow thievery to go on for very long and you're probably lucky that it wasn't them who happened across your lot. You and your former associates would have all been killed before you stepped from cover, after your minds were scoured for every bit of information you had so any other raiders could be rooted out and destroyed. Now that you are living on borrowed time, tell us what you know."

Darius had already surrendered. He was pliable. "Like I said, I only joined them a little while ago, and although they talked of the big hauls, I didn't see anything. We scavenged off the land. You were the first target that we saw since I joined."

Caleb thought as much, figuring the young man had no luck. The fisherman looked to his fellow villager from Trent, raising his eyebrows suggestively.

"Fine! I'll see if Tom can use an assistant" Zeller replied before asking Arnie to pick up the pace. She was tired of being on the road, even more so because of the attack.

"That's settled. We won't mention your role as a raider as long as you promise us that you will steer clear of thieving, and if you hear of anyone thinking that this is a good career choice, you need to let the Elders know so that it can be stopped before anyone else gets hurt. If you lie, Arnie will know. He's probably already been through your mind…" Caleb knew that Arnie wasn't able to read minds like a Hillcat could. The Aurochs was able to talk with the human he was joined with and that was it, but Darius didn't know that.

"I will, honestly, I will. You know that, don't you, Arnie?" the man pleaded.

Caleb raised his eyebrows and looked suspiciously at the younger man.

"Maybe we should drop you off right here. How long do you think you'll survive with a broken arm?" Caleb taunted.

"I'll work hard, I promise. It sucks out here!" Darius looked down and started to cry. The big fisherman had his answer. And if they needed further confirmation, one of the recently arrived Hillcats that had bonded with Tom could and probably would check. Barely more than a kitten, he could still look into the man's mind and see if he was being honest. Caleb was satisfied with that and the fact that Zeller would tell Tom the truth of how Darius came to be his new apprentice.

An apprentice blacksmith with a broken arm? That would be a tough sell, but who better than Free Trader Zeller to make the pitch?

# River Crook

Young Tom knew Zeller was coming because his bonded Hillcat told him. Neeson was large, even for a Hillcat, but that had made him overconfident. He'd tangled with a cold-water croc and come out on the losing end. His back leg had been injured and now the 'cat walked with a severe limp. Neeson could no longer run fast enough to catch most prey and although he could still climb trees, he had trouble getting down. His activity level was low and he was starting to get fat, but Young Tom kept him close and took good care of his new best friend.

When the wagon rolled into the burgeoning village, Tom was there, ready to lift his mate down and carry her home, but Zeller stopped him with a half-smile.

"What's wrong?" he asked, thinking it was something he'd done. He, like Braden, had partnered with a strong woman from Trent, one who ensured that no one person dominated the relationship. Women from Trent were quick to express their dismay, and equally quick to express their appreciation. Tom liked it all and knew how empty life could be without it.

"We have company. Micah's dad is with me, and he's been injured." Tom bellowed for someone and an old man hobbled into the town's main square carrying a large pouch. "And Arnie's been injured, too." Tom lifted Zeller down so she could show him, all thoughts of an injured human taking second place to his mate's Aurochs partner.

The numbweed had done its job and the wound had scabbed over, and Arnie told them that he felt fine. Tom waved the old man toward the back of the wagon while he and Zeller held each other, absentmindedly stroking Arnie's nose as he nuzzled them back.

Caleb had dropped the wagon's gate and was sitting with his legs dangling. Behind him, Darius cowered, fearful of facing the villagers from River Crook.

The old man ignored everything except the two arrow wounds in Caleb's leg. The healer produced a small knife and cut the pants leg, exposing the two swollen, purplish holes. He used a rough plant to scrub the wounds.

Caleb howled in pain, squeezing the side of the wagon hard enough that he threatened to snap the material. Zeller and Tom joined him to provide moral support as the old man continued his ministrations. He poured water, scrubbed some more, and then finished cleaning. He held numbweed on the wounds until he heard the big fisherman's sigh of relief, then the old man sewed the holes closed. He patted additional numbweed on the sutures, then nodded once, packed his things, and walked away.

"I guess I'll be fine," the fisherman said with a brief smile. "Hi. I'm Caleb." He held out his hand, and the blacksmith took it, they shook, heartily as two big men did. The large 'cat worked his way between Zeller and Tom, looking up at the fisherman.

"Well, hello! Who's this pretty kitty?" Caleb said, extending his ongoing battle of wills with the Hillcats.

*'Humans are so droll,'* the 'cat replied over the mindlink. *'The stupid one trying to hide is afraid. He will do as he's told.'* With that, Neeson strutted away, as much as his injured leg allowed.

The big fisherman grunted as Tom helped him from the wagon. "Come on, Darius. We have our confirmation that you weren't lying to us. Now, go forth and do no evil," Caleb said without looking at the young man.

"Hold on there," Zeller started. "Come with us, you have work to do while I get reacquainted with my man." Zeller crooked a finger at Darius. He crawled from the wagon, standing with his head bowed.

"They call you Darius," Tom told him. "You were here recently. How did you come to be in the company of such shady Free Traders?" he asked, earning himself a punch in the stomach from his partner.

"I'm sorry. I shouldn't have gone with them," was all Darius said.

"Raiders," Zeller added, clenching her jaw, instantly angry at the thought.

"So, that's what brings you back? I don't see the others." Tom looked to Zeller. She drew one finger across her throat, then held up three more. "We won't talk about that. No one else needs to know. You now have a new life as my apprentice. I hope you don't mind hard work." The blacksmith slapped the smaller man on the back, hard enough almost to knock him down. Tom and Zeller walked arm in arm toward the forge. Caleb limped after them with Darius holding his head high as he helped the fisherman.

Less than seven turns later, Zeller and Arnie made a quick trip to Westerly and the hills overlooking White Beach to deliver Caleb and the fishing equipment. Even though he was not completely healed, he told them that the sooner he got started, the sooner he'd be able to go home to Mattie.

# The Beach

A large man cast into the surf of the Western Ocean, trying for Caleb's approval, the master fisherman, come all the way from the eastern shore to teach the newcomers how to harvest the sea's bounty.

"If you only had boats, we could do some real fishing, but this'll do. For now, anyway," the older fisherman told the man casting. "Let out more line." The coiled heavy fishing line lay at the man's feet. He pulled a handful and fed it through the eyes of his pole toward the ocean.

The line was yanked across his fingers, leaving a deep gash. He almost dropped the pole.

"There you go! Wrap the line around the stop and hold on. Your first fish looks like it's going to be a whopper!" Caleb exclaimed. They'd been fishing for two days and had donated a great deal of bait to the underwater denizens, but had yet to bring one ashore.

The transplant from the village of Westerly, on the plains east of White Beach, did his best to maintain his composure as he struggled with the pole. At times during the battle, he thought the fish was winning as it pulled him toward the surf.

"I better get the gaff. We don't want to lose this one. C'mon, let him know who's in charge! Drag that slimy beast in here and let me jab this iron hook through his gills. Come on, now, pull him in!" Caleb encouraged the new fisherman as he tried to position himself in the surf, but not too deep, just in case their fish turned out to be a shark. He continued to guide the man, who worked his way back and forth along the beach while he continued to wrestle with the pole. Caleb grimaced as the salt water stung the arrow wounds in his leg. They were healing, but he was still miffed at how much they hurt.

The tip drooped as the man barely had enough strength in his arms to hold the pole upright.

"I can see it!" Caleb cried aloud. "It's as big as a boat. Now's the time, laddie, pull with all you've got." He moved thigh-deep in the surf, keeping his legs spread to give himself leverage to drive the gaff home and help his student bring the monster ashore.

Caleb had never seen such a fish. It was flat, with its eyes on the black and green mottled top. Underneath, it was all white. A wide tail thrashed the water as the great fish decided it didn't want to come ashore. The fisherman was pulled to his knees and almost lost the pole. With a monumental effort, Caleb jumped into the surf and drove the spear tip of the gaff between the creatures eyes. The old fisherman landed on the fish, slid off, and toppled into the ocean.

He sputtered as he lunged back to his feet, regaining his grip on the gaff. He pulled it and expertly twisted the hook-end underneath the fish. Caleb stood upright, pulling the gaff into the creature's head, then backed out of the surf, dragging the massive fish with him.

He pulled until it was on the dry sand above the lightly rolling surf. The fisherman in training was on his hands and knees, panting like a dog as he looked sideways at his catch. The pole lay forgotten in the sand before him. Caleb had collapsed in the sand, his injury aching from the salt water. The weight of the fish challenged him, but in a good way. He sat next to the monster, trying to catch his breath.

He looked at the man they called Digger and grinned. "No greater fish has ever been caught, my friend!" Caleb said. When he finally stood, he reveled at the great creature before him. "Tonight, we feast!"

Caleb pulled a knife and started cleaning the fish, right there on the beach. He found the meat on the flat top to be thick. He cut numerous steaks and piled them on the inverted skin he'd used to cover the sand. Then he flipped the fish and started on the bottom side.

"We'll need a proper fish cleaning station and a cart to move sea monsters like this," Caleb quipped, looking at the other man who was now sitting in the sand, his arms hanging uselessly. "Give us a hand. It's going to take all we've got and then some to move this where we can cook a little for now and smoke the rest for later." Digger finally stood, wobbly and weak, but he was standing.

"Let's get to it, then, but, I'm pretty sure I'm done fishing for the day," he chuckled.

"What?" Caleb exclaimed. "Just when they started to bite, too…" They laughed together as the surf behind them started to churn. The two men didn't notice anything until they heard the sound of grinding sand and water dripping. An ancients' oceangoing vehicle crawled up the sand behind them, stopped, and the front started to open.

Caleb wanted to run, but his body wouldn't move. Digger stood upright, mesmerized by the sight of the metal monster. A large flat panel at the front dropped into the sand. The inside contained smaller metal creatures of various designs, some rolling from the vehicle while others hovered as the Tortoid did. One, humanoid in shape, but bulkier and squatter, approached Caleb and Digger and used its metal arms to grab them by their hands and lead them back to the vehicle. It dragged them through the fresh fish, ruining the day's work.

*What a shame!* Caleb thought to himself, distracted from the plight of his abduction by the loss of the what he considered the greatest catch ever. *I really wanted to know what that fish tasted like,* were his last thoughts as he drifted toward nothingness.

# Bad News

*'Good afternoon, Braden!'* Holly said pleasantly via Braden's neural implant. *'If I may have a word, in person, I would really appreciate it, and alone, if that's okay?'*

Braden stood by the oasis with Micah, their children, and a mass of their friends representing the other intelligent species on Planet Vii. Ax and 'Tesh were chasing Klytus and Shauna, their half-Hillcat bonded partners. The 'cats easily avoided the screaming children as other Hillcats, full bloods from the north, lounged lazily in the sun. Bounder and Gray Strider were with them, visiting from the nearby Wolfoid town of Livestel.

The Hawkoids, Skirill and Zyena, perched in a tree above the lake. They and Aadi, First Master of the Tortoise Consortium, were the only original companions who claimed that they lived full time at New Sanctuary, but the others visited often enough that they could have called it home.

*'Sounds dire, Holly. I'll be right down,'* Braden replied, not worried. The Artificial Intelligence known as Holly was stretching his digital legs, seemingly in an effort to become more human in how he was perceived by the others. He often practiced on Braden.

Since their return from the north these past three moons, things had been going very well. Trade was accelerating with Free Traders joining the routes as soon as Old Tom could build another wagon. With each new one, new Free Traders hit the road.

"Holly wants to see me for some reason," he told Micah out loud. "I won't be gone long." He looked at the menagerie on the small beach around the lake. He spotted the Golden Warrior among some of the newcomers with Treetis, his young protégé, attached to his hip. Braden tried to get the 'cat's attention, but stopped when he realized that G-War probably already knew that he was going. The 'cat didn't like anything underground and wouldn't go unless it was an emergency, then he'd complain the entire time.

Braden walked alone to the elevator building, where he waited patiently as a couple survivors from Cygnus VI exited and headed somewhere. They generally didn't like being in the sunlight and ventured out infrequently and only for short periods of time.

When Braden walked from the elevator into the New Command Center, he could sense the tension. Holly instantly appeared and escorted Braden to the wall covered with monitors. With a nod, nine of them combined to show a single video, taken by one of the satellites orbiting the planet, zoomed in to show a higher level of detail.

It was White Beach. Braden had been there before. He knew that Caleb was there, teaching new transplants how to fish.

He watched as the surf turned white and a vehicle crawled out. Two dots on the beach were escorted into it. Braden saw dots leaving the vehicle and assumed they were the people gathering Bots. Holly sped up the video showing the Bots returning with other humans in tow. The vehicle then slowly retreated into the surf and disappeared.

Braden stood in silence while the others working in the Command Center waited.

"Caleb?" he finally asked.

"We believe so," Holly answered softly.

*'Micah, you better get down here,'* Braden told his mate over their mindlink. *'The so-called sea monster is back and it's taken your father into the Western Ocean.'*

Without answering, Micah started running. She intercepted Heloysis and Luciana to ask the two Rabbits to watch the children, something they did as a matter of course whenever the toddlers were at New Sanctuary.

Micah tore through the elevator doors and into the darkened spaces of the New Command Center, where Holly replayed the video for her. Braden hugged her as she stood motionless. Her face tightened as she watched the vehicle disappear into the ocean.

"Holly, last time you were able to talk with the vehicle. Why didn't you do anything?" she asked accusingly.

"They have changed their access and I was unable to penetrate the system before they were gone. I shall review my copies of the attempt and see where I can improve for next time."

She nodded as a way to apologize to Holly for thinking he didn't do what he could to prevent her father's abduction. The AI had always been there for her and Braden through the best and worst of times. Even though she could see he was a projection, to her, Holly was real. "We need to go there, Holly, to White Beach. Get ourselves captured and go under the sea where we can find all the people, find my father, and rescue them."

"I might caution against that," Holly started, using the human expression he found to be most tactful when suggesting a course of action different from what Braden or Micah was leaning toward. "If the Bots take you, they will take all your equipment. Once in the undersea facility, you may not have access to what you need in order to escape. The facility could be under two thousand meters of water, that's twice as high as the decks on the Traveler. You would have no way to get to the surface and be trapped there with the other survivors, assuming they are all still alive."

Braden rolled his eyes at Holly, who grimaced when he realized what he'd just said. Micah ignored them both as she tried to think through other options to rescue her father. At Micah's subtle but firm request, he'd gone to White Beach to teach the new settlers how to fish. She felt like it was her fault and that it was her responsibility to get him back. Micah did not want to tell her mother, as Mattie would insist on joining them in their search.

"Options, Holly," Micah commanded, sounding presidential as she squinted at the images on the various monitors filling one whole wall of the New Commander Center.

"I am currently working on bringing a self-sustaining floating laboratory close enough to shore that you will be able to climb on board. I believe the ship will be able to take you where you need to go. There should be two mini-submarines on board. If those are unavailable, then we'll try to use the underwater communications on board the Warden to talk with the undersea facility. Proximity will be important if that course of action is to have any chance of success."

"How long have you had control over this Warden?" Braden asked, miffed that Holly hadn't told them about an important piece of Old Tech that was floating around the Western Ocean.

"Only a month, Master Braden," Holly said soothingly. "The scientists from Cygnus VI and I have been working on it, but didn't have a use for it before now. We simply don't have the people to send on long voyages at this point in time."

"That's not your decision!" Micah yelled, instantly furious.

"No, Master President," Dr. Johns said as he stepped forward. "But I made that decision and I'm sorry. I should have told you." Micah let out the breath she was holding and shook her head.

"I'm sorry, and no, you don't need to tell me everything. You know that I prefer that you don't." She tried to smile, but couldn't. "I want my father back." She looked from face to face.

"Bring the Warden to White Beach. We'll meet it there in ten turns' time," Braden said, looking at his partner, then back to Holly. "Set us up, Holly. Firepower, gear, anything you can think of to help us on this one. I have no idea what we'll need. We trust you, Holly. And you, too, Dr. Johns. We're going after Micah's father, and we won't return without him."

*'I hate the ocean, but I know what happens when you're left alone, so I'll be joining you, and Treetis, too, and Fealona,'* G-War said, inviting his favorite 'cats to join them.

*'And us, too,'* Skirill added joyfully.

*'You all know we're going under the water, right?'* Braden asked over the mindlink.

*'Of course we do,'* Aadi chimed in. *'That's why you need us, and Caleb and Mattie are our friends, too. We would go to the ends of Vii for our friends.'*

*'And beyond,'* Micah added, with a sad smile as she and Braden headed

for the elevator. They'd taken the companions all the way into outer space, where they had fought together.

Braden and Micah were on their way to the armory, because Micah had just declared war on the Bots of the Western Ocean. She hoped that her father and the others from White Beach were still alive, otherwise there was no limit to what she was prepared to do. Braden had witnessed that side of her and didn't want that person to see the light of day, but knew that he wouldn't be able to stop her if Caleb was injured. Braden suspected that he'd probably join her in the inevitable conflagration.

# Preparing for War with an Unknown Enemy

Once in the Armory, they stood and looked around, not sure what they should take. "Holly, do you know if they have Security Bots at the undersea laboratory?" Braden asked as he started to think about what their possible enemy might look like.

"There is so little information available regarding the laboratory and the undersea facility that I hesitate to guess," Holly started. Braden and Micah waited, knowing that Holly would continue. "They had everything they needed to build them, from what I can see on the manifests. Part of their equipment list included an industrial-sized fabricator along with enough Development Units to build anything else. They could have an entire city down there by this time."

"If they have Security Bots, how do we fight them?" Braden asked, concerned that their newest enemy was invincible.

"I have a couple items that you may find useful. One is a field generation device. It is a little bulky, but it will disperse the defensive force field of a Security Bot. If there is no nearby field, then it will provide protection with a field of its own, just like the Bots have. The second is a device that is a power grounding unit." Micah looked where Holly directed them to.

"This looks like a fishing spear," she said.

"Once the security field is neutralized, fire the spear into the Bot, and it will ground the unit, rendering it powerless. You do not want to get into a blaster battle with a Security Bot," Holly cautioned. "It would be best to avoid battle with the Security Bots in entirety. You must win over the intelligence that runs the undersea facility. I suspect since the Development Units are programmed not to harm people, it is most likely that you will find a thriving population in the facility on the ocean floor. I don't know if there are ancients there or whether the computer system that is inevitably there realized sentience or not. The scientists of that era were very bright, so I suspect sentience."

Holly stood with his arms behind his back, trying to project calm. Even with Holly's assurances, Braden had grown comfortable blasting things into oblivion. An undefended Security Bot would probably deliver a most gratifying explosion. Braden was more comfortable with a blaster than even his recurve bow. Still, a Security Bot would be a challenge.

"They didn't hurt people as they were taking them," Braden started. "But we take no chances. We need two of everything, Holly." Braden picked up the spear and handed it to Micah. She hefted it easily, practicing aiming it. Braden did the same with his. The field generation device was a big, heavy brick. They decided that one of those was enough, otherwise they'd be too loaded down to move.

"And here's something you should have with you, too. This design came from Earth, but as soon as I knew you'd be going to the Western Ocean, I had the fabricator produce a number of these, one for every member of your party." Holly looked pleased with himself as a Server Bot approached carrying a stout box filled with strange looking contraptions. There was bar laterally across the front of what looked like a nose piece, with two round protrusions beneath and to the sides. There was a clear square pouch at the back of the strange Old Tech.

"What do we do with these things, Holly?" Micah asked as she examined the new devices.

"These will help you breathe underwater for a short period of time. Open the pouch at the back of the mask. It is a plastic bag that goes over your head, cinching around your neck, as tightly as possible without choking yourself, of course. Unfortunately, we don't have any big enough for Brandt Earthshaker, King of the Aurochs."

"There must be twenty in here, Holly. How many people do you think are coming?" Braden asked, looking at the hologram, who shrugged in reply.

Micah finally smiled, still angry and slightly overwhelmed, but a real smile. "Holly knows us too well."

"Rally the team, G. We leave as soon as we're outside. I think Malo and Denon are grazing the fields, along with Max and Speckles. Let's see if one of them would like to pull the cart, and then we can ride the horses," Braden said aloud, conveying his thoughts over the mindlink as well.

Holly nodded and raised his hand as if he wanted to speak. Braden pointed at the hologram impatiently. "We have another one of the new wagons ready, well several actually, but I know you wanted to wait to roll them out until you divulged the existence of New Sanctuary to the people, all the people."

Braden and Micah did not want to have that conversation again, because they knew Holly was right. Even though the Council of Elders was split on revealing the existence of the Old Tech stronghold, they both felt it was the right thing to do. Give the people hope for a better future. It would start with addressing the kidnapping of people from White Beach. The people deserved to know that Old Tech was alive and well, and that it was nothing to be feared, just something to be managed, like taking a herd of water buffalo across the Great Desert.

"When we get back, Holly, we'll take the kids on a tour of every village and make them all aware that the ancients are alive and well and working in the people's best interest. When we get back, we'll know what to say. Maybe we can leave some Old Tech at each village, a communication device to show them how Old Tech can help them? Between now and then, we have a ways to go and some work to do. It's been a while since I've been on a boat, but it'll come back to me. I was raised at sea." Micah lost her smile as she thought about their trip ahead, into the unknown ocean to find something an interminable distance beneath them.

"This ship won't be like anything you've ever seen before. It is far more advanced than even the RV Traveler. It has living space for a crew of nearly one hundred, with all the support that would entail, including laboratories both above and below the surface," Holly said, grinning broadly. Micah was in no mood to explore the wonders of the ancient world.

"I don't care, Holly, just as long as it will get us where we need to go. It will do that, won't it?" she asked pointedly.

"Yes, Master President, it will do that, in style. I'll have it waiting for you just off shore. I'm afraid it has a rather significant draft and you may have to swim for a bit to get to it. Once it's closer, I'll see if any of its ferries are functional. Getting on board could be hard or it could be easy. I cannot tell you which at this point."

"I can't see G-War swimming into the ocean for any reason," Braden said matter-of-factly.

*'Neither can I. We're ready if you can find your way out of that place,'* the 'cat told them over the mindlink.

"Shall we, partner mine? Let's see who "we" means and then let's get down to the business of saving Caleb," Braden stated, stepping toward the elevator. Micah joined him, wondering why she was carrying the field generator and he was carrying the box of breathing devices, which weighed nothing compared to what she was carrying.

Once on the elevator, she gave him the stink-eye until he put the box down and took the field generator from her.

# Leaving New Sanctuary Behind

When they arrived at the lake, the companions were gathered, waiting. Malo, one of the larger bulls from the Toromont Aurochs, stood impatiently, ready to run. He'd heard about the new wagons that didn't seem to weigh anything, and he wanted his chance to pull one. Denon stood nearby, ready to go as well.

The Rabbits held the children close, their 'cats at their feet, comforting them as they knew their parents were leaving.

The Hawkoids watched, ready to fly ahead and scout the way. Bounder and Strider confidently flexed their Wolfoid hands on the hafts of their lightning spears. Aadi floated serenely over the lake, blinking slowly and watching events unfold, as he usually did. Braden spotted Max first. Even the horses had joined the parade.

"So, G, who's going?" Braden asked, rather than undermine the 'cat's best laid plans.

*'Us,'* he said simply. Braden should have expected that, gritting his teeth and reviewing his mental list. Tortoid, Hawkoids, Wolfoids, 'cats, an Aurochs, and Rabbits, but Heloysis and Luciana had come to New Sanctuary to live. They both nodded their small heads at Micah.

*'Not us. We will stay with these two delightful creatures. And then there's those two,'* Luciana said, tipping her nose toward the half-Hillcats that had grown bored with comforting their humans and were now trying to hook their claws into Bounder's tail. With a well-practiced move, he kicked the two away from him. Not to be deterred, they launched their small, furry bodies toward Strider's tail. They crashed face first into her spear as she twisted it in front of them.

Braden started to laugh, but Micah cuffed him across the arm.

"If there is a garden on board that ship, Rabbits could make sure that it produced, although I hope we're not on board long enough to see a full cycle of a crops," Micah said.

Dr. Johns walked up behind them with two more scientists in tow. "Can they join you, maybe permanently man the floating laboratory, the Warden? There's so much that we don't know about our own planet!" the old man said excitedly.

"Do they get seasick? No matter. We'll ask for you, Dr. Johns. You two, get your trash and meet us here. You have about thirty heartbeats," Micah ordered, skipping introductions. She didn't know their names, but her father needed her help, and she wasn't getting any closer by standing there.

"But we have all our equipment!" the middle-aged woman proclaimed.

Micah's eyes narrowed and her lips pursed. "We're leaving," she said in a low and dangerous voice. "Malo!" she yelled as she stormed away to hook the Aurochs to the wagon.

Braden stepped close to Dr. Johns. "We'll be taking the rainforest road. If you take Denon and head due west, past Livestel and then up the coast, you should be able to get there before we do. Load your wagon and go. If you can pick up Loper and Sunny Day, then they will make sure that you don't have any problems. Tell them what it's for. They will join you and help you." Braden shook hands with all three and jogged after his partner, stopping to rub the noses of the two horses.

"I'm sorry Max, Speckles, but we have to go fast. This isn't a trip for you, but when we get back, all of us will go somewhere, I promise."

*They are happy to hear that, Dad, and look forward to your return.'* Ax said in his little thought voice.

*'And you tell Max and Speckles both that none of this would be possible without them. None of this. They are the heroes of our generation!'* Braden always liked to heap praise on the horses. They were simple creatures, but that didn't mean he had less respect or admiration for them. They both whinnied and threw their heads as Ax relayed Braden's positive thoughts. The horses danced away and trotted toward the fields.

The wagon had magically appeared, undoubtedly delivered by one of Holly's metal minions. Micah had Malo in place and was strapping him in. She stroked his nose once she finished and thanked him for helping her. He bowed deeply to her, in deference to the King of the Aurochs' friend.

Bounder and Strider leapt into the back, joining the two 'cats already there. Braden looked for the noticeably absent G-War, before finding him under Malo's nose. The two seemed to be engaged in deep conversation. Braden suspected they were negotiating the terms that would allow the 'cat to ride on the Aurochs' head. Malo was nowhere as big as Brandt, but he was still a large creature, dwarfing those around him. Braden turned his attention to their load out. Holly had already filled the wagon with food and water, though the field generator hadn't made it yet. He looked back toward the lake and saw it there with Klytus sitting on top of it. Shauna was rubbing her body on the frame while the Rabbits and the twins were in the bushes looking at something. Braden chased the two 'cats away and lugged the device to the wagon, carefully putting it inside.

If they were to fight a Security Bot, that one device was their only way to do it. He tied it down as an added precaution.

He looked into the trees where the Hawkoids perched, nodding to both of them. They dipped their heads in reply.

*'Another adventure, my friend,'* Skirill said in his thought voice. *'Too bad we aren't going east, where we might see our hatchlings.'*

*'We might get to see Zeeka, who is traveling with Bronwyn and the Queen,'* Braden told them hopefully. They both ruffled their feathers at him.

"Wagon, ho!" Braden yelled to the few remaining creatures--Denon, two Rabbits, Ax, 'Tesh, and the 'cats. The toddlers came running for one final moment with their parents before they left.

"When we return, we'll have your grandpa with us," Micah promised her children. Braden bent down on one knee next for a group hug with the children. The Rabbits waved with the children as their parents climbed into the wagon and asked Malo to head out, best possible speed to the rainforest road.

He tentatively stepped forward, hoping to get the feel of the wagon, but as he'd heard, it felt as if he pulled nothing. He jogged, then quickly broke into a distance-eating run. Two Hawkoids flew ahead, intertwining in an aerial dance they enjoyed when they flew freely above the planet. Micah watched them for a while, letting the wind whip past her face.

Braden could feel her sadness and doubt, not because he sensed her emotions as she could sense his, but by her posture, the set of her jaw. He knew her well, that she felt helpless until she could face her enemy, lift her sword against them in battle. Braden felt helpless, too, but he was in no hurry to fight Bots. He caressed the blasters at his hip.

"How many times have we left, just like this, armed to the teeth, going to war, dragging all our friends along?" Braden asked.

Micah nodded, slowly, thinking about her mate's question. "Too many times to count, but we've come home every time. So far, anyway."

*'It only takes once, my friend, but that's why we had to come with you. To make sure this time is not the one,'* Aadi interjected over the mindlink.

Braden reached into the wagon to grab the Wolfoid's ear and give it a good scratch. "We are always happy when you join us. And this time above all others. Our family is in trouble."

The wagon quieted as everyone was absorbed in their own thoughts. G-War rode on Malo's head, ears up and eyes watching the way forward as if he expected something untoward to happen at any moment.

"And how many times have you alerted us to danger, my friend?" Braden asked the 'cat.

*'More than you can count and probably more than you deserve,'* G-War said mysteriously.

"Like when Brandt and Arnie almost tipped the wagon over up north? But we ate well that night, didn't we, G! I like the open road," Braden said, looking at the clouds. He stood, balancing with a wide stance. "I'm Free Trader Braden and I like being on the road!" he bellowed to the sky.

Micah nodded. "All we have to do is throw the kids in the wagon and we'll get back to being Free Traders. One village to the next, but we'll carry news, news of New Sanctuary and what we've done to prevent a future war, how everyone can share in what the ancients left behind."

Braden agreed, squeezing Micah's hand and leaning closer to her as they settled in for the long ride ahead.

Malo ran tirelessly to the rainforest and then in, without hesitation. He didn't run as fast as Brandt, but his pace was steady and the riders weren't jostled as they would have been at a faster pace. The Aurochs continued to run without pause. The others ate and slept, wondering when Malo would tire, knowing that he would run himself to death because the Aurochs bulls were in a constant state of competition. They all wanted to best Brandt Earthshaker in one contest or another. It took Micah convincing G-War to get into Malo's head and encourage him to stop.

Maybe it was the image of how the 'cat brought the King of the Aurochs to his knees when he was running out of control at Toromont's Run that finally convinced Malo to stop and get something to eat. Despite the long run on the rainforest road, it had yet to start raining. Braden and Micah counted their blessings since a downpour was inevitable. The Old Tech wagons that Holly produced made the trip comfortable for the riders. The Aurochs would suffer the weather, although they seemed unperturbed as they raced through the rain along the well cared for road.

Zalastar wouldn't allow anything less and was leading his people to be less afraid of humans and the other intelligent species. Braden and Micah had seen a number of Amazonians on their last trip. They passed one along the side of the road already on this trip, both waving in greeting. As they stretched their legs, a group of Amazonians approached. Bounder and Gray Strider watched the Lizard Men warily, the war fresh in their minds. The numerous attacks along the rainforest road haunted them.

When the shadows cleared and the Lizard Men were visible, Pik Ha'ar's unique face came into focus. Braden and Micah rushed to greet him. The Lizard Men towered over the humans. Green, broad-chested, and heavily muscled, they were physically intimidating.

*'My friends, it is good to see you!'* Pik told them as he approached and offered his hand to the humans. *'What brings you this way?'*

They told him. He nodded, then waved another Lizard Man to him. They talked together in their unique soundless way before the other ran off.

The Hawkoids swooped in close to say hello to their old friend. Bounder and Strider also greeted the Lizard Man warmly. He nodded to them all.

*'We have had success developing what we call a "skin suit" to wear when we are outside the rainforest. We have tested this, albeit briefly. I will run it through its paces when I join you to save Micah's father,'* the Lizard Man said.

"Pik! I don't know what to say, but salt water is different than rain. I'm not sure about this," Micah replied.

*'What I've learned from you is free will. We have the freedom to choose our own destinies, do we not?'* the Lizard Man asked.

"You do," Micah conceded.

*'Then my choice is to come with you. I will be able to help. Is there any way I can get a blaster?'* Pik asked innocently.

Braden and Micah looked at each other and started to laugh. "No," they said together.

"I'm sorry, Pik. The last time you had a blaster, it didn't turn out so well," Braden chuckled.

When the skin suit arrived, Pik showed it off proudly. It was made of a thin, rubbery outer coating to stretch and flex with its wearer. It contained spongy material on the inside that would hold water in. It had vents that could be opened as the user desired to let the suit breathe. The only thing he needed was water to moisten the interior, then he could put it on and be healthy in a drier climate. They didn't know how long the suit would retain the water north of the rainforest, but the Amazonians hoped one fill would last an entire daylight.

Pik climbed into the front of the wagon with Braden and Micah, where he'd still be exposed to the rain, whenever it started to fall. The others piled into the back and they were off. Malo had only met Pik briefly on a couple different occasions, so he spent the happy reunion between old friends eating and resting. When they were ready to go, he was stiff, but knew that he'd work his muscles out as he ran. Only two turns remaining. His goal was to best Brandt's record-breaking run.

And no one kept records, but the Aurochs all knew about it. The humble King's exploits were fodder for the Aurochs' trough.

# A Rolling Stone Gathers Moss

It took Malo two full turns to make it to Greentree, the closest village on the north side of the Amazon. Braden and Micah confirmed that he had tied the great King's record and should be so remembered!

Pik walked around in his skin suit, seemingly comfortable and healthy, although the villagers shied away from the Lizard Man. Braden and Micah kept him close to them, kindly introducing him to the good people of the village, hoping they would be more accepting.

The village Elder, Ditarod was in the fields, helping the Rabbits Patrice, Delavigne, Ferrer, and Brigitte. It wasn't long before the five returned to see their friends.

The Wolfoids roamed among the people, greeting them with taps of their paws on shoulders, receiving neck and ear scratches in return. The Tortoid floated serenely throughout, nodding at one person or another as they passed. The Hawkoids stayed in the trees, perched where the people could see them and wave.

Bigotry was shunned and shouted down quickly as the menagerie that roamed the village of Greentree had risked their lives to save humanity, to bring peace to the south, making it possible for these people to return to their village. The story was recounted at every gathering by those in the know. A couple villagers from Greentree had died in the Amazon during the trip where they accompanied Braden to find the Overlords. Everyone's sacrifices were remembered whether human or a human creation, even though the people had not yet been informed that was where the intelligent species came from. Soon, though.

As was the new custom, whenever Braden and his partner rolled into a village, there was always a celebration. Since they came to Greentree and Coldstream more often than other places, the celebrations tended to be more sedate. Braden always appreciated a warm greeting and a freshly cooked meal. It was the way of the Free Trader, something he'd always been and would always be, even though he now served the people in a different capacity.

They celebrated, although Micah was ready to go. Malo needed to rest in order to take them to Coldstream where they'd ask Brandt for help in getting the wagon to White Beach. No Aurochs was ever forced to pull a wagon, so the traders always asked and then pampered those who agreed to join the traders on the road.

A Hawkoid appeared in the distance, diving toward the village and back-winging to a landing on the branch with her parents.

Braden and Micah didn't have to wait long before they could feel the ground shaking from the thunder of pounding hooves. Braden and Micah both chuckled, knowing only one Aurochs who could make the ground move.

People scattered as the King of the Aurochs slid into the Market Square.

*'You have returned!'* he said in his booming thought voice. The humans winced at the onslaught. *'I shall join you as my friend, Caleb, needs my help. I've never been on a ship and you left me behind when you could have used my help on the Traveler, or so the little orange man has informed me. And you, and you,'* he said, dancing as all three 'cats attempted to jump on his face and climb to the top of his head.

Another Aurochs ran into view, the Queen with Bronwyn riding her. When the great beast stopped, Bronwyn climbed down and ran to Micah, who no longer had to bend down to hug the young girl. Then Braden greeted her and pushed her to arm's length.

"Have we been gone that long?" he asked. Bronwyn shook her head.

*'No, but the Queen makes sure that I eat, too well, I think. No matter where we go, it seems like everyone is trying to fatten me up!'* her thought voice still sounded like that of a little girl. She greatly preferred using the mindlink, because it allowed her to do other things, like hug the Lizard Man and the Wolfoids, pat Aadi's head. She waved to the 'cats, who nodded politely in return.

Braden was amazed how G-War treated certain people, when the one whom the 'cat had known the longest was dismissed with a wave of one furry paw.

*'Get over it,'* G-War intruded on Braden's thoughts.

*'Ass!'* Braden replied instantly.

*'If you get me wet on this trip, I will make you regret pulling me out of the water all those turns ago. I didn't let you save me just so you could throw me back in,'* the 'cat informed them all over the mindlink. Micah stifled a laugh with a snort.

Braden turned to his partner. "Did he not hear the part where we might have to swim to the ship? What part of swimming is so hard to understand?"

"He heard it and understood what Holly meant, lover, clearly, but he discounted it, knowing that you will move mountains to ensure his comfort." She smiled. "And mine, by the way."

He couldn't argue with her logic, but that didn't mean he was hiding a way to get to a ship at sea without a boat or without getting wet. There was nothing in his pouch or backpack that Holly had provided. He had a few turns to think about it, but he relied on the scientists coming from New Sanctuary to have a solution. There was no way they were swimming with their equipment. Dr. Johns was the one hiding a trick or two, he suspected.

"We shall see," Braden said, feeling more hopeful than he had just a few heartbeats before. Thinking of Brandt swimming with a menagerie of creatures riding him as if he were a big, brown island made him laugh. He heard the others laughing, too, over their mindlink. The King of the Aurochs didn't think it was very funny.

"We shall see, my large friend. No matter what the price, we'll pay it to set Caleb free."

They settled in for a celebration, eating and drinking well, because with the sunrise, they'd leave. Malo said that he was coming along, too. The Queen said that wherever Bronwyn went, she would go. Micah didn't relish taking the teenager with them into harm's way.

Not again, but Bronwyn wouldn't be dissuaded. They figured if nothing else, they could leave her on White Beach with the Queen and encourage them to go back to Westerly.

With Bronwyn in the front of the wagon with Braden and Micah, Brandt pulling, two Wolfoids, the two Rabbits Ferrer and Brigitte, a Lizard Man, and a Tortoid, another two Aurochs running behind, and two Hawkoids flying ahead, they departed Greentree. Braden understood about the twenty breathing masks.

They hadn't gotten as much sleep as they wanted, but that didn't matter. Time was of the essence, and they left with the sunrise. Micah opened her neural implant to talk with Holly.

*'Holly, is there any vehicle of the ancients that might make this trip go faster? Once we've let the rest of the people know that Old Tech is alive and well, I would like to waste less time traveling when there's an emergency,'* Micah pleaded with the AI.

*'Of course,'* Holly replied instantly. *'We have everything we need to build hover cars. You could make the trip from New Sanctuary to White Beach in approximately one day using the vehicle,'* Holly informed her.

*'Do it,'* she ordered and closed the link. She looked away from Braden, hoping that he hadn't seen her. She was ashamed, because she had talked Braden out of everything Old Tech, yet when it came down to it, she was the first one to give in completely.

The potential was immense, such as Old Tech to build schools so the children could get an education above and beyond anything contemplated since the war ended over four hundred turns before. People could learn how to do more with less, how to live like the ancients, and thanks to the safety protocols they'd put in place, they wouldn't learn how to die like the ancients. That gave Micah some comfort for what was the impending revelation that she and Braden would deliver to the people.

Bronwyn looked at Micah closely, while Braden was lost in his own thoughts. "It'll be okay," the teenager whispered.

*Mature beyond your years, and yes, you are right. I think it will be okay, because it has to be,* Micah thought to herself. Brandt started walking easily, but it wasn't long before he was running, not as fast as he was capable of, but fast enough that Malo and the Queen had to work hard to keep up. He maintained that pace until midday had passed and they found themselves approaching the fields where the water buffalo grazed under the watchful eye of their Aurochs shepherds.

They made a quick stop in Coldwater so Braden could trade for sweetened, smoked pork. Then they were off again, heading west toward the setting sun. Brandt slowed as darkness covered the Plains of Propiscius, but he didn't stop. He kept going until almost midnight, when he finally pulled up next to a stream, drinking deeply even before the humans could unhook his harness. The other Aurochs joined Brandt muzzle-deep in the stream. Brandt suggested that Malo pull come the new daylight.

The others climbed out of the wagon and stretched. Pik unfastened his skin suit and waded into the stream, lying down in the cool water to rehydrate the suit and himself. The rest of the companions lined up alongside the stream, drinking and refilling flasks. No one talked. They were too tired. Most of them collapsed under the wagon, some slept inside.

And that was the routine for the next two turns until they reached River Crook. There, they stopped for nearly a full turn as the trio of Aurochs grazed and rested, even getting some special treats from the fields where a number of Rabbits were helping the harvest to greater and greater yields. It turned out that a couple of the master gardeners were Ferrer and Brigitte's offspring. Braden could never keep them straight. There had been over one hundred Rabbits born on Vii to the few adults who transferred from the Traveler.

Of all the souls that Braden had touched, the Rabbits were the most gentle and loving. They reminded him of Bronwyn, an entire species just like her. But the Rabbits could also be fierce in combat when they had to be, to defend their loved ones. Braden wished that more people could be like Ferrer and Brigitte, who were simply happy to be alive.

The fireworks started when they talked with Zeller and Young Tom. They told Braden and Micah about the raiders and that Caleb had been injured. Even though it had happened nearly a full moon previously, Micah drew her sword and looked around, hoping to see her enemy. Tom's new apprentice Darius looked shocked and then excused himself.

*'It was him,'* G-War told Micah. *'He was one of the raiders, but Caleb forgave him and Tom doesn't want you to know.'* Micah was furious and started going after Darius, who ran when he saw her.

Braden tackled his mate and almost got a handguard to the head for his efforts.

"It's how Caleb wanted it!" he shouted at her. She continued to struggle, but not as vigorously.

"Caleb convinced Zeller who convinced Neeson," Tom said, petting the large scraggly looking 'cat at his side. G-War looked at the young 'cat.

*'There must be something you can do for him? Maybe Holly...'* G-War pleaded with Braden. He looked at the 'cat, knowing that G never asked for anything unless it was important. Besides food, that was.

Braden opened his neural implant and asked Holly if there was anything he could do. Holly made Braden look closely at the 'cat's leg, both sides, up and down, so the Artificial Intelligence could review the injury, before reaching a conclusion. *'Yes, that can be fixed. On board the Traveler, there is everything needed to repair the 'cat's leg back to normal. Surgery to replace damaged bone with titanium components and cloning technology to replace the muscles, nerves, tendons, veins, and those kinds of things. Yes, that can be done and it will take approximately two weeks. The 'cats have exceptional healing powers so it may take even less time.'*

"I think you're going to have to take a trip, Tom, to somewhere you never imagined existed, if you want to help Neeson. He can be healed, as good as new."

The blacksmith started to cry as he hugged the 'cat to him. Neeson struggled to extricate himself from the large man's grasp. Zeller thanked Braden and Micah profusely.

"Once we get back, we'll make everything clear. We told you that Old Tech exists. Zeller drives an Old Tech wagon. Well, that is a drop in the bucket to what's really out there. I'll leave it at that. WHEN we return," Braden made sure to emphasize the word 'when,' "we will help you and

Neeson and for that, all we ask is that you help us get the message out when the time comes. We don't want anyone to be afraid of Old Tech or envious of it. It is just another tool to help them live better lives, that's all."

Young Tom tried to hug Braden, but settled for a handshake so they didn't fall into a small campfire they'd made between Zeller's wagon and their own. The Wolfoids, 'cats, and Rabbits snuggled in close. Pik stayed farther away, because of the flames, not the heat. He liked it hot, but hot and wet. Aadi stayed close to Braden and Micah, but remained on the outside of the circle.

The Aurochs were somewhere else. Arnie, Brandt, Malo, and the Queen were grazing and enjoying the free flow of the river, warily because of the threat from a rare cold-water croc.

Although Crabby and the other leaders from River Crook wanted some of Braden and Micah's time, they let them be alone with their fellow Free Traders. With the morning, Braden and Micah would meet and greet everyone. They enjoyed the people from River Crook, and held a special place there because they'd helped the people to establish it.

They were always happy to see Yellowfin as he grew into a strong young man, barely older than Bronwyn, who caught him glancing in her direction on more than one occasion. She found ways to steer clear of the village and stay with the intelligent creatures she considered to be her best friends.

Once they retired for the night, Braden and Micah dropped the side of the wagon to create a bed for themselves. It was a feature of the Old Tech wagon that they appreciated and took advantage of on occasion. It came in handy when they had as many companions as currently traveled with them.

"How do we get into these situations? If I understood Holly right, the ship might have two mini-subs, enough for four total people, if they squeeze in tightly. Yet we have a small army with us. Who chooses who goes to the undersea world?"

"We do, as always, but I suspect there's more that Holly isn't telling us. I think since he allowed us to bring everyone as well as all the equipment, he knows of a way where no one is left behind. If the facility is as he expects, expanded and heavily populated with Bots and abducted humans, then we'll need our friends if we are to win them over," she whispered.

Braden figured the same. There was no way Holly would encourage them to take such a broad range of species, only to leave them on the beach.

"We'll see what tomorrow brings," Braden replied before kissing and hugging Micah, but going no further as Bronwyn was in the wagon, an arm-span away, along with the Wolfoids and the Lizard Man. Micah finally relaxed. If her father had forgiven Darius, then who was she to hold a grudge. And Arnie and Zeller had killed all three of the real raiders, which made Micah more accepting, too.

Braden took it better than Micah would have expected. He was furious in the north when they were attacked while traveling the open road. The thought of the trade routes that he had pioneered being plied by raiders should have driven him into a mindless frenzy. But he listened to the story, nodded, and thanked Zeller for taking care of it.

She had to know as his mind hadn't been clear on what he was thinking. She perceived that he'd been happy hearing about it. "Why weren't you angry when you heard about the raiders?"

"What?" Braden asked, having already fallen asleep. She nudged him.

"Angry? About the raiders?" he asked. "Zeller took care of them. That's exactly what we tried to instill in the new Free Traders as we traveled back and forth, that they fight for themselves and for what's right. We can't keep bad people from raising their ugly heads, but we can make sure that the good people aren't afraid to stop them. It is everything I hoped it would be. The south is still safer than Warren Deep was when I left the first time and when we returned. That's because of us and what we taught. Angry? Not on your life. I'm proud of what we've built. You want to know what really concerns me? How do I get G-War to the ship without getting him wet and me scratched?"

Micah's eyes sparkled in the darkness as she appreciated her mate that much more.

# The Open Ocean

They stood on the beach, sixteen strong, and looked at the sea. A long ways out, they could see the spire of an ancient's dream. It looked like something from one of Holly's projections of the future past. Although it seemed to be coming closer, no one was going to swim that far into the ocean to catch it. Skirill and Zyena flew to it and around it, sharing their view with the companions. It had decks open to the weather and enclosed spaces, too. The windows glistened and decks sparkled.

One main structure rose into the air, a vast structure called a sail that was filled with decks, spaces, windows, furniture, and equipment. The black of solar panels graced the upper surfaces of the sail, those open to the sky. A blade turned at the top of the vertical structure.

"There must be a Maintenance Bot or something that is on board and functional," Micah stated. "There's no way a ship can spend any time on the ocean and not get dirty. My father spends one day a week scrubbing the scum from his boat, making sure the keel is clean so that it travels cleanly through the water."

The Hawkoids circled carefully and Zyena landed on a handrail at the top of the ship, which was generally round, with the sail in the middle where the various decks above sea level were located. It arced gracefully upward from the wide base. They could see another deck just below the surface that looked to be a garden, with leaves from robust plants pressed against the glass.

Underwater, the fore and aft sections of the ship were visible from Zyena's perch. It was shaped roughly like one of the boats from Trent, but so much larger as to be beyond comparison. *'You will be very comfortable once on board,'* she passed over the mindlink. *'We cannot look inside as we don't see a way to open the hatches and doors.'*

Braden accessed his neural implant and contacted Holly. In moments, the upper level door opened and both Zyena and Skirill landed on the deck outside, then hopped through the door before it closed behind them. Their daughter Zeeka stayed outside, just in case.

They explored as much of the ship as they could while the rest of the companions stood on the beach and watched by way of the mindlink.

"It looks like someone could walk through one of those doors at any moment. Are you sure there's no one on board?" Braden asked.

*'No. There are no sounds of people or things. Only the mechanical noises of the ship sailing itself toward you and even those are very faint. We don't smell anything or see any sign of a human. It is clean, but we suspect there's a Bot in here somewhere,'* Skirill replied.

They hopped when they had to, flew when they could, and searched the ship from the garden deck to the top of the spire, where the controls to manually drive the ship were located. Skirill wasn't a fan of Old Tech, but he was impressed by the size and design. The top of the sail was an impressive distance from the ocean, where a non-flying creature could get a view such as the Hawkoids always had. He could see how humans could live their entire lives aboard this one ship and never be bored.

*'It even has a fabricator, Master Braden,'* Skirill said when he passed through the galley, which was a kitchen, and dining area.

Braden found it hard not to smile. Micah punched him in the shoulder. "Hey! Who says we have to travel like beggars just because we are going to war?" he stated, making his point that he appreciated the finer things that Old Tech offered. Micah couldn't disagree as she thought of the hover car that Holly was building. Then she pushed that thought to the back of her mind. Her father was somewhere under the ocean. This ship would get her closer.

One step closer.

*'We have company,'* G-War told them. The others assumed fighting positions as they prepared for an unknown enemy, but all they saw was Denon running toward them from the south. He pulled an Old Tech

wagon with the two scientists waving at them with broad arm motions.

"How are we going to get them to the ship?" Braden asked rhetorically. Treetis raced up the beach toward something that moved through the sand. He pounced, then jumped back. The 'cat circled his prey, then pounced again. When he jumped back the second time, a crab, claws gripping tightly, was attached to his 'cat face. Treetis hopped around, pawing at the crab in a feeble attempt to make it let go.

G-War looked at Fealona, then back at the ocean before sitting down. The female 'cat sighed audibly before running off to fix things. *You two orange abominations are going to be the end of me,'* she told them all.

*'You wouldn't want it any other way, partner mine,'* G-War replied.

Bronwyn waded into the ocean, holding her hands up as if she were speaking with the clouds. Braden sloshed into the surf after her as she went deeper and deeper, until she was swept from her feet and thrown into him. He held her up and stood there as a fin appeared in the water before them, then a second. The creature's rounded head broke the surface and blew mist from a hole in the top of its head. The smooth gray skin glistened as its dark eyes locked with Bronwyn's

The creature opened its mouth and chittered with a high-pitched voice. Braden was torn. The row of sharp teeth in that mouth and the sheer size of the creatures scared him. He wanted to run from the ocean, but Bronwyn wouldn't let him.

"They are Dolphins!" she cried, as the two gray creatures inched closer until she could stroke their heads and snouts. They dove into the water and swam circles around Braden and Bronwyn until they leapt out of the water, smacking their tails. "I love them!"

Braden chuckled. "Of course you do." Bronwyn jumped into the surf and started swimming, until the Dolphins swam close, urging her to grab their dorsal fins. With one hand on each, the Dolphins, side by side, powered forward. The teenager bounced on top of the water as the Dolphins headed to sea.

"Maybe you shouldn't go too far out there…" Braden started.

*They won't let anything happen to me. They are so kind! We are going out to meet another friend. You said you needed help getting to the ship? I think my friends have a solution.'* Bronwyn continued seaward, far past the breakers. Braden looked back at the companions and held his hands up in a sign of helplessness.

The Dolphins slowed, treading water with Bronwyn until a great head breached the surface of the water, lifting higher and higher, dwarfing the girl and the Dolphins. It was like a building had just appeared from the ocean and towered over the others there.

Braden staggered back and fell as a waved rolled over him. Sputtering, he got back to his feet, then returned to the beach with the others who watched, mesmerized by the sight.

*'Wow, that's a big brute!'* Brandt said, loud enough for half the planet to hear.

*'She is gentle and kind, not a brute! She's a Whale, that's all,'* Bronwyn replied. *'And she'll give us a ride to the ship, if you'd like.'*

"A ride to the ship?" Braden said, suddenly unafraid and welcoming.

Treetis yowled as Fealona ripped the crab from his face, kicking it away until it scuttled into the water. The young, orange 'cat looked both angry and embarrassed. Fealona walked away without looking back at the wayward younger version of her mate. She saw the great creature rising from the ocean.

*'What did I miss?'* she asked. G-War looked at the Whale and imagined himself riding atop the great head.

Denon stopped, expecting the two scientists to climb down and unhook him. They were riveted to their seats, amazed at the sight before them. Dolphins and a Whale, not just any Whale either, but a massive version of an old sperm whale, the DNA having been brought on the Traveler and genetically modified for life on Vii. The same thing for the Dolphins. The scientists had read the briefing on the sea life of Vii.

"So much knowledge that we've lost!" lamented Patti May, a clone and survivor from Cygnus VI. She and Chrysalis, Dr. Johns' cloned son, had volunteered to conduct research aboard the Warden. When they saw the Whales, they knew they'd made the right decision.

"I can't wait!" Chrysalis cried, finally deciding to join the others standing near the surf.

*'Human,'* Denon started. *'Unhook me. I need eat.'*

The clones were oblivious to the Aurochs, so Braden and Micah came to his rescue, rubbing his nose as they unhooked him. The strap marks on his side suggested that he had been strapped into the harness for an extended period of time.

*'How long have you worn this harness?'* Micah asked over the mindlink, concerned about the rubbing and blisters.

*'Since home,'* the gentle creature replied simply.

*'Did you run all this way, straight through?'* Braden asked.

*'Almost.'*

Micah was furious. She stalked toward the group and grabbed Chrysalis from behind, throwing him to the sand. He looked shocked and covered his face with his arms. With a handful of collar, she yanked him back to his feet and dragged him to the now-free Aurochs. Brandt was trailing close behind, snorting loudly. Micah shoved the man's face to within a hand's-breadth of one of the wounds on Denon's side.

"See this! Do you see this? That's because you never unhooked him to let him rest. What do you have to say for yourself?" Micah demanded.

"But we were behind and couldn't miss this opportunity," Chrysalis whimpered.

"They are our equals! Weren't you paying attention the past couple cycles?" she screamed in his face. He tried to cover his face with his hands, but Micah reared back to punch him. Braden dove toward her, catching her arm as it was cocked for a massive blow. As he struggled with his partner, Chrysalis crawled away, only to be stopped by Brandt's massive horns.

"Apologize to him and rub numbweed on those wounds, you idiot!" Braden advised. Brandt nudged the man while Patti May looked on, trying to look invisible. "And you help him!" Braden pointed at her without looking.

The two scientists scrambled to Denon's side, apologizing profusely, before realizing they didn't have any numbweed. Braden held his pouch at arm's length for Chrysalis to take.

"Treat them with respect and we'll treat you with respect. Treat them like they're beneath you and you'll get a beating you will never forget, do you understand me?" Micah growled, face to face with Chrysalis as he reached for the numbweed.

"It's so brutish out here," he replied meekly. "We should not be threatening to beat people, and especially not you, Master President."

"This is the real world and the greatest insult you can make toward me is to demean any of the intelligent species of Vii. Why did you treat him like that? Look at him! You insulted me and all the creatures of Vii." Micah inched closer, resisting the urge to twist his head toward the wounds on the young bull. With his head down, he lifted his eyes toward the injury.

"I'm sorry, Denon. We were too caught up in our own thoughts to put your needs before our own. That won't happen again," he said sincerely.

"And that's all I want," Micah stated calmly, putting her hand on his shoulder. "You're right. I shouldn't choose violence as my first choice. I should have simply turned you over to him." She nodded her chin toward Brandt, who lifted his head high to look down on the humans. She laughed as she walked away.

Braden forced the numbweed into Chrysalis' hand. "Use it generously." He joined Micah, hand in hand, as they returned to the menagerie watching Bronwyn, the Dolphins, and the Whale frolicking beyond the surf.

*What are their names, dear?'* Micah asked over the mindlink, with no trace of her previous anger.

*'This is my friend, Chlorophyta and her mate, Rhodophyta. I call them Chlora and*

*Rhodi! And this, the greatest of all creatures on Vii, is Rexalita. She is magnificent and she tells me that there are very few like her close to shore as they like the deeper water,'* Bronwyn answered.

*'We are pleased to meet you, Chlora, Rhodi, and Rexalita!'* Micah said. They answered at the same time in a mass of high-pitched thought voices. Bronwyn sorted them out and guided each so only one spoke at a time. They sounded like the Rabbits and judging by Ferrer and Brigitte's reaction, they thought so, too.

*'You said that you may be able to help us get to the ship, Rexalita?'* Micah asked.

*'Yessss,'* the Whale said, dragging out the last letter, pounding her words into the listeners' minds. She was much louder than Brandt. *'Inlet, that way, that's deep enough for me to get close. You climb on and I will swim you out there. Easy for me.'*

Micah squinted at the ocean, trying to figure out how Rexalita was pointing and in which direction.

*'To your right,'* Bronwyn added helpfully. *'Not far, I think.'*

"We'll go that way right now," Braden said out loud.

They watched as Bronwyn straddled one of the Dolphins and held tightly onto the dorsal fin while it raced along the wave-tops. The second Dolphin jumped in and out of the water beside Bronwyn, almost as if serenading the teenager. The Whale swam along behind, exuding a carefree air.

"Malo!" Braden yelled, even though the Aurochs was only a few strides away. "Could you bring the scientists' wagon, please?" The young bull agreed and was quickly strapped in to the harness that Denon had just vacated. Braden even helped the scientists back into their wagon, although they expected subterfuge of some sort and hung on as if Braden was going to dump them on the ground.

G-War sprinted toward Brandt and with a mighty leap, landed in the middle of the King's lowered head. Treetis came running as well, one of his lips still bleeding from where the crab's claw had cut it. When he jumped,

Brandt turned a horn into his path. The young 'cat crashed into it, scrabbled for purchase, then slipped and fell into the sand. Fealona casually walked to Micah, who picked her up, petted her, and put her into the wagon that Brandt agreed to pull. The Queen walked ahead majestically, leading the way. The Wolfoids dispensed with the ride and dropped to all fours for a brisk run up the beach.

The Rabbits weren't too proud. They hopped into the back of the wagon along with the Lizard Man, Pik Ha'ar. Aadi floated in and nestled against the gate.

"Aadi, you've been unusually quiet. Any words of wisdom as we start the next phase of this adventure?"

*'No, Master Braden. I think everything is going well. I wondered about the problem of swimming to the ship. You know that the Golden Warrior planned all along to ride on my shell to the ship, or on Skirill?'* Aadi replied.

"I knew he had something planned. He trusts me, but he trusts himself more," Braden laughed.

*'I'm pregnant, you know,'* Aadi added.

Braden almost fell from the bench as he turned to look at his old mentor. "Aadi! You carry the extra weight so well!" Micah punched him for that, recognizing the implication.

*'I know you jest, Master Braden, but the eggs are making me unusually tired. I will do my best to keep up, though.'*

"Congratulations, Master Aadi! I'm so happy for you. What do we need to do?" Micah asked.

*'Warm sand closer to the end, then I'll need some time to see them hatch and after that, I want to show them the world!'* Aadi said, excitement tinging his thought voice, which was usually calm and stately.

"You let us know and we will dig the holes for you," Braden added.

Brandt congratulated the Tortoid, while G-War simply harrumphed, with an off-handed comment about "more children." The others were supportive and even Bronwyn joined the chorus of well-wishers.

The group headed up the beach, running after the Queen and the Wolfoids, who were racing to an unknown inlet. Braden opened his neural implant and asked Holly for help. With a quick search using the satellite imagery, Holly identified a promontory another hour north from where they were if they maintained their current speed.

Braden couldn't get his head wrapped around how long an hour was, but understood it to be a fairly long way. The Wolfoids finally tired and waited for the wagon so they could climb in. Brandt and Malo maintained a steady pace. The riders were pleased that the sand closer to the surf provided one of the smoothest rides they'd ever had.

The Hawkoids finished their exploration of the ship and declared it devoid of intelligent life, although the two Bots maintaining the ship chased them around until Braden contacted Holly to add the Hawkoids to the ship's register as authorized inhabitants. That was the trick to get the doors to open when they approached. Once outside, they noticed that the ship was moving rather quickly, parallel to the wagons on the beach.

With Zeeka, they flew ahead of the ship, swooping close to the Whale and the Dolphins to greet them appropriately, before continuing to the inlet that everyone was racing toward.

Bronwyn enjoyed the ride, but was getting beaten up by the waves. She tired quickly and lost her grip, torn from the back of the Dolphin in the next swell. She went under and couldn't right herself. Rhodi was there instantly, driving the girl to the surface. Bronwyn sputtered when she broke into the open air and gasped, trying to catch her breath. The group racing up the beach slid to a halt, as one, waiting for word on Bronwyn's health. Once reassured, they continued, but at a much slower pace.

Rexalita dove underwater and the Dolphins swam to the side, leaving Bronwyn by herself as a great head moved in below her, gently touching her feet and lifting her out of the water. Bronwyn sat down, then laid down, spread-eagled on her stomach to maintain her balance on the Whale's broad head. The world seemed to fly beneath her as she became one with the Whale.

G-War was envious that Bronwyn had the greatest seat on the planet.

Those on the beach knew it when they saw it: a finger of land extending into the sea, where the sheer sides of a rock formation stood high above a dark blue that suggested deep water. Braden looked at the cliffs over his head, unsure of how to get the people and equipment on top and then to the Whale.

"We really could use that hover car right about now," Micah said. Braden looked at her oddly. "Okay, I can't keep it a secret. I asked Holly to build a hover car for us to make these trips more quickly. There! Are you happy?" Micah snipped.

Braden knew when to discuss issues and when they were best left to later. "I didn't say anything. I agree, a hover car would make this much easier." He studied the landscape before him, looking for a way up.

A tidal surge threatened to swamp the group as Rexalita swam up the inlet toward them. Despite the deep water, she filled the space. She wedged herself against the shore, then leaned toward the rocky outcropping. Bronwyn effortlessly stepped across where three Hawkoids flew around her and landed nearby. She bowed to them.

Braden cupped his hands and yelled upward, "Wait right there. I have an idea!" Micah looked at him and held her hands out in a sign of surrender.

*'Thought voice, lover. There's no need to yell,'* she said over the mindlink. The Wolfoids snickered nearby.

*Damn!* Braden thought to himself as he pulled a length of the Amazonian rope from the wagon. He tied a piece of driftwood to the end and tossed the rope past the young girl. She wrapped it around a rock and tied it off as she'd learned to do with the Aurochs harnesses. Braden tested it by being the first to climb up. When he reached the top, he bowed.

"Now, send up the equipment from the scientist's wagon," he yelled back down. Micah shook her head, resigned with the fact that her partner was fascinated with yelling.

Chrysalis waved off Micah. "We will just use our raft to get there. The equipment is sensitive and we don't want it bouncing up those rocks. We'll get ourselves to the ship."

Micah clenched her fists. She'd had about enough of the scientists and the knowledge that they selectively shared. They didn't have enough common sense to know to unhook Denon when they rested and they didn't think it important to tell the others that they had a boat. She closed her eyes and took deep breaths until she could think without fixating on the thought of punching a scientist in the face.

"Hey, look!" Braden yelled as he pointed seaward. The ancients' ship was slowing as it navigated the inlet toward them. It was much wider than Rexalita so it could enter only as far as the mouth, but it was within a stone's throw. All the rigmarole with the Whale and the boat and Dolphins, when the original plan of swimming to the ship was sufficient since it rested this close to them. G-War climbed onto Aadi's shell while Zyena offered Fea a ride. Treetis begged until Skirill landed.

The Hawkoids took a running start to get airborne, beating hard to lift above the sand and the sea, then gliding toward the wide deck of the ship. They slid to a landing, the 'cats jumping away before touchdown and running when they hit. Aadi swam slowly through the air, while G-War crouched atop the Tortoid's shell.

The Rabbits used their small hands to help pull them up the rope to join Braden on the outcropping. Next was Pik, an accomplished climber as all Lizard Men were. Their taloned feet found toeholds between rocks as easily as on rainforest trees. And finally the Wolfoids climbed the hill. As they stepped onto the patient Whale, a loud bugling filled the air. Brandt's head was raised and he was bellowing his dismay.

*'What about us?'* he asked, demanding an answer.

*'Can you swim?'* Micah asked, having never seen the King of the Aurochs in water deeper than his knees. The Aurochs looked at each other and shrugged in their way, waving their horns about.

*'Never tried,'* Brandt finally answered.

Braden stepped back onto the rocks and climbed down to the sand.

"Come, my friend. We'll swim together. It's like running, for you. Take a deep breath so you float and before you know it, we'll be there."

Braden and Brandt waded into the surf behind the Whale until Braden was swimming and Brandt was up to his neck, then his head. He kept walking boldly forward until he was completely underwater.

*'Braden!'* the great King cried in his booming thought voice. Braden dove under the water, but couldn't budge the Aurochs. A massive black wall came at them, and Braden cringed as he expected the impact to be painful, the surge of water before Rexalita's tail softened the blow as she scooped Brandt out of the water. Brandt sucked in air through an open mouth, making it look like he was screaming. The Whale backed slowly out of the inlet, wiggling as the Aurochs crouched, terrified of falling off the broad, flat tail and disappearing into the ocean's depths. Rexalita also struggled as the Aurochs was far heavier than she imagined any of the land creatures would be.

Braden stayed back from the Whale as she created her own tidal surf that threatened to swamp him. He stroked his way wide of Rexalita's deliberate motions while she worked to get the King of the Aurochs on board.

When the Whale deposited Brandt on the ship's broad flat deck, he danced away from the unguarded edge, staying as far from the ocean as possible, the whites of his eyes visible as he looked at the ocean in fear.

Braden finally made it, swam up to the deck, and climbed aboard. The deck was only slightly above sea level and had no hand rails. It was flat and wide enough to, with a long and deep keel, stabilize the ship.

'We'll wait here, my King, for your courageous and triumphant return,' the Queen offered. The three remaining Aurochs stepped away from the ocean's surf. They'd planned on swimming to the ship. Seeing that Aurochs didn't float, they changed their plan.

The ship slowly backed out of the inlet, giving the Whale space to turn and dive until her head was even with ship's bottom deck. One by one, they stepped onto the deck, all of them dry and thankful for the ride. Bronwyn stayed on Rexalita's head. The others looked at the two scientists struggling to unload their gear. Braden was soaked and preparing to strip out of his wet clothes, when Micah cocked an eyebrow at him. He looked at Bronwyn, then stopped.

But that wasn't what Micah was thinking. "The longer they take the longer it will be before we can go find my father."

Braden walked back toward the edge of the ship and dove from the deck into the water, making sure to splash water toward G-War as Aadi finally approached. Two drops hit the 'cat.

*'I will cut you. While you sleep, I will cut you,'* the 'cat threatened.

*'No, you won't, partner mine. Any time you want to board the ship, I have some loving I need to share with you,'* the white 'cat purred.

Brandt snorted and blinked his eyes clear. No matter the danger, leave it to the 'cats to keep life in perspective.

Braden waded ashore, growing more and more impatient with each step. He told the scientists to put their boat together while he unloaded the wagon. The Aurochs looked at him and shrugged.

No hands.

He carried each progressively heavier item to the place where Chrysalis and Patti May stood looking at a bright yellow square. Braden could tell by the expressions on their faces that they were accessing their neural implants. Holly must have given them limited access to facilitate aspects of this trip since the survivors had been blocked from direct access to Holly. As Braden thought about it, this was the first time any of the survivors from Cygnus VI had ventured beyond New Sanctuary.

They must have been terrified, and Holly, by giving them access, provided them some level of comfort. He relaxed and waited, but only a few heartbeats before Chrysalis leaned down and pressed a button on a small panel. The package popped open and hissed as it started filling with air. Braden jumped back and watched.

"You had to talk with Holly to push one button?" he said in disbelief.

The boat, little more than one person wide and twice as long, filled quickly. They attached a small motor to the back and pushed it into the surf, then Braden handed them equipment a piece at a time until the boat was filled. Rexalita had moved to deeper water and the ship now stood within the opening to the inlet. Braden wanted to toss the equipment onto the deck, but the scientists would have had heart failure.

Two trips later and the equipment was aboard the Warden. The raft was safely secured aft of the tower where the well deck was. The two wagons looked abandoned on the shore, well above the water line. The three Aurochs stood, watching. Finally Bronwyn climbed off Rexalita's great head onto the deck where she stroked the creature's forehead. She waved goodbye and the Whale sunk below the waves, disappearing from sight.

The ship turned and slowly accelerated from the inlet toward the open ocean. The Dolphins easily kept pace and then swam into the ship's well deck, an area of the main deck directly behind the sail that was open to the sea, gradually deepening the farther aft one went. It allowed for boat launch and recovery protected from the open ocean. Bronwyn dangled her legs in the water as the Dolphins propped their bodies half out of the water, wedged onto the deck next to their favorite human.

Braden and Micah opened their neural implants. *'Where are we going, Holly?'*

*'Why don't you ask your new friend if she knows where the undersea city is?'* Holly suggested. Micah passed it to Bronwyn, who chose to ask the Dolphins instead of the Whale.

*'Yes, but they don't go there. It is very dangerous. They kill sea animals that stray too close.'* Bronwyn shivered. *'They say that there is an island very close to the undersea city, and they are willing to take us there, if you'd like.'*

"An island?" Braden wondered. He asked Holly, who searched the images for anything that might be the island in question. He explained his reasoning.

*'The undersea tractors that transported the people from White Beach have a limited speed. I've calculated a maximum arc based on that speed and the length of time the people could survive inside. Then I've cross-referenced all images and hello, here we are.*

*Due west of you, about two-hundred fifty kilometers offshore, is an island that I've not charted before. Not saying that it wasn't there, but it was low profile. We are now turning all sensors toward it and would you look at that!'* Holly paused as if Braden and Micah were supposed to actually be looking at something.

*'Holly, whatever you're looking at, we can't see it,'* Micah said in an exasperated tone.

*'Oh, that was one of my new human expressions. No, obviously you can't see it. I shall remove that phrase from my lexicon. What I'm looking at are low-level emissions coming from the island, the type that suggest there is some type of ancients' power source and equipment. There are numerous hot spots that indicate both human and animal inhabitants. I think your best course of action will be to visit the island first,'* Holly suggested.

"There's no doubt about that," Braden said out loud. "The island, Bronwyn. We would love it if Chlora and Rhodi can take us to the island. I think we'll find something there, maybe we'll even find what we're looking for."

Bronwyn started chatting with the Dolphins while the ship seemed to set itself on a course that Holly had already determined. Brandt stayed on deck, swaying gently as the ship rocked through the waves. A salty breeze drifted past as the other companions started exploring their new home.

Braden climbed the stairs to the top of the sail, the main superstructure above the water. It was roomy and comfortable. When he reached the bridge, he noted that it looked similar to the bridge on the RV Traveler, but to a greatly reduced scale, with positions for three people, but the glass bubble was the same and the workstations seemed to have a variety of Old Tech needed to drive the ship.

Braden sat in the captain's chair. It embraced him and rolled gently with the ocean swells. Ahead, the open ocean awaited.

# An Ocean Voyage

The first to get sick was Treetis, followed closely by Ferrer and Brigitte. Braden was amazed that a white Rabbit could look green, but they managed, and not just because they were tending to the garden deck that they said was already well cared for.

Then G-War fell under the spell of the wind and waves. He yowled like a lost kitten to express his misery of being at sea. Fea seemed unaffected and took the opportunity to highlight the weaker sex when it came to 'cats.

Brandt made a monumental effort not to throw up, but refused to eat and even stopped moving about the deck. He stood frozen in a half-crouch, as if trying to look like a statue, while he focused one hundred percent of his attention on not getting sick.

Bronwyn was completely indifferent to it, spending a great deal of time in the water with the Dolphins. Aadi stayed on the first deck. He floated above the fray, hanging onto a rope to keep from getting blown away. He watched the ocean calmly, although he much preferred the heat of the desert.

The Hawkoids spent time either flying or outside perched on one of the many railings. The swaying of the ship didn't bother them either.

The two scientists disappeared the second they came aboard. It appeared that the ship had a freight elevator that went up two levels into the sail and down five levels to the sections under the sea where the laboratory spaces were located.

Pik stood on deck, mesmerized by the sight of the ocean all around. He tried taking off his skin suit, but quickly discovered that despite the water, the sun and salt dangerously dried his skin, threatening his very life. He rehydrated his skin suit using one of the many available fresh water spigots, once Braden showed him how they worked.

Braden took advantage of the fabricator, but everything had a fishy taste to it. Whereas a fabricator on land used soy and a variety of other plants, the ship's fabricator must have used fish and sea life. Braden asked the fabricator about various fish dishes and he tried a little of each until he found one that tasted like something Mattie made. Even Micah liked it.

Holly informed them that they should arrive at the island in a mere twenty-six hours, by tomorrow evening. Braden asked Holly how long they'd been underway. He said four hours. Less than the length of an afternoon and already most of the companions were incapacitated. It felt like they'd been on board forever. With Holly's help and a three-dimensional map of the Warden, they found the docking area for the mini-submarines. Both ports were empty. Micah threw up her hands in frustration and kicked the bulkhead.

*'Holly, do you have any way of finding where the mini-submarines might be?'* Braden asked.

*'If they were transmitting, we would have already picked them up. I'll search the Warden's records and see if they documented their last trip.'*

"Let's find our room. The captain's quarters?" Braden wasn't dissuaded by the discovery that the mini-subs weren't on board. He had never expected them to be. He figured there would be a way, even if they lowered a communication device to the undersea facility so Holly could communicate with it, take it over like he did the RV Traveler.

"Don't look so down. If there's a power source on an island that Holly didn't know was there, what do you think that means?" Braden asked.

Micah brightened up. "The island is connected to the undersea facility."

"My thoughts exactly. We'll know tomorrow. In the interim, I suggest we find ways to avoid the pukers." Braden nodded suggestively and once in the captain's quarters, they couldn't get their clothes off fast enough. It was rare to have such time alone.

Braden woke early, having slept like a rock in the captain's oversized bed. He walked through the spaces of the ship alone, barefoot and bare-chested. His first stop was the galley, as it was named, for some fabricator-produced coffee. It didn't have that fish taste, as they'd ordered a broad range of food the previous daylight to clean out the system.

While Braden sipped his coffee, he checked on the others. Pik relaxed on the deck, not far from the King of the Aurochs, who appeared to be sleeping. Pik nodded as the human passed.

The 'cats had found their way to the garden deck, which took up the entire space just below the surface of the sea. It was a massive space that Braden took a while to work his way through. The 'cats, Rabbits, and Wolfoids found solace in each other's company as they slept close together, nearly in one big pile. Braden wished them well and hoped they awoke with their sea legs and could function. Fea raised her head and blinked her big green eyes at him, then nodded slightly. She had her two boys, G-War and Treetis, right where she could keep an eye on them.

*'Thank you for coming for us,'* she said softly in her thought voice.

*A 'cat with manners,* Braden thought. *'My pleasure and I'm happy that you joined us.'*

Braden continued below deck, where he found sterile corridors and laboratory spaces with great windows to the undersea world. It was dark outside so he could barely see anything except what ambient lighting showed. Small fish had taken a liking to the ship and darted in and out of the light in front of the window. Braden watched for a while, finding the motion of the fish to be peaceful, even hypnotizing.

He shook it off and continued into the bowels of the ship, noticing that the motion of the sea was much less down here. He found where the scientists had stayed, only because their clothes were clean and neatly piled outside their doors and the space was labeled, "Technical Staff Billeting."

"Of course, there is a Server Bot to take care of the absent-minded scientists," Braden said out loud to himself as he walked away, making no noise in his bare feet. The material on the deck was soft and non-slip. He enjoyed walking on it. He wondered if the ancients also walked barefoot. *Probably not,* Braden thought. *The ancients seemed to take everything for granted.*

Braden made it to the lowest deck, five levels below the sea. It was dark. A row of viewing cubicles with clear windows made up the sides of the level. There were mechanical systems down there that launched the scavengers to pick the materials used by the fabricator, Bots to clean the hull, and the empty bays where the mini-subs were located. One could dive into the water of those docking bays, and swim straight down to get outside the ship. Braden had no idea why the water didn't flood into the deck, and he refused to ask Holly. He didn't care how the ancients' technology worked. He simply accepted that it did.

That didn't mean he couldn't be amazed by it. He found the elevator and took it as high as it would go, to the second level in the sail. He climbed the three remaining flights of stairs so he could sit in the captain's chair as the sun rose behind the ship, lighting the endless ocean before them. He felt a quiver in his stomach as the immensity of it all momentarily overwhelmed him. He couldn't fathom the distances involved.

When they were on board the RV Traveler, he didn't feel like he was in space. It felt more foreign and vast on the Western Ocean as the ship ventured far from shore.

He heard the padding of feet behind and saw Micah, dressed in a bathrobe and also barefoot. He turned to get up, but she held him down, letting her robe drop.

"Again?" he asked hopefully. Micah nodded as she helped him out of his pants. They christened the captain's chair appropriately, expecting that the stodgy ancients would have been appalled.

A sunrise at sea was a magnificent affair as the waves radiated with the new dawn, sparkling far and wide below the rising orb. As it transitioned from a dark orange through yellow to a blinding white, the sea changed from black to a deep blue.

Braden no longer felt overwhelmed. Maybe Micah had sensed something from him and helped him past his anxieties and insecurities. She made him more aware of everything around them.

Such as, he had coffee and she did not. They went to the galley where they found three hungry 'cats. Braden ordered coffee for Micah, and they all waited until the familiar ding signaled the cup was ready. G-War's patience was wearing thin, which signaled that the seasickness was only temporary. Braden wondered why the 'cats had gotten up. They seemed to be sleeping so peacefully only a short time ago.

*'Really? You have no idea, do you? Now get us food,'* G-War demanded.

"I have just the thing. I found this yesterday. Mr. Fabricator, one salmon tartare, please." When Braden pulled the small plate from the fabricator, G-War's ears perked up. When the dish was on the floor, Treetis dove toward it, only to get slapped away by the Golden Warrior. Fea stepped between them, hissing at each, then casually settled in to eat her breakfast.

Braden ordered two more and the fabricator delivered. Treetis was standing, pawing at the door of the ancients' device. "That doesn't make it go any faster," Braden told the young 'cat. He hip-checked the orange creature out of the way so he could retrieve the two dishes and set them on the floor. G-War and Treetis dug in like the ravenous carnivores that they were.

*'Hungry,'* G-War told Braden after inhaling the first dish. Braden put the three dishes back into the fabricator, then ordered three more. Treetis pawed at the door again.

Braden turned to Micah, holding his hands up and shaking his head. "Did your mother drop you on your head too many times?" he asked the 'cat. "If you want to hunt, maybe the Dolphins can help you, but you might get wet." Treetis hesitated for a moment, then pawed afresh at the fabricator.

"Hungry," Micah said with a smile. G-War held up a furry paw, giving her the 'cat finger. Braden delivered the plates to the floor and ordered the human favorite, omelets with ham and cheese.

They tasted like omelets with fish and seaweed.

The Hawkoids snoozed on deck, perched on a railing. They'd had great luck catching fish that the ship seemed to readily attract. They shared a number with Pik, who reveled in the taste of the fresh catch. Pik had gone to the well deck to chat with the Dolphins. He enjoyed their company, considering them to be his wet brothers, even though they had nothing in common besides both being genetically engineered by the ancients.

Brandt was lying down, sleeping peacefully until Bounder poked him with his spear, chuckling as the Aurochs leapt forward, sliding on the deck. The King turned and appeared ready to charge, but Bounder surrendered.

*'Do you think you can eat, my big friend?'* the Wolfoid asked. Brandt thought it over, took a few steps, then nodded, waving his horns dangerously.

The two Wolfoids disappeared down the stairwell and returned with armloads of greens, followed by two Rabbits with more freshly picked from the garden. The King of the Aurochs ate tentatively, not wanting to devour the offerings in two gulps.

Bounder and Gray Strider joined the others in the galley, where Braden worked the fabricator while Micah retired to her quarters to get dressed.

Bronwyn finally made it to the galley, looking shriveled from having spent so much time in the water. She wore a broad smile, happy to be with all her friends, both old and new. She greeted each warmly and hugged them tightly, even the 'cats, who tolerated her doing so. Even Micah didn't enjoy such a privilege.

Braden wondered where Aadi had gone. "Aadi?" he shouted through the hatch to the outdoors. An outside deck circled this level, so Braden stepped through and looked around. He saw Aadi at the very back of the deck at sea level, trying to walk forward. Braden ran, taking the steps down three at a time, hitting the deck hard and racing to his old friend's side.

"What's wrong, Aadi?" Braden asked, concerned for the Tortoid, believing that there was something amiss as part of the pregnancy.

*'I'm afraid that the ship is moving faster than I can swim. Get behind me and I'll show you. Be ready now,'* the Tortoid said mysteriously. When Braden stood at the edge of the deck, the ocean close behind him, Aadi floated upward and was instantly swept into Braden, nearly knocking him down. One leg went into the sea as the human pushed Aadi forward and crawled back aboard.

"I see," Braden said. He jogged back into the sail, dripping from his wet pant leg, and returned with a short length of rope. Aadi held it in his beaklike mouth as Braden pulled him back toward the sail where they could secure the Tortoid inside, make sure he didn't float away. The ocean was a big place.

They made their way up the stairs to the galley where Bronwyn tapped his shell. *There was nothing to worry about. Rexalita is with us. She would have saved you and brought you back to us,'* the girl told them all over the mindlink while she enjoyed her omelet. Braden was surprised that she didn't question the taste.

With the companions together and chatting, Braden opened his neural implant to check in with Holly.

*'Good morning, Master Braden!'* the AI said cheerfully. *'I am following your progress closely. Current projections show that you won't arrive until tomorrow. I am re-routing you to the south to avoid a nasty storm that seems to be brewing. You will miss the weather, but the seas could get rough.'*

*'I won't share that part with the others. It seems they've only just recovered from the pukes that equally affect both the strong and the weak,'* Braden replied. *'We think that the island and the undersea facility must be connected. Is there any way you can confirm that? Find us a way in that doesn't requires the mini-submarines?'* Braden stood at the railing, watching the undulating ocean. He understood why Caleb kept going back to sea, even though his people were doing most of the fishing while he managed the trade and the village. The sea called people to it, so they would know how small they were in comparison, and then learn how to work with it, but never dominate it.

*'That is a most logical conclusion, Master Braden. I have redirected available sensor systems. At this time, I don't have any additional information, but we won't have all the data until later today. Before you arrive, I will have everything I'm going to get and will share it before you go ashore,'* Holly stated.

*'Thanks, Holly. No surprises please.'* Braden closed the link, certain that Holly kept information from them until they had no choice but to continue. Braden wondered if there would be Androids.

He hated Androids.

G-War also hated them because he couldn't sense them. Pik said he harbored no ill will toward the biomechanical creations, but Braden doubted his sincerity. Micah was merciless when it came to Androids, despite Holly's protests.

*'Why are you thinking about Androids?'* Micah asked over the mindlink. He wondered where she was. *'Our room, I'll be out in just a couple heartbeats.'*

*'It just feels like the work of Androids,'* he told her.

*'We have our blasters. If we see an Android, we kill it first, no matter what. Holly will want to have a conversation, but I'm not good with that. We kill it and all of its Android buddies except for one which we'll turn over to Holly, then we go find my father.'*

*'Sounds like you've already thought about this. What if they have Security Bots with them?'* Braden asked.

*'Then we use Holly's devices to finish them off,'* she declared. *'So, we won't get there until after tomorrow's sunrise. I'm looking forward to another night in that bed,'* she told him, sharing an image of naked, sweating skin.

*'I don't know what's happened to you, but I like it!'* Braden exclaimed. *'Maybe we should make trips on the Warden a regular thing. Next time I talk with Holly, we'll see what we can arrange. We need a harbor closer to New Sanctuary, though. Yes, I think a survey of the areas in the south are in order!'*

"Once we have my father in hand, then we'll take a look at what's next," she said aloud, startling him. Her mood darkened, but only for an instant. "I like the motion of the ship, the sound of the sea slapping against the hull. There's something magical about it all, reminds me of growing up. My father was always there, ready to go to sea, he said for fishing, but I suspected it was more than that. Much more. He loves the ocean."

"We'll get him back. We're on our way to the ends of Vii for him, and we'll go farther if we have to. Whatever it takes, because I want to take you to sea on a vacation where there's nothing to worry about except what we're going to eat next!" Braden hugged his partner tightly, enjoying the smell of her hair, the curve of her neck. He liked how the sea drew him in, too.

# The Storm

Clouds darkened the daytime sky and despite the ship's increasing speed, the storm was faster. It circled the ship and as the evening dark approached, the sea started to rage. Braden wasn't sure what to do. Micah had been through storms at sea, but they had no control over the ship. Micah contacted Holly.

*The ship has survived over four-hundred years of storms at sea without a scratch. It will be fine, but you, on the other hand, I suggest you find someplace to strap yourselves in. It could get rough. I suggest the garden deck or one deck lower. If you've put anything out, I suggest you tie it down. Good luck!'* Holly signed off before Micah could ask any more questions.

*'We need everybody down below. Brandt, I'm sorry, but we're going to have to tie you down up here so you aren't swept overboard.'* While Micah and Pik positioned Brandt next to the sail and started running ropes and straps, conveniently provided by a Maintenance Bot, around his body, Braden went below to find the scientists. He yelled at them to secure their gear, which they had just finished unpacking and set up. They started to argue, but he waved them off and told them when the equipment was destroyed, they weren't going back for more. Then he stormed off, trying to slam the door on his way out, but ancient technology wouldn't allow such a demonstration.

He bounded up the steps, past the garden deck where the Rabbits hopped to and fro, securing both plants and equipment.

"Less than two nights. We've been here for less than two nights. How much stuff do we have?" Braden yelled at the bulkhead as he kept running, holding the railing as the ship started to gyrate unpredictably. Brandt was strapped in and miserable. Pik took a position next to the great King and stood, holding a hand grip on the bulkhead, the other wrapped around one of Brandt's straps.

*'The girl,'* Pik told Braden without elaboration. The whitecaps of the waves rose high above the deck, crashing across at irregular intervals. Brandt stood tall to keep his head above water, while Pik remained stalwart, unmoving as he was pounded by the ocean. Braden went hand over hand along a railing that led to the well deck, where he found Bronwyn hanging on to the Dolphins as they fought to keep her head above the water.

Braden dove in and breast-stroked hard to get to Chlora and Rhodi. He gripped a dorsal fin and tried to talk, but the waves kept overwhelming him. The Dolphins kept swimming just to stay somewhat within the confines of the well, which was now a full body length under the water.

"We have to go inside!" Braden finally managed to yell. Bronwyn shook her head, eyes wide in terror.

*'Can you get us close to the hatch? We can hold on there until the ship heaves out of the water, then we can get inside,'* Braden asked the Dolphins, finally remembering to use his thought voice.

*'We can and we must. We have to get into the open ocean if we are to survive, get to a place where we can dive below the fury of the waves. Listen, little one. You must go inside,'* Chlora pleaded. The Dolphins powered forward, dragging the two humans along a surging wave, riding high, then diving into a trough, only to be overwhelmed by the next massive wave. The Dolphins raced downhill, building enough momentum to fly up the next swell where they bounced off the railing of the sail's second deck. Braden threw himself over, bracing himself behind the railing while he held on to Bronwyn with his other hand. As the wave continued past, the Dolphins disappeared into the darkness.

Bronwyn reached futilely into the space where her friends had been before turning and letting Braden pull her onto the deck next to him. They waited for two more waves to pass before they opened the hatch and jumped inside. Bronwyn shivered as they slowly made their way down the steps, bouncing into the bulkhead as they descended. They stopped often as the steps turned from a climb to a dangerous fall and back to a level walk. The ship twisted and jerked violently.

The crashing of the waves. The anger with which the ship was tossed. And yet, it was quiet inside. The ship rode the turbulence, became one with the motion. In the case of the Warden, it appeared that the ancients had worked with nature and not against it. The ship was built to ride out the storm, not to bully it or bend its will to that of the ancients. It didn't need to power through the raging sea, only wait until calm returned. Then it would continue on its way.

Braden and Bronwyn finally made it to the deck below the garden level where the mass of companions huddled in one room that looked to be specifically built as a place to weather the storm. It was well padded, without hard furniture, and with plenty of handholds and places in which a person could wedge him or herself. The 'cats were clinging to one piece of furniture that would probably have to be replaced. Their claws had dug deeply as their bodies were yanked back and forth, although the motions there were nowhere near what they were on the second level where Braden and Bronwyn had just been.

Brandt suffered mightily. He was thrown hard one way, then the other. The straps and ropes cut into his hide. He couldn't maintain his balance. He puked green mash, again and again until only bile came up. He felt weak as a kitten. Pik Ha'ar never wavered. He stood tall against the storm, seemingly immune to the deck's constant motion. Brandt focused on the Lizard Man, taking strength from his nearness. The companions shared their support over the mindlink while they were bounced around within the padded room.

Braden couldn't stop thinking about the Aurochs on deck, or the Lizard Man. As he and Micah held each other, he had an overwhelming urge to check topside, but Micah wouldn't let him. She was right. There was nothing he could do up there except be swept overboard. Aadi remained inside on the first level, keeping himself centered so he had the smoothest ride of all.

At least they had light. On the deck, darkness seemed to surround Brandt and Pik, press in on them despite the deck lights having been turned on, blazing into the storm.

The sea continued to rage well into the night.

No one realized when the storm had passed as they'd fallen asleep.

Braden woke first, as usual, while the others were passed out from exhaustion. Braden's first steps were stiff and sore, his body abused from fighting with the ship against the raging sea. He left the room and jogged through the corridor, quickly climbing the steps past the garden level to the main deck.

The King of the Aurochs was on his side, soaked through and through. Braden's breath caught, until he saw the chest slowly rise and fall. Trying not to disturb the great King, Braden unlashed him, loosening the bonds and wincing at the raw flesh beneath, already white around the edges from constant exposure to the salt water.

Pike Ha'ar was leaning against the bull's leg, sound asleep, skin pale from starting to dry out. Braden ran into the sail and up to the third level above the deck where the captain's quarters were located. He recovered his pouch of numbweed, noting that the quarters had already been straightened and cleaned.

When he returned, Pik was up and stripping off his skin suit. There was an on-deck shower that Braden guessed was to rinse a person who had gone swimming in the ocean. Pik turned on the water, adjusted the temperature as Braden had shown him, and stood beneath the spray, turning slowly to let the fresh water bring the joy of the rainforest to him.

Braden started rubbing numbweed into the King's wounds, taking care to do the worst ones first. Micah and Bronwyn appeared, and joined Braden in taking care of the Aurochs. Brandt's eyes fluttered open, the whites bloodshot. He tried to focus, but found it difficult.

*'My friends,'* he said softly. *'I don't think I've ever been so tired in my entire life.'*

Bronwyn put her hands on his head, helping to relieve some of his pain. It wasn't as great as they thought for he was mostly bone weary. Even though Holly told them that they'd arrive at the island that morning, Braden and Micah agreed that they needed to recover from the storm. The King needed time to recover. Pik looked ready to go, even though he continued to stand in the shower's spray, letting its healing waters run over his body.

*'I feel better already,'* Brandt told them as he struggled to stand.

"Food?" Braden asked. The King nodded with a snort.

*'As much as you can carry, my friends!'* he said, his thought voice rising in volume. Braden slapped the great creature on his uninjured shoulder.

"Your will shall be done, my King! By the way, you know that when you get wet, you smell really bad?" Braden added.

*'The cows love the smell of a wet bull, my friend. You should rub some on yourself and see the change in those around you,'* Brandt replied without hesitation. Micah coughed and covered her mouth with a fist, shaking her head vigorously at her partner.

With a final slap, Braden and Micah went to the garden level where they met the Rabbits, who were unwilling to share as much food as the King required. They reluctantly parted with all the injured plants and about a third of the vegetables, but no more. Once they carried that upstairs and turned it over to Brandt, Braden went the galley, where he ordered a couple different vegetable dishes.

It turned out that the King of the Aurochs liked the meals from the fabricator, so Braden and Micah took turns ordering food. They wondered if they could shortcut the system and get a mass of edible sea plants directly.

# The Evil Ones

The remainder of the companions made an appearance, leaving the padded recreation room behind to enjoy the calm of the morning sun.

The Hawkoids took to the air as soon as they were outside, flying high into the air, circling the ship, and floating on the ocean breeze.

The 'cats wanted nothing to do with the wet deck or the ocean. They suggested that if Braden and Micah ever tried getting on board a ship again, they would die mysteriously in their sleep before they could take one step away from shore.

Aadi slowly made his way up the stairwell, deciding to stay indoors so he wasn't left behind as the ship sailed ahead. The Wolfoids walked onto the deck, stretching and smiling into the sunshine.

*'I hope you don't take this the wrong way,'* Strider said in her thought voice, *'but you have dragged us on some of the craziest adventures. There we were, in our village, roast pork almost every night. Nothing out of the ordinary ever happened, then all of a sudden, here comes the humans and since then, one adventure after another, each trying to kill us in a different way. Next time you go to sea, it's okay if you don't tell us about it,'* she chided.

"Come on, Strider! You wouldn't have it any other way. If we went without you, next thing we know, we'd be the ones getting chased at the next blooding of the pups. And if anything happened to us, you'd feel bad and you know it," Braden told them as he took the time to scratch behind her ears, hugging her neck in the Wolfoids' sign of affection.

She nuzzled him back, squinting into the sun.

*'How long until we get there,'* Bounder asked. Braden shook his head as he opened the neural implant.

'So good to hear from you, Master Braden! I trust all is well?' Holly's good cheer was always expected.

'We're fine, no one went overboard, despite the Western Ocean's best attempts. All here, all alive, all is well. How long to the island, Holly?'

'You were pushed off course, so you should arrive later this afternoon. I promised the latest information and here's what I have. Nothing. We don't know if there is a direct link to the undersea facility or not. We believe that there are twenty people and hundreds of animals. I can't tell you if the animals are intelligent or not.'

'That's more than we had, Holly. We'll take care of things. Let us know if you find anything else.' Braden minimized his window without closing it, which allowed Holly to contact him at any time. He had grown used to having the small window at the periphery of his vision.

"This afternoon, according to Holly," Braden stated, loud enough for all to hear, all except the scientists. He didn't know if they would ever see them topside or anywhere else for that matter. The laboratory levels were completely self-contained with a fabricator, rooms, and facilities.

The plan for the day was to rest and do nothing. There was some excitement when Rexalita arrived and made a celebratory circle around the ship. She swam alongside as she was far too large for the well deck and the Warden's stern extended much farther behind the ship than anyone realized. Bronwyn took a full run off the deck and jumped into the ocean, dog-paddling until the Whale eased the girl onto her head, then lifted her skyward as she used her powerful tail to propel her forward. The ship picked up speed as if it seemed to know that the Whale wanted to race.

Bronwyn howled and pumped her fist from atop the Whale while those on deck leaned into the wind as the ship accelerated. They cheered as they encouraged the Warden, but the ship was no match for the largest creature on Vii. The Whale surged ahead, leaving foam and the Warden far behind.

The ship slowed as it conceded the race. It assumed a leisurely pace northeast toward the island where Braden and Micah hoped to find answers regarding the disappearance of her father and all the villagers from White Beach.

The Dolphins appeared in the water between the Whale and the ship, returning with a splash by leaping and dancing on their tails. The Whale dipped into the sea, turning Bronwyn loose to join her small friends. As she swam, two new fins appeared in the water, black, cutting the water as they headed directly for Bronwyn. The sea dance stopped, and the Dolphins shot like arrows toward the girl.

Rexalita vaulted nearly completely out of the water, crashing back in and sending a tidal wave with Bronwyn surging away from the new fins. The Dolphins came in from behind and leapt over her head, landing in the water between her and the newcomers. The fins split up, two became four and Bronwyn screamed.

The Dolphins abandoned their blocking maneuver, turning to swim forward, catching the girl as they sped toward the Warden. The fins lined up as they pursued. The entire ocean to the side of the Dolphins seemed to rise up as Rexalita broke the surface again, opening her mouth, sharp teeth sweeping under and over Chlora, Rhodi, and Bronwyn.

The Dolphins swam out the other side of the Whale's open maw. Then she clamped down, trapping the sharks. Three of them disappeared into that huge gullet, while the fourth made a sharp turn, swimming away from the Dolphins and the young girl. They continued to the ship and around aft, swimming smartly into the well deck and depositing Bronwyn where she could easily climb from the water.

*'We are so sorry, little one! We didn't see the evil ones until it was too late,'* Rhodi apologized.

*'There's nothing to be sorry for,'* Bronwyn said happily as she jumped back into the water to hug the snouts of her two friends. *'You saved me from them, and you, too, Rexalita. You were all magnificent!'*

Micah hugged Braden as they watched and listened. They always had friends with them, friends willing to fight to keep them safe, just like they'd done, so many times.

Pik appeared next to them carrying his skin suit. He pointed to them and to his own chest. Since Pik was a clone, the terrible wounds he'd suffered fighting the Androids weren't there. *'I died for Aadi, just like I would have for any of you. And I'd do it again, too,'* Pik said matter-of-factly.

Braden choked up, not knowing what to say.

G-War interrupted their thoughts by projecting an image of Treetis pawing at the fabricator and yowling.

# All Ashore Who's Going Ashore

The rest of the daylight was spent resting, eating, recovering, and preparing for the unknown. Holly had no additional information once the weather passed, even though he could see the island clearly through available sensors. He'd engaged the survivors from Cygnus VI to provide a human touch and still nothing new.

*'I think every place we've ever gone into, we had to rely on what we had with us. This time, there are sixteen of us, including three Hawkoids and three 'cats! There is no one better to show us what waits beyond the next tree, over the next hill. Don't worry, Holly, we'll be ready,'* Braden said as he touched up his blasters, cleaning them, checking their charges, ensuring that they rested easily at his hip. Micah was doing the same thing. They were anxious, although they wouldn't go ashore until the new daylight.

Skirill, Zyena, and Zeeka spotted the island first. Braden had anticipated something the size of New Sanctuary, but it was much larger than that. A central peak dominated the landscape. The emerald green of the foliage stood in pleasant contrast to the blue of the sea. The cover was near complete and the Hawkoids were challenged to see anything beneath the leaves and vines. Beach sand outlined the entire island, except for one point in the south where a rocky outcropping cut into the sea. One tree stood alone at its end, a rebel taunting the open ocean.

*'Don't get too close. You remember what happened when that Security Bot took a shot at you from New Sanctuary! Nothing like the smell of scorched tail feathers to wake you up,'* Braden told the Hawkoids.

*'You never told me that you fought a Security Bot,'* Zyena accused Skirill.

*'It was nothing, my love,'* he answered bravely.

Braden and Micah laughed. Skirill had run like a rat on fire as soon as the Security Bot sent its laser beams skyward. Even G-War was impressed by Skirill's changed history, so much so that he shared an image of the Hawkoid diving for cover, smoke trailing behind him.

Zyena flew close to her mate and cooed soothingly to him. The 'cat was miffed by his failed attempt to poke fun at his friend. Fea had a good laugh at G-War's expense.

"We'll call this one a win for you, Ess!" Braden announced as the Hawkoids finished their stand-off tour of the island. Skirill led the way as they returned, in a mini V formation, flying as if on a mission. They flared as one, landing on the railing together, then turned around to face the ocean.

"Did you see room between the trees where Brandt can walk?" Braden asked.

*'Yesss,'* Zyena replied, thinking as she talked. *There was room. The trees are tall and have wide branches, but they aren't too close together, not like the rainforest. There is room for all of us.'*

"Bronwyn, do the Dolphins think we can take the ship close enough to walk ashore?" he followed his original question as all the companions stood on deck. Even Aadi had come outside as the ship slowed. He still held onto a rope tied fast to the sail, just in case.

*'Chlora and Rhodi will let us know. They are going to swim around the island and take a look. Rexalita will also try some of the approaches. I'd go with them, but they are going to check it out from under the water, maybe share what they can of the undersea city, but they don't want to be seen,'* Bronwyn informed them as she watched the Dolphins swim out of the well deck and away.

Braden looked up at the massive superstructure of the ancients' ship. If anyone on the island had been looking, the ship would have already been spotted. It cut an imposing figure against the blue sky.

The ship's presence was no surprise, but what they brought ashore would be, because they were coming in force, ready to fight. If a Security Bot guarded the island, then they had Holly's gear to hopefully stop it. Braden looked at the clunky objects the AI had given them, two spear guns and one heavy block of technology, and shook his head. Holly wanted them to go to war carrying a brick. And Braden would carry it, too. He wasn't afraid of much, but the apparent invincibility of a Security Bot concerned him greatly.

"Why are you fixated on Security Bots?" Micah asked. "I didn't get the impression they were there, only that there was a remote chance. Holly didn't even talk about them until you asked. Don't you think he'd see them using one of his sensors? Sure, we'll carry that equipment, but I don't think we'll have to fight anyone. I think that the people he saw are our people, abandoned on the island and forgotten. Let's collect them and leave." Micah was confident in her assessment as she fiddled with her equipment, waiting for the Dolphins and the Whale to return.

Aadi swam slowly through the hatch and joined Braden and Micah on deck. Now that the ship wasn't moving, the Tortoid didn't have to worry about getting blown overboard.

"What are you thinking, old man?" Braden said kindly, but the words still earned him an elbow in the ribs from Micah.

*'What is your plan, Master Braden?'* Aadi asked.

"We go ashore, find who lives there, talk to them and get more information. We don't know anything. There are signals from that place which Holly says indicates a presence of someone using ancients technology. Outside of that, twenty people, hundreds of animals, and those animals could be intelligent. What we don't know far outweighs what we do know. Our goal is information, then we make a plan."

*'An intelligent goal.'* Aadi blinked slowly as he waited. Braden didn't know what else to say since he didn't really have a plan. *'We shall deal with whatever we come across, assuming that we are not in a hurry.'*

Micah looked up sharply. "My father may be there and if he's not, then someone will know where he is. We can't delay any longer!" she said passionately.

"Aadi, what would we do without you?" Braden asked with a bow. "We have to go slowly, look around, be careful we don't get ourselves into something we can't get out of." He looked pointedly at Micah before continuing.

"We have to be patient, lover," Braden insisted. "We'll find Caleb, in due time. That's what we're here for, so let's get it right from the start. We don't need to burn down the entire jungle on this island. Who knows? This could be another long lost colony and they found the cure for stretch marks!"

Micah launched herself at Braden and tackled him. Lying on the deck, she straddled him and pulled his face close to hers. "What are you trying to say?" she whispered.

"I'm saying that I'm the luckiest man alive and that we have to take our time on the island. That's all. Please don't beat me up," he said with a smile, sticking his tongue out at her. The rest of the companions watched, hoping for a throw-down similar to the great battle of wills between Caleb and Mattie. They were disappointed when Braden surrendered so quickly.

Micah helped Braden up and they went from one companion to the next. Pik was armed with his spear and wore his skin suit. The Wolfoids carried their lightning spears, while the Rabbits had their small laser pistols on their belts.

Braden was always taken by the absurdity of a Rabbit with a weapon, but he'd seen them in action and when defending their loved ones, they were merciless. He'd talked with them and asked if they would protect Bronwyn. Braden once again built his plan based on Bronwyn's ability to talk with all creatures. She needed to talk with the animals that they encountered. He was using the girl again, but she was old enough at fourteen to make her own decisions. She was on the road by herself, but not by herself as she'd always had the Queen by her side and Zeeka, the Hawkoid.

*'Hey, G, why didn't a Hillcat bond with Bronwyn?'* Braden asked over the mindlink, as he couldn't see where the 'cats were hiding.

*'It's the opposite. All the 'cats wanted to bond with her. She told them unless they could work it out, she wouldn't accept any of them. So, they're still working it out,'* Fealona interjected. *'While here, I will stay be her side. I can't trust this cretin.'*

Braden suspected that she pointed to Treetis. G-War had saved Braden's life too many times to count. Braden trusted G-War to protect them all, with his life if needed.

*'Thanks, Fea. That means a lot to us. We'll be going slowly, so any insight you get, anything you see, please tell us. All surprises are bad, until we know otherwise,'* Braden replied over the mindlink.

"I get it. We go slowly. You lead, I'll be right behind you," Micah murmured. Her chest hurt because her heart threatened to pound through it. She could feel her father close by. She didn't know if it was real or not, but sitting here next to the island was taking its toll on her patience.

With a splash, the two Dolphins frolicked their way up the well deck, stopping when they reached its end. They danced out of the water, bobbing their heads and chittering as they talked with Bronwyn. No one else could hear them as they directed their thoughts to the girl alone.

Once finished 'talking,' they departed with graceful backflips into the water, and a race back to the open sea. Rexalita's massive head rose slowly from the ocean behind them. Bronwyn ran next to the well deck until she reached the point furthest aft, where she extended a hand toward the Whale, who was still too far away.

Braden ran after her to make sure she didn't jump into the ocean.

*'This ship can park next to the rocky point. The deck will be almost on the shore,'* Rexalita's loud voice resonated within their heads. *'I will show you.'*

Braden opened his neural implant. *'Holly! Follow that Whale!'* he called, cutting off Holly before his usual joyous greeting.

*'Yes, Master Braden, I see where she is taking us. Once we clear this reef, I'll get a better view with the sonar. Wait one moment,'* Holly advised.

*'Holly, half the time, I have no idea what you're saying, but I expect it means something.'* Braden chased Bronwyn as she ran for forward to stand on what passed for a prow on the Warden. It was barely higher than the round deck that encircled the sail, but it had a small railing that they could hang onto. Bronwyn waved as the Whale's tail rhythmically stroked the water,

propelling the great beast forward and around the island to the rocky outcropping, where she swam aside the wall of stone, nearly to the white sand beach, then turned and swam back out. She waited patiently for the Warden to pass as Holly expertly guided it into the protected cove.

*'This is almost perfect. It looks like we'll be able to anchor the ship within a few meters of the shore. Brandt will be able to wade through the water to get to the beach. The rest of you will have no problem,'* Holly said, quite pleased with himself.

*'Once we go ashore, I'll need you to take the ship back to sea. I doubt our scientists will be able to defend it should someone not us want to get on board,'* Braden advised.

*'You are right, Master Braden, that it will be best to take the ship back to sea. I will do that. Simply call me and I'll bring the ship back to the beach as soon as possible,'* Holly said, waiting for a reply. Braden was satisfied and without answering, closed his neural implant.

"Even you, Brandt! Holly says if you jump off the deck, you'll be in shallow water and then can wade ashore. That's our plan, anyway."

*'Did you forget about us?'* G-War added. Bounder chuckled.

"Where are you?" Braden asked as the ship maneuvered into position beside the rocky point and the beach.

*'And your keen eyes are going to keep us all out of danger?'* the 'cat answered sarcastically. Braden looked around until he spotted the three 'cats looking through the railing from the deck above.

"Just get down here. We're ready to go. I thought we might wait until the dawn but since we can walk ashore, we'll see what we can see now and return to the ship by nightfall," Braden told them all. The 'cats meandered along the walkway above and disappeared into the galley. They soon arrived on the main deck where they joined the others.

"G, you, Pik, and I take the lead, Micah and Aadi behind us, and Ferrer, Brigitte, Bronwyn and Fea behind them. Bounder to the left of us and Strider to the right. Bringing up the rear, Brandt, I want you and Treetis to make sure no one gets behind us. Skirill, Zyena, and Zeeka, we'll need you flying overhead, in front and to the sides, but don't get too close. We don't want to alarm the natives." Braden looked from one face to another, happy that no one had been seasick for a while.

Treetis vaulted to the King's face and ran to the top of his head, where he perched proudly. Aadi hovered closer to the deck so both G-War and Fea could climb onto his shell. He rose into the air and started swimming across the deck and over the water. Pik jumped into the ocean without hesitation, going completely underwater before bobbing back to the surface. He swam ashore with a few quick strokes.

Both the Wolfoids jumped in and dog-paddled the short distance to the shore.

The Hawkoids continued to circle back and forth over the beach, ready to give warning should any of the local fauna appear.

The Rabbits looked at Braden and Micah. "Don't tell me. You can't swim?" Braden asked. They both nodded, their noses twitching. The humans looked at each other as Bronwyn dove into the water and swam easily until she could stand, then she walked ashore. The 'cats jumped from Aadi's shell as they arrived, and they stood to either side of Bronwyn, looking warily into the trees.

Braden and Micah sat on the edge of the deck, their feet dangling in the water. "Come on, you two. Climb up here and let's go see what this island has to offer."

Ferrer and Brigitte both squealed as they climbed onto the humans' backs, sharing space with backpacks and other gear. Braden grunted. Micah gasped. The Rabbits were as heavy as a human twice their size.

"You have to get off. We'll sink to the bottom." Braden opened his neural implant.

*'Are you seeing this, Holly? How do we get the Rabbits ashore?'*

*'I didn't want to say that I was amused by the transition from ship to shore, but there are life vests in the cabinet in the sail on the main deck.'* Braden got to his feet and went inside to find the flotation devices.

*'Holly, you mean to tell me that Bronwyn and I were out here in the storm, and these things were right here?'* Braden was angry.

*'It was all contained in the safety briefing that I sent you while you were on your way from New Sanctuary,'* Holly countered.

*'You sent me so many files I couldn't even see them all, let alone read them. You know I didn't read them!'* Braden shook his head and took the life vests outside to the Rabbits. He also gave them a flotation ring that they could hold onto, just in case.

Brandt stood by, in no hurry to jump into the water. He wrestled with the fear that started to grip him. Bronwyn stood on the shore, calling him to her. Chlora and Rhodi showed up and skimmed across the surf, scraping their bellies on the sand as they smacked their tails to escape the shallows of the shore. They were enjoying themselves, but they were also there to help.

Brandt pawed the deck, then started running. He leapt from the edge of the ship and cleared half the distance to the shore in one great bound. When he hit the water, he came down hard, sinking up to his knees in the soft sand. As he dipped, a mini tidal wave surged over him, peeling Treetis from his head.

When the water settled, it wasn't even shoulder high, so Brandt strolled boldly ashore, while the young orange 'cat swam through the surf until he reached the beach. Fea and G-War stopped their tree watching to see their adopted son overcome adversity. He shook when he made it to the dry sand, but that didn't help. The saltwater made his skin itch, so he rolled in the sand. G-War shook his head and turned back to the trees. *'Really? We had to pick this one out of all those who came south with us? The 'cat nation is doomed,'* G-War said with a forlorn tone in his thought voice.

Braden and Micah jumped in and found that they had to tread water as they called the Rabbits to them. They stood with their ears drooped, arguing back and forth. Finally, Ferrer stepped to the deck's edge and hugging the ring closely to him, he jumped. He hit the water with a smack, sending a shower over the two humans, but he didn't sink past his neck. Micah grabbed his life vest and swam toward shore. Brigitte followed and soon the companions were on the beach and none the worse for wear.

# The Island

As Braden had directed, each assumed their position while Skirill flew under the branches and through the trees ahead. He zigzagged with the hard flying that tight spaces demand. By the tree trunks, there were broad lanes of sand that gave way to dirt and grasses. Brandt had far more room than he needed. Skirill gave up trying to fly near the top of the canopy and flew close to the ground where he could clearly see the way ahead.

Zeeka flew near the companions, perching on branches here and there where she could see to the sides of the group as they moved ahead. Zyena flew overhead, high above the jungle.

Braden kept looking down at G-War, who walked casually, cocking an ear every now and then. He suddenly stopped and crouched, pointing into the trees to their front and left. *'A group comes, animals and humans.'*

Braden waved everyone to a stop. They crouched. The Rabbits held their laser pistols at the ready as they pressed in on both sides of the teenage girl. Fealona stood in front of them, hackles up, snarling.

The Wolfoids pointed their spears toward the trees. Zeeka took off and flew that way, but Braden yelled at her to come back. She promptly climbed into the branches, taking a position over Bounder's head.

Bronwyn twisted her face as she looked confused. Micah went to her.

"What's wrong? What do you hear?" she asked.

"It's jumbled. They are all talking at the same time and none of it makes sense," she said out loud, trying to clear her head of the noise from the approaching strangers.

Braden had never imagined what he saw as the group stepped into the open. There were a dozen beings, some animal, some human, all misshapen. From extra legs to missing legs, from slanted heads to claws for hands. They all carried weapons of some sort, mostly sharpened sticks, the rest clubs. One creature, a three-legged Wolfoid-looking beast, simply carried a big stick in its mouth.

"Hold!" Braden called in his best Free Trader voice, raising his empty hand, palm outward.

"It talk like the Professor, it do. Should we eat it?" one creature, as big as a horse, but with swollen hands for feet and a human face atop the long and thick neck, asked while twisting its head back and forth.

"We don't eat the Professor, but we eat the beasties!" another creature said, looking like a man, but with arms like octopus tentacles. It thrashed its arms, hitting another one of its group with the club it clutched.

"Watch, Bongo, knucklehead!" the other wailed, dropping his spear. He sat on the ground and started to cry. Bronwyn tried to run to him, but Micah held her back.

The man with the octopus arms started stroking the other's head.

"Take us to the Professor, please. We wish to speak with him. And put those ridiculous weapons down before somebody else gets hurt," Braden told them.

"No, you!" another said angrily, thrusting his spear awkwardly. "NO!"

The creature next to the spear wielding man looked like a boar with a man's head, tusks making his spoken words unintelligible, but he made his point by taking the spear away from the other and throwing it on the ground. He nodded to Braden emphatically.

Braden looked at Micah and slowly shook his head, rolling his eyes. Micah shrugged. She walked toward the group, holding Bronwyn's hand. Her other held her blaster. Braden raised his weapon casually, not wanting to alarm the misfit band.

Bronwyn walked first to those crying and touched them on the head. "There's no need to be sad. We're your friends," she said, gently and warmly. The Rabbits stood close by and seemed to be readily accepted by the other creatures, not even earning a second look. The humans took all their attention.

"You hold!" the man-horse creature said. "We hurt it, eat it," he threatened. Brandt snorted and pawed the sand. They ignored him, too, even though he towered over them.

The girl looked at the man-horse with raised eyebrows. Micah followed closely as Bronwyn approached the creature. He raised his head and loudly snapped his jaws shut.

"Now, now," Bronwyn started, "those look like they hurt you a great deal. Let me help." She pointed to his feet. He let her touch his shoulder, then sighed as the pain seemed to fade from his body. He sat, looking like a great dog, and then he rolled to his side. Bronwyn took a knee and scratched his belly. Micah gave her a handful of numbweed for his feet. She applied it and wished him well, then she walked from one to the next of the misshapen creatures.

"How have you come to be here?" Braden asked. They didn't know— they shrugged or shook their heads, each looking adoringly at the girl.

Micah kneeled next to the man-horse creature. "Can you take us to the Professor? We'd like to meet her or him," she said in a low voice, calmly, while stroking his neck.

He looked to Bronwyn for guidance. "Yes, please. Take us to the Professor," the girl said, nodding to Micah. The man-horse stood, testing his pain-free feet, and waved to the others.

The creatures gathered into a group surrounding Micah and Bronwyn, their weapons forgotten on the ground as they pointed the way into the woods and started limping, stumbling, and shuffling away. Braden and the others followed, still spread out, suspecting a trap, but certain that if there was one, it would not have been set by the group they followed.

The Wolfoids stayed to the sides, while the Hawkoids took turns flying ahead, then finding places in the branches where they could watch the odd procession.

Braden, G-War, Aadi, and Pik stayed close to the group, confused. Braden opened his neural implant. *'Any ideas, Holly?'* he asked after explaining what the greeting party looked and acted like.

*'I don't know, but suspect human interference. Natural evolution does not make such changes to a body. I think you'll find the Professor is a scientist, and not a very good one, judging by what I'm seeing,'* Holly replied.

Braden didn't have a follow-up question, so he closed the link with the AI. *'Anything, G?'* he asked the 'cat.

*'This bunch is more dangerous to themselves than us. I sense some tasty creatures not far,'* the 'cat suggested hopefully.

*'Not yet, my friend, but soon. We'll make a quick stop to see this Professor, then we'll return to the ship, come back in the morning and talk more after we've had time to think about it all.'*

*'I'm not sure what there is to think about. We're stuck on an island with a pack of idiots.'* G-War closed their mindlink emphatically as he looked forlornly into the brush, hoping for a chance to hunt fresh game.

# The Professor

*'I see a compound up ahead. It looks similar to that of the Overlords,'* Skirill told them. He shared what he saw with the others. Braden was instantly alert.

*'Not idiots, G, failed experiments,'* Braden said. Bronwyn started to slow down, grabbing Micah's hand. The creatures seemed to grow more excited as they approached the compound nestled beneath the branches of great trees, concealing it from the overhead sensors that Holly counted on to see the world.

Bronwyn stopped completely. *'I don't want to go any further,'* she said over the mindlink. Micah pulled her blaster and kneeled. The creatures left them behind and entered the area near the buildings, cheering, grunting, and chanting Bronwyn's name. Braden positioned himself behind a tree, bracing his blaster against the trunk as he aimed toward the buildings.

G-War was alert. *'I don't sense anything, but I know someone is there,'* the 'cat offered. Treetis stood atop Brandt's head, hackles up and back arched. Fea leaned against Bronwyn's leg, keeping herself between the unknowns of the compound and the girl. The Wolfoids watched for an ambush, but they expected the real danger would come from one of the buildings.

Pik remembered the Overlords. His thoughts centered on that day, seemingly so long ago and that battle, how he'd killed them, mercilessly. He saw it all happening again, right before his very eyes. He turned away as vertigo seized him, putting his hand on a tree to keep from falling. Aadi came close, nudging him and talking to him in the unique Lizard Man language that the others couldn't hear.

While Braden was distracted by Pik's discord, an elderly man walked from behind one of the buildings, using a cane to help him as he went from one of the misshapen creatures to the next, greeting them kindly and touching each on the head. Micah crouched as the man looked into the trees, squinting to make out the newcomers in the shadows.

The man-horse creature tried to speak louder than the others, but the cacophony was unintelligible as each vied for the attention of the old man. He nodded knowingly as he slowly made his way toward Braden, Micah, and the companions.

Bronwyn tried to inch away. The Rabbits stood shoulder to shoulder in front of her, protecting her with their bodies as they held their laser pistols in their small hands.

*What do you see, Bronwyn?'* Micah asked.

*'Darkness,'* she answered, not elaborating. She ducked behind the Rabbits, peering out from behind their big ears. She shivered, clutching their harnesses as she pulled herself closer to her guardians.

Fea had had enough. She raced forward, sliding to a stop before the man, arching and hissing with one paw raised and claws fully extended, threatening to rake the man's flesh.

Braden was shocked from his reverie by the sound of a 'cat ready to fight. He jumped from behind the tree, making plenty of noise to distract the old man.

"I'm Free Trader Braden, and we're here on a mission of peace." Braden spread his arms as he talked, forcing a smile against the hostile emotions that raged all around him.

"Peace, you say?" the man responded in a rich baritone. "With blasters and laser pistols? Lightning spears and engineered creatures with claws bared? I am but an old man and can't understand why I would warrant such aggression on your part."

*'He knows things he shouldn't. Why is his mind closed to us?'* Micah asked Braden in her thought voice. The old man waved as if he heard her and discounted what she was saying.

*'He's one of the ancients,'* Braden replied, holstering his blaster. Micah kept hers trained on the old man. Braden walked at an angle, putting himself between the Professor and Micah.

"I am descended from the ancients, yes, just like you," the old man said, confirming that he could hear the other humans' thought voices.

"We're looking for the people who were taken from White Beach, across the ocean, east of here. They were taken by an ancients' vehicle and ancients' Bots operating from the undersea research facility. We'd like our people back," Braden said icily, dropping all pretense at civility. One of the creatures came at him, but Braden easily parried the punch, sending the attacker over his hip and face-first into the ground.

"That's enough of that," the old man said, holding his hand up to prevent any more actions by members of the misfit band. "They call me the Professor. A small group lived here as part of the undersea research facility, as you've already surmised, when the war came. But the fighting never came here. The people on the island were no threat to anyone. When they were cut off from the rest of the world, I'm afraid my ancestors had to make the best of a bad situation."

As the Professor talked, he wandered closer to the companions. He looked at Strider as if examining her. She didn't let him get closer than the end of her spear as she kept it leveled at his chest. The Hillcat received the same treatment, then the Rabbits, who kept their laser pistols trained on the man. He looked at Pik and nodded.

"A Lizard Man, but one of the originals, not the later evolved versions." He leaned close to Pik Ha'ar, who also used his trident spear to hold the man at bay. "And what do we have back here? Are you one of the Aurochs? My, they never used to be that big. And could this be a Tortoid? I am happy to meet you."

"How do you know these things?" Braden asked.

"I've studied the records, the knowledge that we used to have. I'm glad it's not lost on you. Are you connected with your AI?" the Professor asked suddenly.

"I think we'll return to our ship now," Braden parried, unwilling to engage an ancient without talking to Holly. "We have much to think about. If you would be so kind, meet us on the beach tomorrow morning. We'll return then and have a nice sit-down conversation. Is there anything you miss, from the continent you called it? We could bring it ashore. We have a most excellent coffee," Braden offered, resuming his Free Trader persona in order to disengage from the Professor. The old man gave Braden the creeps.

"I'm afraid not, but the company of new people is most welcome. I look forward to resuming our conversation. Until tomorrow," the Professor said dismissively.

"If you'll be so kind, Brandt, to lead the way back to the beach." Braden pointed at Micah and Bronwyn to follow with the Rabbits and 'cats joining them. Braden, the Wolfoids, Pik, and Aadi backed away from the old man.

"Which beach are you talking about?" the Professor inquired pleasantly.

"I would be surprised if you didn't know the answer to that question." Braden had no intention of playing the old man's game of innocent ignorance. The misfit mob's actions suggested that being armed was a completely new experience for them. They'd dropped their weapons, leaving them behind without concern. "Until tomorrow."

The Professor held the creatures back while he intently watched the companions as they cautiously withdrew. The Hawkoids flew the path ahead, while Skirill stayed behind, watching for anyone following. Braden didn't think they would, knowing that they didn't have to. He suspected the old man had all the information about Braden and his companions that he wanted.

When they arrived on the beach, the ship was already there. Holly had driven the ship even closer, wedging the deck against the sand of the shallow water, before it dropped over the edge of a cliff. Brandt waded out and with a mighty leap, was able to get his front legs and chest onto the deck. He twisted back and forth until he managed to get a back hoof up, then he pulled himself upright and stood on the deck, majestically outlined by the setting sun.

Bronwyn waded through the gentle surf and with a helping horn from Brandt, she was pulled onto the deck. Aadi swam through the air near her, in case she needed a friendly shell to grab onto. The Wolfoids and Lizard Man were also there to help, then climbed on board after Bronwyn.

The Rabbits waited on the beach until Braden and Micah could carry them the few steps to the deck and wrestle them on board. Then the humans returned for the 'cats. Treetis hadn't tried to ride the Aurochs as the King clambered aboard. The young 'cat still looked rough from his earlier dunking. The Hawkoids stood on the second deck's railing, watching the woods for any sign of duplicity.

There was none.

Braden helped Micah aboard, and she pulled him up after her. They stood together on the deck as the ship slowly pulled away and backed out of the small cove.

"What the hell is he all about?" Braden asked, screwing up his face as if he'd just eaten something unpleasant.

"He's almost as spooky as the Androids," she replied.

That made Braden's ears perk up. "Did you get a close look at him?"

"Yes, and he looked plenty human to me. Bronwyn, is he a clone?" Micah asked. The girl shivered as she recalled her mind seeing his.

"Yes and no. I can't explain it, but he's not right. We should leave this place." Bronwyn sat on a deck chair, hugging her knees to her chest and rocking. Fea climbed into the chair next to her, rubbing against her and purring. The deck chairs magically appeared and disappeared as the Bots managed the ship as if humans had never abandoned it.

"Did you see anything in his mind about my father, about Caleb?" Micah asked.

Bronwyn shook her head, then wiped her nose on her shirt.

"Impressions?" Braden said, waving all the companions into a circle around them. Perched on chairs, sitting on the deck, standing, or laying, everyone was focused on the matter at hand. "He knew things like Holly would know them. He asked if we had neural implants, although I think he already knew that we did. I wonder if he has one, and then who is he connected to?"

*'I sensed evil, but he has patience. He wasn't ready for whatever he wanted to do. Once he felt my presence, he closed his mind to me as easily as you close a door,'* G-War added.

"Did he get into your mind, G?" Braden asked, unsure what else the old man learned from their minds as they tried to probe his.

*'Please,'* the 'cat scoffed, closing his eyes and feigning sleep.

"Aadi, I think he knows something about those taken from White Beach. I'll keep working on him, but it'll be best if there are fewer of us out there to distract him. I think just G-War and I should go."

Micah pursed her lips, waiting for Aadi to talk Braden out of his ill-conceived plan.

*'I think you may be right, Master Braden. He looked at us as if we were science experiments. The creatures that he surrounded himself with? Those were his attempts to create different species. His efforts didn't work. I think the less he interacts with us, the better off we'll be.'* Aadi floated serenely in the middle of the group, turning slowly so he could look at each one's face. *'It will be best if we stay on the ship, away from the island. Maybe you can use the small boat that our scientists brought to take you ashore?'*

Braden looked at his partner, but she didn't want to argue with Aadi, that she should be the one to go and not Braden.

"Brandt?"

*'I have nothing, my friend. This task requires a delicate touch. If you need someone run over, I'm your Aurochs. Or if we were going to sit down and have a nice chat, I can do that, too. But this? No. I will stay here and keep watch over Bronwyn,'* the King of the Aurochs replied.

"Pik?" Braden asked, going through the companions one by one.

*'He is an Overlord and should be killed as soon as possible. Then we will search the island, find what we came for,'* Pik suggested.

"It may come to that, Pik, but let's see if we can learn something first. Ess, Zee, Zeeka?"

Skirill looked at his mate and their daughter. They all shook their heads. *'We saw no other creatures, nothing special,'* Zyena stated.

"Were you able to see the whole compound?" Braden asked her.

*'Yes and it reminded me of the Overlords' compound in the Amazon. There's a well-worn path heading away, opposite the way we came from. I recommend we explore that more. Skirill can do that tomorrow when you are meeting with the Professor. Zeeka and I will stay here and watch,'* Zyena said.

"I don't think he noticed you Hawkoids, so let's keep you out of sight as much as possible. Skirill, are you up to explore the rest of the island, well, at least where that path goes?"

*'Of course.'* Skirill bowed.

"Ferrer, Brigitte?"

Both Rabbits shook their heads, ears flapping in the gentle breeze as the ship moved away from the island and into the open ocean.

*'Last, but not least, are you there, Holly?'* Braden asked over the neural implant.

*'Yes, Master Braden. I am not at all comfortable with anyone meeting this 'Professor.' I think he is a holdover from the ancients, no better than those who started the civil war that nearly destroyed our world. We cannot trust him.'*

*'Pretty strong words, Holly,'* Braden replied. *'I already knew not to trust him, but what else? My plan is to not leave the beach with the Professor. I don't want to be anywhere we can't overwhelm him with force. He's an old man. What could he do to us if we take him? That band of misfits is no match.'*

*'Just be careful, Master Braden. If he's an ancient, he may have tricks that you don't suspect,'* Holly offered. Braden closed his neural implant.

"If anyone thinks of anything else, let me know. We'll talk again over breakfast." Braden looked at the Golden Warrior, while Treetis with his hair finally starting to settled down, sat next to him. Fea was with Bronwyn, talking. The Rabbits were on their way to the garden. The rest of the companions headed for the galley. Dinner called.

# An Unpleasant Surprise

The morning arrived with a beautiful sunrise that Braden and Micah watched from a balcony on the third level of the sail. They stood, arms around each other, enjoying the salt of the ocean air. The Hawkoids flew high above, circling the nearby island. They weren't looking for anything, just stretching their wings. They loved to fly.

Just as Braden loved to trade. He'd decided that he'd approach this as a trade deal. What did the old man want for information that would help them get Caleb and the others back?

Micah didn't support Braden going, but knew that it was for the best. She would lose patience quickly as the old man dodged direct questions. She'd resort to violence and that wouldn't get her the information. It was better that Braden and G-War go it alone. Micah didn't like it, but accepted it as their best chance.

Over breakfast, no one had anything new. Fea was especially kind toward G-War while Treetis had an annoying habit of pawing at the fabricator when he was hungry, which seemed to be all the time. Braden facilitated the young 'cat's behavior by getting him something every time he did his thing. Braden was just trying to be nice, but Treetis was learning the wrong lessons. G-War shooed the younger version of himself away and ate half of what Braden had gotten from the machine.

The Wolfoids seemed fascinated by the exchange. Braden sat close to the fabricator because it only responded to verbal commands. Skirill sometimes had luck making it work, but generally, it was up to the humans to order food for everyone.

Braden and Micah didn't mind. They would do anything for their friends and usually the smallest things made the most impact. They had all risked their lives, but the little effort was what kept them close.

"That's enough of us milling around and looking at each other!" Braden declared. "G and I are going ashore to work a deal. That's it. We'll be back before you wake up from your morning naps! Holly! Move us close to the shore. Where is our boat?" Braden yelled, giving orders as he expected a ship's captain would.

The companions casually moved to the main deck, where the boat was tied up at the front of the well deck. The Bots must have removed it during the storm as he didn't remember it being there when they were getting thrown around. It didn't matter. He asked Holly for a quick instruction on how everything worked. Holly reiterated at least seven times that under no circumstances was the Hillcat to extend his claws and penetrate the bladders of the small boat, which it relied on to keep it afloat.

When the ship was close, Braden gave Micah one last hug and kiss, and he climbed into their small boat. G-War jumped and was instantly yelled at for using his claws to stop himself from sliding when he hit the wet rubber.

"If you think your paws are wet now, if you sink us, you'll be just like Treetis, a drowned rat," Braden cautioned. "Just stand in the bottom there and I'll get us ashore as quickly as I can." Using the lever that controlled their speed, Braden guided the boat from the aft end of the ship which Holly had conveniently pointed toward the island.

Braden turned the handle a little one way, then the other, getting the feel of how the boat responded. He twisted the handle and the engine hummed, driving the boat faster and faster until they went airborne over a surging wave. The 'cat bounced into the air, almost as high as Braden was tall. He came straight back down, landing hard within the boat.

*Do that again, and I will sink us and drown you,'* G-War growled, unhappy with his human for the entire oceangoing adventure.

"Relax, G! We're almost there." Braden throttled back to slow their headlong rush. He'd almost fallen overboard with their little stunt and didn't want the embarrassment of the boat racing away without him. G-War would never let him live that down.

Braden guided the boat into the small cove where the dark water was clear, but too deep to see the bottom. They cruised across the calm waters and slid the boat ashore. When Braden stepped out and started to pull the boat farther up the sand, away from the tidal pull, G-War spoke.

*'They're here,'* he said. Braden immediately opened his neural implant. He wanted Holly to be included, for the inevitable challenges the old man would bring.

Braden let the boat drop and turned to face a younger man, well built, standing firm.

"Yes, they're here, nothing to fear, all in good cheer!" he said with a big smile.

"Who are you?" Braden asked, surprised at the switch.

"Why, I'm the Professor, of course. Shall we?" the man pointed to a small table and two chairs that had been set up in the shade of a palm tree, similar to those growing at the Oases in the Great Desert. Braden never knew what they were called until Holly told him.

"I thought the man we met yesterday was the Professor," Braden said, confused.

"Yes, he was. That was me. I had worked all night and hadn't had a chance to clean up. I feel like a new man!" the young Professor exclaimed. Braden gritted his teeth. It was never good to argue with a customer who was clearly lying.

*Why the bait and switch?* Braden thought to himself, trying to get back into the right trading mindset. It didn't matter who negotiated, as long as they were willing to talk.

G-War looked into the trees, staring at certain spots but not speaking, because he knew the Professor could hear him, even when he spoke only to Braden. The 'cat didn't like his thoughts intruded upon, although he couldn't understand why people were upset when he did it. He was a 'cat, after all.

"Well, then, shall we?" Braden pointed to the table and started walking that way. The Professor took a keen interest in looking at Braden's boots.

The Free Trader didn't ask as he didn't want to be drawn into any conversation that didn't have Caleb as its main topic.

"I'll start by repeating myself from yesterday. We are looking for humans that were taken from White Beach a few cycles, I mean years, ago and then more people taken recently. We believe they were taken to the undersea facility that is just off shore from this island. You and I both know that's not a coincidence, so let's talk about that and how we can get our people back," Braden said firmly, jaw set as he studied his opponent.

"What a shame that you think I had anything to do with that. I really have no idea who gets taken or when. My work is far too important to get caught up in the mundane," the man replied politely.

"What is your work?" Braden wanted to find common ground with the Professor, who seemed interested, although everything that came out of his mouth was questionable. Braden also noted that the Professor had just confirmed he knew about the undersea facility. The gentle thrust and parry of the negotiation had begun.

"I think it best if I show you," the man said, standing up. He produced a device that looked like the communicator Holly had given Micah. The Professor pressed a button and the window where Holly had been filled with fuzz, blocking Braden's vision. He closed the window and blinked the image away.

Braden looked at the device and lunged for it, but his muscles didn't seem to work right. His legs became thick, then his arms were too heavy to hold up. It became harder to breathe. G-War snarled and tried to attack the Professor, but three different nets sprang up from the sand. He tangled into one and a hidden arm dragged the net over the 'cat, trapping him.

G-War twisted and slashed, hissed and jumped. All to no avail. He didn't give up. He kept fighting against the net until a powder wafted over, instantly calming him.

*'Braden, I've failed you,'* the 'cat shared over the mindlink before he passed out.

"No one will hear your plea for help, you magnificent fighter, you. Look at all those scars. My! You must have been in some battles. And you too, my young friend, you too." The Professor looked closely at Braden, happy that the pin in the chair had done its job and effectively delivered the drug that rendered the young man unconscious.

"You will both add nicely to my experiments, help me get past these interminable hold ups. Come now!" he yelled at the woods. "Take them to the den." The misshapen mob appeared and threw Braden unceremoniously onto a stretcher. G-War received even less consideration as they dumped his unconscious form into a bag.

The Professor pointed to the raft and the man-horse shuffled to it, using a spear to poke holes in all the bladders. He pushed it into the surf where it was dragged backward and disappeared into the depths of the cove.

Skirill was sitting on a branch of the lone tree at the end of the rocky outcropping. He could see the beach and everything that happened, but he stayed silent as he knew the Professor could hear him. He remained unmoving, sitting as close to the trunk as possible, trying to remain unseen. He'd been there since the break of dawn and watched the Professor set up. He hadn't seen any of the traps being put into place. He'd failed Braden, too, but he didn't know that was exactly how G-War felt. Skirill hadn't heard a thing from those on the beach, and that surprised him.

When the mob and the Professor disappeared into the woods, Skirill waited until he was sure they were gone, and then he launched himself skyward, flying quickly to the ship.

He landed and told them what he'd seen. Without hesitation, the two Wolfoids grabbed their spears and ran full speed to the edge of the deck and jumped into the ocean. They started dog-paddling, but the tide was going out. Soon, with Bronwyn's help, Chlora and Rhodi showed up to guide them toward the shore.

*'Holly, get us ashore, now!'* Micah called via her neural implant.

*'I think haste will not get you what you want, Master President,'* Holly cautioned. *'We need more information, otherwise, I fear that all the companions will be captured. The Professor blocked the neural implant and I suspect he blocked the mindlink, somehow, too. The Hawkoid heard nothing from Braden or the Golden Warrior.'*

Micah stomped on the deck and spit angrily. She growled as she talked. "Bronwyn, ask the Dolphins to bring the Wolfoids back, please. We will plan, and then we will return. When we go, all of us will go. The Professor will pay for this. I will make him pay," Micah said through gritted teeth.

# Together We Go

Micah stood looking over the railing, seething at the limited information they'd gathered. The Hawkoids had flown into the tops of the trees, but they were unable to get too close to the compound. No one liked the thought that the Professor could not only hear them when they talked over the mindlink, but he could block it as well.

When the Hawkoids found two other outposts hidden beneath the canopy of the jungle, they flew back to the ship before reporting. They didn't want to be discovered. Micah updated the map that Holly provided by way of the neural implant with the latest information, what they'd seen of the compound the previous daylight, and with all the locations where Holly discovered emissions. After consolidating the information, they realized that they still didn't know very much. The map had a great deal of empty space.

Holly suggested dropping advanced listening devices, but it would take the ship's small fabricator a full day to produce them. Micah didn't want to go in completely blind, but she couldn't wait. She assumed that the Professor was doing the worst things to her mate.

*'Master President, I also suggest you take the field generator. I believe that will mitigate any of the Professor's electronics that he may be using. The only way the neural implant can be blocked is with technology, and the only way your mindlink can be blocked is with biotechnology. Both are within the power of the ancients. If we can mitigate their technology, physically, he is no match for you, even the younger version of the Professor, and no, I have no idea what that is all about. I can only surmise that there are two of them, an older man and a younger, cloned version.'*

"You want me to carry that big brick?" Micah asked.

*'I would have the King of the Aurochs carry it, personally, but if you want to carry it, who am I to argue?'* Holly replied. Micah tried not to deliver an angry retort,

because Holly was right. Since Brandt was going, he could carry it and not even notice he had it. She'd ask him.

The Dolphins swam up the well deck and delivered two dripping Wolfoids, who were not pleased at having returned to the ship.

"I'm sorry, but Holly had a bunch of good points. We can't go storming in after the Professor, he's an ancient with ancient technology. Skirill said he easily captured both Braden and G-War. If we go running in there, he'll take us, too, and then there will be no one left to rescue anyone. It's up to us to get this right because if we don't, we lose Caleb, too."

The Wolfoids hung their heads, shaking with the desire to do something but hamstrung by circumstances and an enemy that was more dangerous than any they'd previously faced. When it came to fighting, their leader who always came up with winning plans, wasn't there. They had to figure it out on their own.

Pik Ha'ar stood close by, seemingly unfazed by the situation. He looked at the shore, unmoving. Aadi swam close to the Lizard Man. *'Tell us, Pik, what are you thinking?'*

*'Let us sail the ship around the island. I wish to look at it from all angles. Then we go ashore, individually, coming at the compound from each of the cardinal directions. If one of us gets taken down, the others press on. Micah's concern was that there would be no one left to come rescue us. We split into four groups. Then there will be three who can come. We need to time our movements so we all arrive at the same moment. We cannot use the mindlink,'* Pik said smoothly and calmly.

"Holly!" Micah yelled. "Take us on a tour around the island, quick as you can, please."

"Aye, aye, Captain!" Holly announced over a loudspeaker.

"How can you hear me?" Micah asked, even though she'd talked with him out loud before on the ship.

"There are a number of sensors. This ship was very advanced at the time of the civil war. It was the best that the ancients' technology could offer, a testament that it could float around the ocean for four-hundred years and still look new when we found it, and that includes the quality of the gardens. While the Rabbits are on board, I've disengaged the Development Unit that would usually tend the foliage."

"Always thoughtful, Holly. Let's look at the island and see what it will take to seize control. Pik has a plan. Do as he tells you," Micah ordered.

"I can't hear Pik Ha'ar when he speaks," Holly answered.

"Fine," Micah retorted. Even Holly knew that when she said 'fine,' it didn't mean fine. Braden and Holly had had many long conversations about the nuances in language use between the human females and males, although Braden admitted that he had minimal expertise, most of which was learned the hard way. "I'll tell you what he says."

The companions gathered on the port side of the sail, on the open deck outside the galley. Brandt stood on the deck below, watching the shore go by. The Hawkoids flew high above, looking for any sign of Braden and G-War. Pik pointed at various points, then asked the Hawkoids if there was a route inland from there.

They all had clear paths into the interior of the island, they were told. Pik was concerned that the ways seemed too inviting.

*'Strider, Brigitte, and Zeeka. Bounder, Ferrer, and Skirill. Brandt, Treetis, and I. Micah, Aadi, Fea, and Zyena. These are the groups. I will disembark last. Judge the time it takes us to get around the island. First ashore, Strider's group to the northwest. You'll skirt the peak and head east.*

*'Bounder's group will land on the north shore and head south to the compound. You will be the closest, which means you'll have to wait much longer before you move. Do you understand?'* Bounder nodded.

*'Micah, you will land over there, on the eastern shore near the stream. Follow it inland and it will take you directly to the compound.*

*'Brandt will land in the cove as it's the only place he can disembark. We will head inland, quickly to the compound. I suggest we do not kill any of the misfit mob. They are innocents in all this. The Professor is the problem. We will close on his position and attack as soon as we arrive. Just like we did in the rainforest.'* Pik looked to each

face, waiting for them to nod before moving on.

*'I am Pik Ha'ar, Commander of the Lizard Men. We cannot stand by while there are those who would do evil in the way of the ancients. There is a new way now and people like the Overlords and the Professor are not welcome here. They change, or they die. And the Professor? He needs to go. Once we have him, the Golden Warrior will rip the secrets from his mind and then we will end him.*

*'Brandt and I will make noise, head up the trail like a herd of water buffalo. The rest of you, quiet as you can. We will storm into the compound first, distract them. The rest of you follow, watch each other, look for anyone who has succumbed to the technology of the ancients. Cover them and keep them safe. The rest of us will converge on the Professors, both old and young. Any questions?'*

*'What about me?'* Bronwyn asked in a small voice.

*'You are the key to making it all work. We need your Dolphin friends to take the teams ashore. And we need Rexalita to make sure that no one approaches the ship while we're gone. We don't know what other creatures the Professor has. And then when we need help, we will call you. You will be the only one left.'*

*'But I can talk with them. They'll listen to me!'* Bronwyn pleaded.

*'Then you go with Micah,'* Pik readily conceded, hoping that the girl could keep the misshapen mob from hindering them as they went after the Professor.

"You sound just like Braden," Micah said, slapping the Lizard Man on the shoulder. She didn't smile. She didn't have it in her. She encouraged her father to teach the villagers of White Beach how to fish, and he was taken. Then she let Braden go ashore alone to be taken as well. Her father was missing and her partner was captured by a man Bronwyn said was filled with darkness.

She readied her gear for the tenth time. Everyone was fully loaded with food, water, and weapons. Brandt had the shield generator tied to his back with Amazonian rope. He was still healing from the storm's gashes and rubs, but he didn't complain. He was the King of the Aurochs and his friends were in trouble.

Pik asked Micah for a blaster, but she didn't have an extra one. He said that he'd be fine with his trident. Pik assumed that he'd be bait for the Professor, opening the way for the rest of the companions to take him down.

Micah knew what Pik was thinking, but didn't have a better plan. She gave the Lizard Man's plan her full support. As she thought about it, she wondered where the scientists were. She headed below.

She found them in the lab, so engrossed in a project that they didn't even hear her enter. Micah cleared her throat, then louder. They didn't lift their heads from examining whatever was on the table.

"Oh, for heaven's sake," she grumbled as she walked behind them and grabbed a handful of each, pulling them roughly away from the table.

"Hey!" Patti May looked put out. Chrysalis knew better than to argue with Micah, so he kept his mouth closed.

"Braden has been taken by an ancient still living on the island. Bronwyn described his mind as 'dark.' He knows all about the intelligent species, that they were engineered by the ancients, and he can block our mindlink and the neural implant. He's dangerous. He has Braden and G-War and we're going after them. You two are staying here, but you have to be ready in case we need you!" She emphasized the last few words, but couldn't imagine what the scientists could do if things got ugly. She wanted them to participate in some way, even if only to wish them well.

"What do you want us to do about it?" Patti May said with a sneer. Micah took a calming breath.

"I want you to be ready to come ashore. If we find a laboratory, you may want to examine it, but I don't think the Professor is very good. There's a group of creatures on that island that are misshapen with low intelligence. I think they are his failed experiments."

"A Genetic Engineer from the old school. We didn't do any of that on Cygnus VI. We cloned, but that was standard technology, not any kind of research. When can we go look at the lab?" Chrysalis asked.

"We have no idea where the lab is or when you can come ashore. We haven't gone ourselves, yet, but we have a plan."

"Good. Let us know when things are safe for us to look at the laboratory," Patti May said as she returned to the bench where she'd been working. She waved one hand dismissively as she resumed her study. Chrysalis shrugged and mouthed the words, 'thank you.'

Micah walked out of the lab and opened her neural implant. *'Holly, would Dr. Johns be put out if I killed his son and that other scientist that we've been saddled with?'*

*'Master President, I never know when you are joking. I don't think anyone should be killing anyone else. Those two are established scientists. They are very good at what they do. You shouldn't have any problems with them,'* Holly said soothingly.

*'So, yes. Dr. Johns would be put out, is what I hear from you. We need help and they aren't helping. They don't even seem interested in helping.'*

*'Master Micah, Pik Ha'ar's plan is tactically sound and has a very high probability of success. I think you underestimate your abilities,'* Holly added, sounding confident.

*'I think you overestimate them,'* Micah replied, closing the link.

Pik asked to meet the two Wolfoids and Micah on the bridge. Once there, he used the navigation board to show a three-dimensional image of the island. The Wolfoids were never good with two-dimensional maps, but they seemed to completely grasp the representation that Holly provided.

Pik ran through the plan afresh, talking about how long it would take each group to travel through the jungle. They estimated the time between drop off and when they should start walking. Then he changed things. Once south of the island, the ship would turn around and head the opposite direction, which changed the delivery sequence, but Pik wanted to reduce the predictability.

The ship would circle the island a second time, dropping each group into the ocean on the starboard side, away from where someone on the beach could see them leaving the ship. With the Dolphins' assistance, thanks to Bronwyn, they'd swim the teams close to the shore, then return to the ship for the next group. Pik absolutely didn't care that the 'cats were going to get wet, although Fea didn't complain. Her mate had been captured, too.

The female Hillcats were the hunters when they ran in a pack. Fea was no different. She watched over a great number of 'cats, the matriarch of a large group that had left the 'cat enclave in Warren Deep and ventured to the south to reestablish themselves as predators and not surrender to a life as a shepherd. And bonding with humans was encouraged, to help humanity along a better path.

Fea was going after her mate, just like Micah, and wouldn't return without him. *'I don't think you can hear me, Ax, but just in case, I'm coming for you.'*

Micah put a hand on the white 'cat's back, hoping they'd be ready for whatever the Professor had in store. Micah had her sword slung across her back and two blasters. She carried a length of rope, one flask of water, and only a little food, energy bars as the fabricator referred to them. And that was it. She would be ready to fight with each heartbeat as they traveled inland.

The ship swung around the south end of the island and the first group prepared to go into the water. The Rabbits wore their life preservers and the Wolfoids had an extra flotation strap around their necks, to keep their heads out of the water.

The ship sailed past the cove, where Brandt's group would disembark last. First up was Micah's group. She let a strand of rope trail behind her that Aadi could hang on to as the Dolphins took them ashore. Micah carried Fea in her arms, hoping she'd be able to keep the 'cat from completely submerging. Bronwyn carried her own food and water. For a teenager, she'd seen too much, been a part of things no one her age should have to be a part of, but thanks to G-War, she was stronger and Micah was happy to have her along. Bronwyn would be able to keep the creatures from attacking them while the Professor was taken care of.

Pik didn't say anything. He simply pointed at the ocean and nodded.

The Dolphins magically appeared next to the ship. Bronwyn and Micah climbed directly onto their backs as Fea wrapped herself across Micah's shoulders and Aadi clung to the rope from her pack. The Dolphins veered away from the ship, lolling in a trough to put distance between themselves and the ship. Once it was well clear, they started swimming.

# Micah Ashore

Aadi tried to stay as close to the water as possible, not wanting to be easily seen, but every time a wave hit him, Micah was almost yanked from the Dolphin's back. Fea clung to Micah's neck like a huge scarf, draped to her waist. The 'cat was mostly dry and Fea wanted to stay that way. Bronwyn was soaked as she frolicked on Rhodi. Chlora was all business, carrying a heavier load and dragging a sea anchor.

The Dolphins took them into the surf then swam parallel to the beach until they were in waist-deep water for Micah. She slid off Chlora, thanking her for her help, turned, and ran for the beach with Aadi still hanging onto the rope. Fea dropped to the sand when they were past the tide. Bronwyn did the same, taking longer to come ashore as she watched Rhodi and Chlora dive through the surf and race to catch up as the ship sailed into the distance.

Zyena was perched in a tree, intently watching the jungle. Micah and the others stopped below her and waited. They'd agreed not to use the mindlink. The Professor had to know they were coming, but the details of the plan were different from the execution. Now that they were ashore, silence was king. Micah had turned her neural implant completely off as Holly had encouraged.

Zyena used her wing to point to a path and then nodded. She took off and flew ahead, staying under the jungle's canopy, landing where she could see Micah as well as the approaching trail. They'd asked for her to screech in warning if anyone or anything appeared.

Fea melted into the undergrowth, popping up not far away, her all-white head standing out against the greens prevalent on the island. She sat calmly and, with all her senses, watched.

Bronwyn leaned close to Micah, but only to watch the jungle, study it, listen to its sounds. She didn't seek comfort. She'd learned a great deal about the world in her short time on it, and she realized that some people weren't compatible with the rest. She discovered that the humans and the Overlords could not coexist. In her mind, the creature that called itself the Professor was in the same category. She expected that when night fell, he'd be gone and she was good with that, because she believed that it needed to be done. She looked at Micah, smiling, knowing that Micah wasn't afraid to kill him herself.

Micah noticed the teenager looking at her, but didn't speculate on why. It only mattered that the girl stay out of harm's way. Micah waved to Zyena, then pointed at her own eyes and stabbed her fingers forward, pointing down the trail.

Zyena understood. Scout the way ahead. She launched and flew forward, weaving left, well away from the trail, then right, crisscrossing the trail at ninety degrees as she looked to make sure the others weren't walking into a trap. A ways forward, she ran across a built-up mound, with a door inclined against it, as if opening to a stairway down. The Hawkoid resisted the temptation to project a mental image of the door. She flew around it, and not seeing anyone or anything, she returned, landing on the sand next to Micah. With her talon, she drew a rough map of the trail leading ahead, then meticulously drew in a door and a mound. It was little more than a stick figure as this was her first time drawing, but she pointed emphatically to the circle and door.

Micah nodded, but the only thing she understood was that there was something man-made up ahead. She didn't know if it was a trap or a building or what. What mattered most was that they knew it was there. Bronwyn put her hand on the Hawkoid's shoulder, nodded, and then looked to Micah.

"There's a door set into a small mound. It looks like it leads underground," the girl whispered. Bronwyn was gifted in ways that Micah could only guess. She hadn't used the mindlink, so however she learned the information, Micah was pleased to know the particulars. She wanted to check it out before they moved toward the compound. She waved at Fea and Aadi, signaling that they were going.

Aadi hovered nearby, the rope still in his mouth as he tried to stay out of the others' way. He was ready to do what he could, a focused thunderclap at the forefront of his thoughts.

The 'cat disappeared into the undergrowth, reappearing down the trail as she crouched low, listening and watching.

Micah picked a route to the side of the obvious trail. With a blaster in one hand and her sword in the other, she walked carefully, expecting a trap. Bronwyn was right behind her, stepping where Micah stepped, moving slowly and deliberately.

Zyena perched almost directly above the mound, watching in the direction of the compound. Micah wondered if she'd moved too close to her ultimate target. She took a knee behind a bush, not far from the door. She put her sword in the scabbard across her back and drew her second blaster. She rested one in the bush and held the other loosely as she settled in to wait until the others were on the island. Then she'd figure out what this place was all about. If she had to, she'd burn them out of the underground, send flame into the hole as if destroying a nest of ground wasps.

## Bounder Ashore

Bounder vaulted into the wave, missing Rhodi completely. His head dunked for less than a heartbeat as the flotation device around his neck helped bring him back to the surface. Rhodi dove and came from below, easing him onto his back. He used his Wolfoid hands to grasp the Dolphin's dorsal fin as he straddled him with his back legs, scratching Rhodi in the process. Wolfoids were ill-suited for riding Dolphins.

Ferrer was terrified to go into the water, even though he wore a life vest. Holly watched it all using the external sensors and slowed the ship so they didn't go too far past their drop off point. Pik finally offered a hand to help the Rabbit off the deck and onto Chlora's back. Ferrer let go only after he had one hand firmly on Chlora's fin. He couldn't get where he was comfortable on the Dolphin's back as his back legs weren't made for gripping. He had no time to adjust for as soon as he let go of the ship, Chlora veered toward the open ocean.

The ship immediately sped up as Holly wanted to get back on schedule for the final two deliveries. Ferrer closed his eyes, shaking as he hugged himself against the Dolphin's slick back. He held the fin with both hands, getting wetter and wetter as she swam toward shore. Finally, the Dolphin stopped swimming and rocked gently from side to side. Ferrer opened his eyes and blinked rapidly as salt water dripped into them, burning.

He saw that they were beyond the surf, in the shallows. He brought his outside leg over and pushed off Chlora's back so hard that she rolled upside down into an oncoming wave. Ferrer splashed into the water that was chest-deep to him and ran as hard as he was able to get out of the god-forsaken water, and kept running once he hit the beach. There was no predicting the direction a terrified rabbit would run.

Bounder was already ashore and could only run after the Rabbit, watching over him in case a threat appeared. He carried his spear in his hand, slapping it into the sand as he ran on all fours. Skirill flew ahead, under the jungle's canopy, but still as high off the ground as he could manage. He bobbed and weaved between branches and trunks as he tried to keep one eye on the Rabbit and one on his way ahead.

Ferrer stopped, eyes wide as he looked for an escape route. Bounder tackled him, both of the wet creatures rolling through the sand. He made to hop up and run, but the Wolfoid wrapped his big feet in a bear hug. This earned him a Rabbit kick in the chest, which launched Ferrer away from Bounder and into a tree trunk. He collapsed, dazed and covered in sand.

Bounder stood up and shook, sending sand flying. He tried to brush the rest off, but it clung to his wet fur. He shook his head and adjusted his grip on the lightning spear. He poked the Rabbit in the chest none too gently. Ferrer's eyes popped open.

Bounder crouched near him, putting out both hands as a calming gesture. The Rabbit's eyes darted one way and then another. Bounder gripped Ferrer's head in both hands and rubbed noses, looking into the Rabbit's eyes. At one point in Vii's history, a Rabbit would have wilted in fear being nose to nose with a Wolfoid, but not anymore. They were friends, allies in the cause of freedom.

Ferrer blinked to clear his eyes, then patted Bounder on the shoulder to show that he was okay. Ferrer stood and shook, sending sand in an arc over Bounder, who shook in return, making sure he sent sand flying Ferrer's way. Skirill watched it all in amazement.

He thought they'd gone ashore to rescue Braden and G-War, not undergo a male bonding experience. He leapt from the branch and dropped toward the ground before extending his wings. As he approached the two other members of his party, he back-winged, slapping both Bounder and Ferrer in the head repeatedly before landing.

He used one wing to point the way inland. Then he pointed at Bounder, sending him behind a tree in one direction. He selected Ferrer and pointed him toward a bush in the other direction. Then the Hawkoid pointed repeatedly at the sand. "Stay put and wait," he was telling them. Skirill flew back into the trees and tried to look inconspicuous. Other birds flew about, but they were nowhere near the size of a Hawkoid.

Bounder's group had the shortest trip to the compound, not shortest distance-wise, but short in that there was a wide path that led straight through the jungle. Skirill spotted a way to the open sky where he could fly above the trees and tell the others when the ship had arrived at the cove. The other Hawkoids would be doing the same thing at regular intervals to coordinate the attack on the compound.

They settled in to wait.

# Strider Ashore

The last two groups watched in shock as Ferrer panicked.

They knew that they would have to go into the ocean next. Strider made Brigitte go first so she could 'encourage' the Rabbit from the deck. Holly prepared to slow the ship, just in case.

They added an extra flotation ring around each of her small arms. She waddled to the edge of the deck and looked with trepidation as the ocean's waves slapped the side of the ship and splashed the deck. Rhodi angled close, swimming easily alongside the ship as it traveled south, abeam the western side of the island.

Strider encouraged Brigitte, who stumbled as she got close to the edge. She sat down heavily and looked at the ocean. Strider tried to be patient, but couldn't. There was too much at stake. Strider wrapped her Wolfoid arms around the Rabbit, pinning the floaties to Brigitte's side and with a mighty heave, sent them both overboard.

Rhodi and Chlora were ready, stalwart in their assistance to the companions simply because Bronwyn had asked for their help. The Rabbit bounced off Rhodi's back. With the round flotation devices on her small arms, she was unable to grip the Dolphin's dorsal fin. Rhodi bumped her over his head where she lay on her stomach, backed up against his dorsal fin. She wrapped her arms around his head and he chittered happily. Rhodi had free use of his tail so he propelled them quickly along the surface.

Brigitte had a great view and watched in joy as they swam along the wave-tops.

When the Rabbit bounced off Rhodi, Strider went into the water. She sank as she remembered the device she was supposed to wear around her neck was still on the deck. She'd left it behind. She kicked and pawed, trying to get herself back toward the surface. When something big rammed into her, driving her forward, she broke the surface and kept going as Chlora came out of the water with her. When the Wolfoid splashed down, she landed on the Dolphin's back. She clasped her arms around the dorsal fin and they were off, racing to catch Rhodi and Brigitte.

Zeeka was already flying over the island. When the others reached the shore, she flew back to the beach, diving and turning sharply over the others' heads as she zoomed into the jungle along the path they were to take inland. They were to start immediately, while the other groups would be waiting. They had further to go around the hill that rose sharply on the western side of the island.

They didn't need to climb it to get a view since Zeeka could fly high above the jungle and then return to show them the way. From the western side, they didn't have a clear path either. Their way forward was strewn with debris, and lined with gullies and rock falls.

They moved out as soon as they determined a viable route. Strider went first. Brigitte followed as the Wolfoid stayed on all fours and worked her way through the brush and over obstacles. Zeeka crashed through the foliage over their heads in a controlled dive to get below the cover. She spread her wings and glided low to the ground as she zigzagged easterly toward the compound.

Zeeka turned sharply to the right as she discovered a well-worn path heading up the hill. She followed it to a wide opening with a metal gate. She hovered in front of it, beating her wings as she let her eyes adjust to the darkness within.

A wide corridor was beyond with a high roof. It sloped gently downward, turning and disappearing around a corner in the distance. Zeeka returned to the others, wanting to tell them, but knowing that if she spoke, the Professor would know they were there. She was afraid of the man, because the others feared him. With everything her parents had told her of Braden and the Golden Warrior, the fact that the old man had, by himself, taken them both was alarming.

When the others reached the well-traveled path, she'd show them the entrance to the cave. Strider could determine what to do from there.

# Braden Awake

"G? Are you there?" Braden asked, wincing at the pounding in his head. He tested his arms, surprised to find that he wasn't bound. He was in a bed, uncomfortable and rough, but better than in the sand on the floor. G-War meowed and snarled, to let Braden know that he was there.

Braden thought the room they were in looked dark, but found that a cloth was wrapped around his head. When he removed it, he realized there was a patch over his eye, the one behind which the neural implant had been installed. Braden tried to activate it. There was nothing.

"Crap. He removed my neural implant. Why aren't you in my head, G?" Braden asked rhetorically. *He can block our mindlink, too?* The Overlords had nothing on this guy, these guys, whatever the real story was.

Braden threw his legs off the bed, which he found was a simple cot, padded with a thatch-work of vines and leaves. Walls of the ancients surrounded them on three sides and on the fourth, metal bars stood close together, floor to ceiling. The 'cat was in a small cage chained at the front of their prison. Braden found the lock, but didn't have anything to pry it open with. G-War barely fit inside. He and Braden locked eyes, but they couldn't share a single thought. The 'cat looked miserable.

Braden's head hurt less, probably because he was doing something, but he was miserable, too. "I'm right here with you, G. I wonder if they used a gaff hook to take that thing out of my eye. It feels like they split my head open." Braden sat on the cage and G-War yowled, so he adjusted and sat on the floor next to the cage. He closed his eyes and tried to will the pain away.

He heard a slight creak as the door outside their prison opened.

"I hoped that you'd be awake by now," the Professor said. Braden couldn't see the man in the semi-darkness using his one eye. The patch covered the other and Braden hoped that his eye was under there.

"Let us go and we won't kill you," Braden said, half-heartedly, as he held his head in his hands.

"Your friends are on their way here right now," the Professor replied. "I expect that's exactly what they have in mind. What they don't know is that we've had four-hundred years to improve how we defend ourselves. Remember that we were cut off because of the war. We never knew if or when they were coming for us. That means that we are more than prepared for your happy band of cavemen and their pets." The old Professor moved close to the bars and looked at Braden.

"Do you think just because someone put a neural implant in your head that you are an equal to those who came before, a peer to a person like me? I'm the Professor, and compared to me, you are no higher on the evolutionary scale than those creatures you met on the beach!" His lip quivered as he spoke, eyebrows pulled downward as he tried to control his rage.

"If you've had four-hundred years to improve, why couldn't you take out the implant without tearing up my eyeball? And if you're so good, how come that mob of misfits even exists? You think you're smarter than you are and that's how you're going to fall. Just like the Overlords, at the end, you'll be begging for your life, begging your betters to have mercy." Braden's head throbbed with his efforts to think.

He leaned against the cage, putting a couple fingers through so he could touch G-War.

*That's more like it. Now how are you going to get me out of here?'* the 'cat said clearly into Braden's mind. He sighed and turned toward the Professor.

"I'd like to rest now, if you don't mind. Show some compassion. That'll make it easier when your time comes," Braden said, unable to stop threatening the man.

"I've already gotten what I needed from you. The females will provide the rest, but a sample from each of the species will give me enough to work with for the remainder of my lifetime, which is beyond what you can imagine," the Professor taunted. He dropped a flask to the floor and kicked it through a gap at the bottom of the bars. "Drink it," he said, hesitating for a moment before turning and walking from the room.

The door closed lightly behind him. Braden saw a corridor beyond, lit by the artificial lights of the ancients, but that was all he could see before the door closed. He couldn't judge how wide the corridor was or whether there were cells on the other side. All he knew was that he was trapped in here, but at least if he touched the 'cat, they could talk.

That was his sole comfort. G-War seemed to appreciate it, too, although his misery at being in the cage dominated most of his thoughts.

Braden opened the flask and sniffed, expecting to smell a strange concoction, but there wasn't anything. It tasted like water. Braden fed the mouth of the flask into the cage to make sure G-War was able to drink, too. The 'cat drank more than half the flask, but Braden didn't care. He'd do without. Once they finished the flask, he staggered back to the bed, hoping that sleep would bring relief.

He fell asleep quickly, but his dreams were dogged by images of the Professor sticking needles into him, cutting pieces from his body, and laughing at him the whole time.

# Pik Ashore

Holly expertly maneuvered the great ship around the rocky outcropping and into the cove, driving the ship gently onto the shore where Brandt leapt from the deck and landed knee-deep in the water. He waded ashore as Pik slipped over the side, splashing into a small wave rolling past the ship.

Pik walked onto the beach without hesitation, expecting that the Hawkoids had seen the ship enter the cove. He watched the Warden backing out to where it would wait for the companions' return.

Treetis crouched atop the King's head, watching the trail and wondering why the misfit mob wasn't there to greet them. He thought he was ready to go to war. He'd killed much game as G-War had taught him how to hunt, and he expected those lessons would translate directly to fighting a human. Even if they didn't, he'd figure it out when the time came. He wasn't worried. He was a Hillcat.

Pik waved the King forward as he walked, then started jogging along the trail to the compound. Brandt followed, matching the Lizard Man's speed until Pik held up his trident, signaling for a halt. They stopped and listened. The Lizard Man pointed to Treetis and held up his hands. The 'cat looked at him for a few heartbeats before he understood.

Treetis closed his eyes and tried reaching out as the Golden Warrior and Fealona had taught him, trying to feel if others were near. He sensed the presence of smaller creatures, not intelligent, before he found the misshapen creatures, blocking the trail ahead.

Once he knew they were there, the challenge was to communicate to the Lizard Man and the Aurochs what he'd seen. He climbed down Brandt's face and jumped into the sand. He scratched a line forward, then pointed along the sandy trail. Brandt and Pik both nodded. Then Treetis stabbed a claw into the sand a dozen times on the trail ahead of them. He raised a paw and staggered around on his other three, then again pointed up the trail.

Pik nodded and tapped Brandt on the nose. It was time to execute the plan. Brandt would run at them full speed. They creatures would dive out of the way, and Brandt would continue to the compound, where Pik would hunt down the Professor. The Lizard Man was confident that the Professor held no power over him, like he'd been able to dominate Braden and the 'cat.

Pik joined Treetis on Brandt's broad back. With a gentle tap, Brandt knew they were ready. He pawed the sand and launched himself forward, running faster and faster toward the compound. As Treetis had seen, the creatures stood in the way. They'd recovered their spears and clubs and shook them at the oncoming Aurochs. Only for a moment, though. As Pik had guessed, they threw their weapons away as they dove into the brush, frantic to get out of the way of the great King.

Brandt dodged slightly to miss one who was slower than the others, bumping the creatures aside as he raced passed. He continued running, slowing as he approached the compound. Pik slid down the King's side before he came to a stop. With his trident before him, Pik Ha'ar burst into the building from which they'd seen the Professor emerge the day prior.

Inside, he found a living quarters with books, many, many old-style books. There was technology, too and a door that was locked. Pik jabbed at it with his spear, but to no effect. He bolted from the small building and went to the next, a larger structure, with windows open to the side. Pik jumped in front of the window and looked in. It appeared to be a laboratory, similar to the facility he'd awoken in on the RV Traveler. Old Tech dominated the space. Pik ran around the building to find the door, entering when he did.

He made a quick tour around the facility, and not seeing any weapons or the Professor, left without touching anything. The third building looked to be a barracks of sorts. It had two rows of bunk beds, all recently slept in. On the other side of the room, there was a long table with bench seats and a fabricator set into the wall. A small restroom was off to the side. Brandt's bugling and stomping alerted Pik to a danger outside. He opened the door and looked into the compound.

The mob had returned. This time, they remembered their weapons. They were trying to form a circle around Brandt, but he was swinging his great horns from side to side and pawing at the ground. The mob hadn't seen Pik as they menaced the King of the Aurochs. Urged on by the man-horse, one darted toward Brandt's exposed flank and jabbed his spear into the Aurochs' hip. The point didn't penetrate as it wasn't sharp enough.

Brandt jumped around, swinging his head violently at the attacker, hitting him, and sending him flying into the nearest building. The misfit crumpled to the ground. Brandt completed his turn, chasing back another misguided adventurer. Pik used his spear to drive the creatures back as he entered the circle. Since they were already there, he used his mindlink to talk with Brandt.

*'There's no one inside, and where are the others?'* Pik asked Brandt. Brandt bugled again and again, to let everyone on the island know that he was engaged with the enemy.

*'Don't answer me. We're in the compound and no one's here. Watch out!'* Pik said over the mindlink, unsure of whether the others would hear or not.

# The Underground Complex

Micah had heard Pik's call as they left their positions and moved past the door in the mound. The others wanted to run but Micah stopped Fea and waved her back. She brought them together and whispered, "If there's no one in the compound, then maybe they are hiding. A place like that--" Micah pointed to the mound. "--looks like somewhere an ancient would hide."

Aadi thought it made sense and he nodded. Fea didn't care either way. Bronwyn was concerned with the creatures that Brandt and Pik faced. She knew that they were mostly harmless, and she had confidence that she could control them. When she tried to speak, Micah put her finger to her lips.

Micah led Aadi to the door. Fea stood to the side. There was a hand-pad next to it. She put her hand on it, expecting a red light indicating that she wasn't authorized access. It didn't light up at all. She pulled on the door and although it was heavy, it opened after she used both hands and braced herself. Aadi and Fea stood close by, ready to protect Micah if someone lurked below.

They peered into the darkness. The 'cat's eyes adjusted the quickest, and she nodded and walked in. Micah followed, pulling Aadi behind her. Bronwyn watched them go, then turned and ran for the compound. Zyena watched from her perch above the mound. Unwilling to fly underground, she went after the girl to watch over her.

Fea continued down a long set of stairs that led far below the surface of the island. The ancients' lighting system seemed to be half-functional. Every other light panel was dark. The heat of the island's day, although not bad, didn't penetrate to the depths as it cooled considerably on their way down. When they reached the bottom, they found a corridor that led in one direction. The poor lighting showed doors at various intervals.

Micah shrugged and pointed. Fea went first, running ahead, only to stop, listen, and then run some more. Micah walked carefully, a sword in one hand and a blaster in the other. She wanted to be ready for anything. Aadi watched, unblinking.

As they came to the first door, Micah looked at Fea and nodded. The 'cat shrugged. She couldn't feel whether anything was inside or not. Micah turned to tell Bronwyn to stay in the corridor with Aadi, but the teenager wasn't there. Micah panicked and ran to the stairs, wondering if Bronwyn had sensed something that made her afraid and stopped.

The steps were empty. The door remained open at the top, casting light into the shadows.

*Bronwyn's gone to the compound to talk with the misfits,* Micah thought, then opened the mindlink, even though she knew it could alert the Professor to her presence. *'Bronwyn is on her way to you, but not us,'* Micah said over the mindlink. Pik confirmed he heard her and they'd watch out for the girl. Micah also hoped that Zyena had heard and was with her. Zyena was large for a Hawkoid and could intimidate the misfits if they became hostile toward Bronwyn.

Micah returned to the doorway and shook her head. She knew exactly where the girl had gone. She suspected that they should have sent her with Brandt in the first place, but in the original plan, she wasn't going ashore. Aadi thought the same thing.

None of that mattered at that very moment, where they stood in an underground corridor, not knowing where the Professor was, or Braden or G-War for that matter. And she wanted to find them.

Micah grabbed the handle and yanked the door open. The lights inside came on, showing a store room of sorts. It smelled musty and dank. Dust lay undisturbed on the surfaces of boxes on shelves. She shut the door and signaled that they needed to move on. They hurried to the next door and the next. This was a storage area, off the beaten path. She didn't need to see what was in the crates, that wasn't her purpose in being there, and checking empty rooms was wasting their time.

She pulled the group together and whispered, "If we don't find something soon, I think we need to go back outside." Fea shook her head and pointed down the corridor. Aadi shook his head as well. They'd all heard Pik's call that no one was in the compound. Bronwyn would calm the mob. They were convinced that Braden was somewhere in the underground complex, as they were beginning to think of it.

For a moment, Micah wondered if such a complex existed below the ancients' compound in the rainforest. She shook that off. Thinking of more Overlords running around was too foul to contemplate.

She was closer to finding Braden and G-War, because she could say with certainty where they were not.

Fea ran past the last few doors along the sides and stopped at a larger, heavier door at the end of the corridor. She nodded and pointed at it. Micah had put her sword away to pull the first door open, and it was still in its scabbard. There was no way she could open doors and carry the sword. She dialed the tightest beam possible on the blaster and held it firmly, ready to fire.

With a deep breath, she yanked on the door, but this one was secured. She put her hand on the panel and it turned green, which both pleased her and frightened her. How and why did it recognize her?

No time to think, she pulled the door open to reveal another corridor. This one was well-lit, wide with impressive doors arrayed along one side. She pushed Aadi through to face one direction while she jumped in behind him, facing the other way. The corridor wasn't empty. There were boxes along the walls and a Bot stood there, too. Micah didn't hesitate, she fired, hoping that its energy shield wasn't active.

Hope was a lousy plan. Her shot reflected from the Bot and barely missed her head as it flashed past, too fast for her to move out of its way, had it come more directly at her. She looked behind her at the scorch mark down the corridor where the beam had spent its energy.

She crouched, ready to dive through the door and away from the Bot if it fired, but then realized that it was a Development Unit, a smaller version of one, but a Bot that didn't have weapons, only the defensive shield.

She relaxed only slightly as the presence of any Bots suggested that there could be a Security Bot somewhere. She tried the closest door, getting a green indicator from the panel before it unlocked to allow them in. She pulled it open and dropped to a knee, ready to fire. The room was a massive laboratory into which most of the doors in the corridor opened.

Bots and Old Tech. This was a laboratory of the ancients.

# Bounder and Ferrer to the Rescue

Bounder and Ferrer threw caution to the wind once they heard the King of the Aurochs bugling his dismay. They raced together down the path while Skirill flew before them, back and forth across the trail looking for hidden enemies.

What the Hawkoid didn't see was the net buried under the sand, its supports hidden against the trees. The net sprang up as the Wolfoid and Rabbit ran by, wrapping itself around them and bundling their limbs.

Their momentum carried them forward until they both landed in a heap, side by side in the sand. Bounder twisted his head to look for enemies who might attack them while they were held tightly within the net. Skirill circled above the trap, watching, wondering if the two could extricate themselves. Skirill expanded his circles, flying farther and farther from the Wolfoid and the Rabbit. When he was certain there were no creatures nearby, he returned to the trap, back-winging to land next to it, where he started using his talons to pull the net from his friends.

The Wolfoid grumbled his dismay, wanting to howl at his failure, but he stayed quiet and started chewing on the rope before his muzzle. He couldn't move anything else, so Bounder fought back in the only way he could.

Ferrer shivered in fear. Once again, the world conspired against him. He closed his eyes and rocked, thinking of being home in his garden. Even the ship's garden sounded warm and inviting compared to this. He convinced himself that he'd made a mistake in coming.

Bounder started jerking his head as he made way through the rope, hoping it would tear apart. Ferrer made himself as small as possible, keeping his eyes shut. He thought the Wolfoid was panicking.

Skirill found the clasps that held the net closed. He started undoing those, one at a time, and the rest was easy. With the edge of the net held in his claws, he flew upwards and pulled half the net away. Bounder kept scrabbling to get out, but Skirill shook his head. The Hawkoid took the other edge and unfolded it from the top of his two friends. Bounder jumped up, ripping the lightning spear from his hand. He untangled the spear, then grabbed a handful of Rabbit harness with his other hand and pulled Ferrer upright.

Bounder nodded down the trail and with one leap, cleared the edges of the net and started running anew toward the compound. Ferrer leapt as only a Rabbit can, easily sailing over the trap and into the sand beyond. He bounded after the Wolfoid while Skirill flew overhead, encouraging him to catch up.

At that point, they hadn't been too far away. Bounder ran into the area as Pik and Brandt stood back to back facing the misfits in a loose circle around them. Bounder leveled his spear at the nearest and Pik raised his hand to stop him.

The Wolfoid refrained from activating the weapon, but kept it trained on the creature with tentacles for arms.

Bronwyn burst into the compound from the jungle and yelled. "No!" She ran first to the man-horse, stroking his thick neck and cooing to him. The other misfits dropped their weapons as they ran to be close to the girl. Pik and Brandt looked, eleven bodies pressed in on Bronwyn. The twelfth lay crumpled next to the wall, forgotten. The misfits lifted the girl onto the back of the man-horse, who beamed at being the center of attention.

Skirill landed atop one of the buildings and watched the others.

*'Where's Strider?'* Bounder asked.

# Strider is Coming

Strider jogged upright alongside the path while Brigitte bounded along, looking at the foliage. Zeeka was up ahead, vigorously pointing at something. Strider slowed and leveled her spear, but Zeeka shook her feathered head. Brigitte sprinted ahead to catch up, or rather, she sprinted to avoid being left behind.

Strider saw the heavily-used path beyond the Hawkoid. It led directly toward the compound, turning at the point before them and going to an opening in the hill above. Strider indicated that Brigitte should stay there with her pistol aimed down the trail leading into the jungle. Strider dropped to all fours and ran up the hill, stopping at the metal gate that blocked the entrance to the tunnel. It was locked with a device that could be accessed from either side. Strider expected that she could blast it open with her spear, but didn't want to do that.

Not yet anyway.

The plan called for them to converge on the compound. Strider knew that Braden and Micah would want to know about the tunnel. Maybe this was the access to the undersea facility they were looking for. She tried to peer through the darkness, but could only see to the bend. Many feet had gone that way many times. She was wondering who had traveled that path when she heard Brandt bugling in the distance. The compound was further than she'd thought.

She turned and bolted down the hill, waving at Brigitte to follow as she passed the Rabbit.

Zeeka jumped into the air and flew hard down the trail, leaving the others far behind. She realized she'd made a mistake when the rocks started pelting her from above. She dodged and weaved, trying to get away, but one hit her in the head, stunning her. She careened off a tree and into the undergrowth. Strider and Brigitte raced forward, oblivious to what happened to the Hawkoid.

Rocks started pelting them, too, but Strider had seen this before. She leaned back, braced her lightning spear and sent bolt after bolt into the trees, scattering the monkeys in all directions. She and Brigitte jogged forward, carefully watching as they passed. They continued ahead, unaware that a mere two strides away, Zeeka was unconscious and crumpled within a bush.

They saw no more monkeys as they followed the wide and well-used path straight to the compound. When they finally arrived, Bounder and Ferrer were there, with Brandt and Pik. Zyena and Skirill perched on the roof of one of the ancients' buildings. Bronwyn was in the middle of the misfit mob, talking animatedly with them.

*'Where's Zeeka?'* Zyena asked.

*'Oh, no!'* Strider cried. *'The monkeys!'* She turned and ran on all fours back the way she'd come. Skirill and Zyena quickly caught up to her and flew past. They continued along the path until they broke into the opening beyond, at the bottom of the hill. They flew back, meeting Strider at the site of the monkey ambush.

Zyena was first to see her, squawking loudly and hovering directly over the bush. Strider dug in and carefully tore the branches away from Zeeka. When they looked at the young Hawkoid, they saw that her wings were sound and her body seemed uninjured, but one trickle of blood escaped from a cut over her eye. Strider cradled the Hawkoid's head in her hands.

Zeeka came to with a start, pecking the Wolfoid's foreleg. Strider yipped in pain, dropping the Hawkoid's head into the sand. Zyena and Skirill cooed to their daughter, happy to see her eyes open. She turned her neck to and fro, worked out the kinks, then tested her wings. She nodded to her parents as she ran a few steps and launched into the air, but struggled to maintain altitude.

*'Go back to the ship and wait for us there,'* Zyena said, breaking the silence.

Zeeka didn't bother to nod as she slowly climbed, catching an updraft from the hill, then headed southeast toward the easily recognizable sail of the Warden.

Skirill inclined his head toward the compound and the three of them raced back. Skirill couldn't help but feel that he was wasting time. *Where are Braden and G-War? For that matter, where are Micah, Aadi, and Fea? Wasn't Bronwyn supposed to be with them?* he thought.

# The Underground Complex

Micah saw the Professor. Without turning, he said in a voice far too loud, "Welcome to my laboratory. I've been expecting you, although it took you far longer than I thought it would. Shame. I had hoped you were more intelligent, but no matter. Come in, come in."

*'We found him. Zyena will show you the way,'* Micah said over the mindlink.

"That won't work in here, but I appreciate the effort. I will have to more thoroughly examine how that works in the genetically engineered creatures and how a human can use it. So very interesting."

The sound of equipment humming pulled their attention away from the Professor. A Security Bot slowly approached from the side. Unlike the ones at New Sanctuary, this Security Bot was more human in shape, with tentacles and various weapons attached. It even wore rough clothing, making it even more hideous to behold. It reminded her of the misshapen creatures outside, but she was under no illusion about the deadly nature of the Bot.

A dual laser beam looked at her from over its left shoulder. Each arm ended in a vicious-looking knife attached to large, multi-barreled blasters. There was a tentacle that carried another weapon of some sort.

And Brandt was in the compound with the shield generator. Micah carefully put her blasters on the floor and held her hands up. Aadi floated serenely, blinking quickly as a testament to his anxiety. He felt the same way he did when the Androids took him—helpless and afraid.

Fea was gone, having dodged back out the door. The Professor looked at the floor and under the tables. "Find it and bring it back here," he barked at the Security Bot. It opened the door closest to it and moved into the hallway, still humming with the power it exuded.

They could hear popping sounds as it fired a myriad of weaponry in the corridor. Micah hung her head, biting her lip at the thought of Fea getting killed.

The Security Bot returned, the limp 'cat held loosely in the tentacle arm. The Bot hovered past Micah and Aadi until it was before the Professor, where it deposited Fea on the table in front of him.

"She's still very much alive, just rendered unconscious. She'll awake shortly, after I've taken what I need, of course," the Professor said as he put on a pair of glasses and studied the prone form of the Hillcat. He pulled a razor and shaved the hair from a leg, her abdomen, and a spot on her lower back.

Micah watched in horror as he produced a keen knife and number of needles. As he made an incision on the 'cat's abdomen, Micah jumped toward the table, getting caught mid-leap by the Security Bot's tentacle, who held her, dangling in the air as she struggled mightily to break free. Aadi started swimming to the side, away from the Security Bot. When he had his angle, he delivered his focused thunderclap at close range directly into the face of the Professor. The young man flew backward, scattering a table of instruments and equipment, and landed roughly.

Sparks and lightning erupted from the Security Bot. Micah spasmed uncontrollably as the world turned black all around her. Sparks danced across Aadi's shell and over his neck, affecting his ability to float. He started dropping to the floor. A second round of electricity turned him limp. He bounced off the floor once, before settling upright, his thick legs splayed to the sides. His beak-like mouth rested on the floor, his black tongue hanging out sideways.

# The Companions Unleashed

*'Micah and Aadi have been captured by the Professor. There's a Security Bot down here. There's...'* Fea told them, getting cut off mid-thought as she screamed over the mindlink.

The companions looked at each other.

*'Bronwyn, how did they get underground?'* Pik asked.

*'There's a door and stairs down, the way we came,'* she replied, alarmed at the tone in the 'cat's voice and the way her 'shout' was cut short.

Pik looked at the compound. He was furious, but no one could tell. Lizard Men carried their emotions inside. His plan had failed because the Professor had a secret hideaway below ground. He had a Security Bot and he had a way to block the mindlink and the neural implant. Pik didn't know how any of it worked, but he knew what happened when those things didn't work.

Panic and chaos. The only way the companions could communicate was because of the Hillcats and Bronwyn. Pik had already dispensed with their silence, but now was the time for something different since his plain had failed so spectacularly.

*'Brandt, we need the device you carry. We'll take it with us as we go below. Bounder and Strider, Ferrer and Brigitte, and Treetis, you'll join me. Brandt, Skirill, and Zyena, please watch over Bronwyn as you must remain here. There's no room for you below,'* Pik said passionately. They were running out of people and they had yet to make any headway against the Professor. *'Wish us well.'*

Pik shambled through the sand, carrying the field generator in front of him. His spear dragged beside him as he pinned it between his arm and his body. His skin suit was preventing him from moving freely, but without it, he'd dry out and die. He continued running, not fast, but faster than if he wasn't trying to run.

Skirill flew ahead of the group, on the lookout for monkeys and other threats to the companions as they made one final attempt to save the humans. Skirill landed on the branch over the mound, the same one that Zyena had used not long before.

The others came running, stopping to look through the open door at the dark stairway beyond. Bounder hesitated only for a moment, enough time for his eyes to partially adjust. He lumbered down the steps, his Wolfoid legs not made for descending, although he could run up them as fast as anyone. Pik followed, then the Rabbits and Strider brought up the rear. Skirill glided to the sand and hopped to the top step.

*They need me,* the Hawkoid reasoned as he hopped to the next step, then the next, taking them one at a time, hurrying to catch the group as they headed toward the bottom.

Strider saw Skirill coming. Who was she to deny one of Braden's oldest and closest friends? She nodded to the Hawkoid as she continued descending the stairs.

At the bottom, they saw what Micah had seen, but what they didn't have was the keen nose of a Wolfoid, who hunted by tracking the scent of their prey. Bounder dropped to all fours and sniffed the floor. He followed Micah and Fea's trail easily down the corridor, to the first door, but not going in, the second door, and then the rest. They hadn't entered any of the rooms. The door at the end was different, sturdier, bigger.

And it was open. The bright lighting from the corridor beyond told them clearly they were entering a better used section of the underground complex. Pik looked at the device he carried. He usually shunned Old Tech, but in this case, he needed it to work or they would all be at the mercy of the Professor and his Security Bot. He pressed on the spot that Micah had showed him and the thing came to life with no fanfare. One light shone on the simple panel. Green. Pik's favorite color.

He nodded to Bounder. It was unfortunate that they didn't have the spear device that was supposed to work with the field generator to neutralize the Security Bot, but they'd make do with what they had.

Bounder jumped into the hallway and fired quickly when he saw the Development Unit. Unlike Micah's, his shot blasted into the chest of the unit, exploding it from within.

He stalked forward to make sure it was dead. Brigitte squeezed past Pik and went left down the corridor to cover Bounder's back. The Lizard Man entered the bright space, walking slowly toward the destroyed Bot. The last members of the group entered the corridor--Rabbits left, the young Hillcat in the middle, and Wolfoids right. Bounder stood up straight, relaxing, until he realized that the Bot he killed wasn't a Security Bot.

The door beside him started to open and he dove out of the way, rolling to come up facing it with his spear aimed and ready to fire. Strider jumped backward into the wall, knocking the spear from her own hand. Both Rabbits fired their small lasers into whatever was coming through the doorway. Bounder's view as blocked.

Lightning sparks filled the corridor, engulfing the Rabbits and the 'cat. The laser pistols flew from their small hands as they twitched and contorted, falling to the floor and jerking spasmodically.

Bounder thrust his spear around the door and fired at whatever was inside. He kept firing, low, middle, high, middle, until his spear grew hot from his efforts. An explosion threw the door open, crashing against him and sending him flying down the corridor. Strider was in the middle of the blast, getting jammed into the wall. She slid down and collapsed on the floor. Pik was thrown backward through the doorway into the first corridor.

He threw the field generator from him and tried to climb to his feet, but his ears were ringing and his head felt thick. A blazing white streak with brown wings flew above his face. Skirill tucked his wings as he went through the doorway, banked hard right then hard left and through the doorway where the remains of a Security Bot still arced and sparked.

Skirill raced in a circle around the laboratory. The Professor lay on the floor, with blood flowing freely from his head. Fea was on the table, with spots on her body shaved. A cut on her abdomen trickled blood. She was out cold. Micah and Aadi were both on the floor, also unconscious. Skirill circled one more time. He had no idea what he was looking for, but nothing alarmed him more than the sight of his friends.

He landed next to Micah and pecked at her cheek until she twitched. He used his wings to fan her, not knowing what else to do.

Bounder pulled himself upright. He hurt all over, but his mate had been right in the middle of the explosion. He went to her, cradling her head as he whimpered and whined like a pup. Her tongue appeared as she tried to lick her nose. Bounder pulled his flask and dribbled water on her muzzle, onto her tongue. She opened her eyes.

"I'm all right," she said in the spoken Wolfoid language. Bounder didn't believe her. Small cuts covered her chest and stomach. Her eyes wouldn't focus. Bounder licked her wounds, knowing that Wolfoid saliva would hasten the healing. Almost as good as numbweed, he'd told Braden a number of times, although the Free Trader never opted for licking when he had numbweed on hand.

She tried to stand but her legs wouldn't support her. She sat back down, then laid down, head between her front paws. "Go and check on the others," she told him. He left his flask and took her spear, unsure of the charge remaining in his.

When Bounder entered the laboratory, he saw the Hawkoid working with Micah. She was starting to come to. Her head lolled on her neck as she tried to regain control of her senses. Her arms flopped uselessly at her sides. Bounder was unable to use his thought voice in the laboratory. He was sure that there was a piece of Old Tech that needed to be turned off, but he had no idea what to look for. The easy answer was to leave the room.

Pik Ha'ar, using his trident to keep himself upright, staggered into the laboratory. He looked around until he saw the Tortoid. Pik stumbled past Micah, Bounder, and Skirill to get to Aadi. Pik checked his shell, then his body. There was a faint smell of something burnt, but beyond that, Aadi seemed unharmed. Still, he was on the floor, his head and legs limp.

Bounder went to the table where Fea lay, partially shaved and injured. He returned to Micah and removed a small amount of numbweed from her pouch. He returned to the 'cat and applied it, letting it settle, stopping the bleeding and taking away the pain from the small wound in the middle of her shaved stomach.

She jerked once, twice, and then lifted her head. She blinked at Bounder, who stroked her head gently.

'*What happened?*' she asked, much to Bounder's surprise. He stopped petting her and tried to respond, but the mindlink was gone. She looked at his half-hand/half-paw and nodded. He started petting her again.

'*What happened?*' she asked again, stronger this time.

'*I don't know. The Professor had you, but he was stopped. It looks like Aadi finished him.*' The 'cat shakily lifted her head, trying to see around her. The Professor was in the middle of the lab, unmoving. It finally dawned on Bounder to check him.

The Professor was dead.

Fea was trying to roll over so she could stand up. As soon as Bounder put his hands on her, she asked him the hard question. '*Ax?*'

'*We haven't found them yet. Micah is just coming to. Pik is hurt, Strider is down, the Rabbits are down, Aadi is out cold. He hurt us, Fea, but we'll keep looking until we've searched this whole place.*'

Two shaky Rabbits stumbled through the door and looked at Bounder, their noses were twitching and their normally upright ears had flopped down the sides of their faces. They carried the young, orange 'cat. Bounder went to them, hugging both of the Rabbits and nuzzling their soft white necks.

Treetis was still out from the Security Bot's weapon, but he was alive. The Rabbits put him on the floor next to Aadi.

While Bounder touched the Rabbits, he talked. '*I thought you were dead,*' he said in surprise. '*I'm so happy that you are alive!*' He hugged them one last time and went back into the corridor.

Strider was still on her stomach, laying on the cool floor. Her eyes looked clear, but her ears suggested she was in pain. He nuzzled her again and looked for another flask of water. Not finding one, he went into the laboratory and asked Pik for his. He readily gave it to the Wolfoid. Bounder's appreciation was beyond words.

With the second flask, she started to feel strong enough to stand. Once upright, Bounder looked her over thoroughly. Since she was already flat against the wall, that probably saved her from real injury. He expected she'd have a bruise that covered her whole body. She walked, stiffly, then went to all fours where she seemed to be more comfortable. Bounder carried her lightning spear as well as his own.

They entered the laboratory, where Micah was standing, Fea was standing, albeit shaky and weak. Aadi was finally lifting his head. Micah tried to walk and nearly fell, then she kneeled next to Aadi and cradled his head in her hands.

"Aadi, my friend, how are you?" she asked gently.

*I've never felt anything like that before,'* he said roughly, his thought voice fuzzy.

"I have to ask, how are your eggs, Master Aadi?"

*I am afraid, Master Micah, for my children. I don't have my senses back, yet, but soon, I hope, and then we'll know.'*

Pik lifted Fea off the counter and put her on the floor. She staggered a few steps before gaining more control over her muscles. She made it to the corridor before she stopped and leaned against the door.

*'Are you coming?'* she asked Bounder once clear of the field that prevented them from using the mindlink when they weren't in physical contact.

*'Where?'* Bounder asked.

*'To find our mates, that's where,'* Fea replied. She took a deep breath and staggered down the corridor, past the exploded Development Unit and toward a different part of the underground complex.

# The Old Professor

Micah stumbled into the corridor, with Pik close behind carrying Skirill in his arms. Ferrer stayed with Aadi while Brigitte joined Strider, just sitting with her, keeping her company.

Bounder took the lead as he was the only one even remotely healthy. The others shuffled and stumbled behind him. He put his nose to the ground and sniffed his way ahead. There were a number of strange smells, but in the background he found what he was looking for: Braden. He followed the scent, feeling odd as he'd never trailed the human before.

But it confirmed that Braden had been in the laboratory. He couldn't smell G-War, but that could have been because someone carried the 'cat through the corridor. First Braden, then they'd continue searching until they found the 'cat.

The underground complex was huge. There was even a small factory with Maintenance and Server Bots producing mysterious parts and pieces. They found another huge laboratory with large clear tanks filled with fluids of some sort. Half-grown creatures were in most of them. Micah was repulsed by the sight and wanted to shoot the tanks with her blasters, but she didn't want to get splashed with any of it. Without the Professor, she hoped that the creatures would never see the light of day.

She closed the door as they left the large lab, a look of disgust on her face. Bounder made a final turn into a corridor similar to the first one they used where half the lights were off. Maybe that was a conservation measure and not a reflection of poor maintenance.

Micah had kept her blaster ready throughout the entire excursion through the complex and she was wearing down. Whatever beam the Security Bot had used on her had sucked the life out of her. She felt exhausted, enough so that even the smooth stone floor looked like a welcoming bed.

Bounder stopped at one door and nodded. Braden's fresh scent wafted under the door, along with G-War's 'cat smell. Fea yowled as she could smell her mate.

G-War's long cry came from the other side of the door.

"No!" Braden shouted as Bounder opened the door and Micah looked inside. She ran straight to him and reached through the bars, but he only hung his head.

"What's wrong?" Micah asked, looking confused.

"There's nothing wrong," a voice said from the corner. The old Professor stepped out and leveled a strange looking weapon at them.

Micah's blood surged, her head throbbed, and she fell to her knees, spent. She couldn't even lift her arm to fire one blaster shot. It was nothing the Professor did, but the complete failure that she felt. Bounder leapt toward the Professor but was caught by a crackling charge from the Professor's weapon. The old man grunted as the Wolfoid's heavy body slammed into him.

Pik dropped the Hawkoid and rushed into the room.

The Professor had turned, just enough to avoid the Wolfoid's full impact, but he was thrown into the wall. Without waiting, he fired at the Lizard Man, who sparked magnificently. The water in his skin suit magnified the light show from the weapon's discharge. Skirill remained in the corridor, out of sight. Fea stood next to her human, then sat, exhausted from the events of the day.

They found that the mindlink was dampened in the cell area, too. But Braden and Micah were holding hands.

*'Good to see you, lover,'* Micah said without taking her eyes from the old Professor. *'It looks like there were two of them, a mistake that seems to have cost us.'*

*'Don't count us out, yet. Where's the other one?'* Braden replied.

*'He and the Security Bot are both dead, thanks to Aadi and Bounder. They hurt us, but nothing that time won't heal,'* Micah said, looking at her partner through sad eyes. Braden nodded. Fea rubbed against the bars. Braden scratched behind her ears.

*'Tell my mate that I will kill the foul creature, as soon as I have enough energy. Find out where Caleb is, so we can finish this,'* Fea told Braden. He looked into her eyes and nodded almost imperceptibly.

"Don't you look all straggly, just like G-War," Braden said casually. "So, Professor. You never answered my question. Where are the people from White Beach?"

"Why, they're in Atlantis, a quaint name we gave the undersea laboratory that has become an undersea city! It really is quite magnificent down there."

"Will we get a chance to see it, see for ourselves how magnificent it is?" Braden prodded.

"Maybe." The Professor committed to nothing.

"How can you get there? We didn't see any kind of ship or place to dock a mini-sub. Do you have the mini-submarines from the Warden? Can you talk with the vehicles from down there, summon them?"

"Oh my!" the Professor exclaimed. "Do you really think you can escape? I'm afraid that your time is up. Let me crush your final hopes. I am going to take your DNA, rip it from you and all your mutant friends, and then I'm going to build a new civilization, new creatures that will respond to my commands and my commands only. The human livestock in New Sanctuary is the base material and with your new genes, they will become invincible. We will return to the continent and rebuild Sanctuary as I see fit. I have Security Bots, I have Gloria. And you? You have no chance at all."

Braden hung his head, nodding solemnly. He looked up. Fea's eyes showed anger, her ears flat against her head as she worked her way between Micah and Braden. Micah and Fea were talking, but Braden couldn't hear. The Professor had moved closer to deliver his diatribe. An angry sneer split his face, his eyes maniacal as he shook his weapon at them.

"Good-bye now," he said in a low and dangerous voice. A commotion from the corridor made him turn. Skirill beat his wings against the doorway as he powered through, flying toward the Professor's face, talons first. The old man couldn't raise his weapon in time, but he turned slightly. Skirill crashed against his shoulder as Micah twisted, throwing the 'cat upward in one smooth motion.

The Professor pulled the trigger on his weapon, sending a stream of electricity into Micah, the metal bars, and Braden. They both jerked convulsively, but they didn't pass out. The power was spread too thinly between the two humans and the cage.

Fea landed on the man's arm and using her claws prodigiously, she climbed toward his face. Skirill continued to beat his wings, to maintain his purchase on the man's other arm. The Professor screamed as the two companions continued their relentless attacks. The Professor stumbled in his futile attempts to fight off his attackers. Both Pik and Bounder were on the floor, close to his feet. The man had no room to maneuver, no place to run.

Braden and Micah collapsed, but they weren't out of it. Braden yelled as he tried to pull himself upright. All he could think about was getting a handful of the Professor and smashing the man's smug face against the bars.

Fea managed to get a claw into the old man's neck, and with an acrobatic spin, twisted her body around his head, tearing deeply into the Professor's throat as she flew to the floor. The old man fell to his knees. Skirill was thrown to the side as the man went down. Fea jumped onto his back, reaching around his neck as blood spurted from the already open artery. But she was angry and raked her way almost completely through his neck.

Micah fought against the effects of the Old Tech weapon, but she was spent, the second time her body was assaulted by the energy weapons that day. She had nothing left to fight with, and now, she was covered in the Professor's blood, too.

The old man dropped the rest of the way, dead before he hit the floor.

Fea rode him down, standing on his back as he splattered his face on the hard stone. Skirill picked at a couple feathers that had been dislodged during his struggle. He looked at the corpse for a heartbeat or two, then hopped over the bodies strewn across the floor to rub his head on Micah's hand. He didn't even say anything. All he wanted was for her to be okay.

Fea sat and held her bloody paws in front of her, disgusted by the thought of licking the Professor's blood. She tried wiping her paws on the clothes of the old man, but that didn't work very well. The quandary continued as she sat on his corpse, thinking what to do, while she waited for someone to free her mate.

Braden stood at the bars. During his time alone in the cell, he figured out that the gate was controlled by an Old Tech panel next to the door. Someone needed to prop the old man up and put his hand on the pad. G-War's cage was locked with a physical device, requiring a key that Braden assumed was somewhere on the old man. Whatever prevented them from using the mindlink in the cell was still active, so G-War couldn't talk with his mate.

Braden sat down next to the cage and put his fingers between the bars. G-War laid against Braden's fingers.

*'Now we wait, but things are looking better than they were before.'* G-War sounded hopeful.

"Now we wait. I have no idea how long they'll be out and there's nothing we can do until they wake up on their own. Skirill! You and Fea saved us all," Braden said in a tired voice, before closing his eyes and giving in to sleep.

# Recovering

Pik was the first to stir. He twitched and his eyes popped open, but he didn't move. He stayed that way for a long time. Micah was out, having succumbed to the exhaustion from her efforts and being on the wrong end of Old Tech. She was emotionally and physically drained. Skirill had waited, but finally hopped into the corridor and took wing. They expected he was going to find the others, let them know that they found Braden and G-War, but he returned after only a few heartbeats. The door to the cell area was closed and he couldn't open it.

So they continued to wait. Braden slept, awkwardly, but with G-War as a comforting presence in his mind. Fea curled up next to Micah, both of them covered in the Professor's blood, but that didn't matter. Bounder's tongue hung from his mouth as he remained unconscious from receiving the full measure of the Professor's weapon. Skirill stood in the doorway and watched over his friends., unable to do more.

When the door at the end of the corridor opened, Skirill let out a screech sufficient to wake the dead. Braden jumped, as did G-War, but the 'cat only bounced off the top of the cage. Fea was up, hackles raised and back arched. Micah stirred. Pik sat up and looked around as if seeing the room for the first time.

Skirill hopped into the corridor and disappeared. When he returned, Treetis was with him, who bolted into the room as soon as he saw the carnage. He ran to Fea's side, joining her with hackles raised and ready to fight.

"Would you get off me?" Micah mumbled. Fea reached out a paw and with a  movement faster than the eye could follow, she slapped Treetis across the head. He jumped to the floor, then danced around to get out of the sticky, half-dried blood.

Craig Martelle

Strider slowly entered the room, every step deliberate as she pulled Aadi behind her. The Rabbits were last, their laser pistols held loosely in their hands. Their noses twitched and their ears perked upright, until they saw the mess inside. Strider nuzzled her mate, and he finally lifted his head, smacking his Wolfoid lips as he tried to moisten his dry tongue.

Micah pulled herself upward until she was standing. "What next?" she asked.

"Put the Professor's hand on that panel," Braden pointed. What she should have been able to easily do by herself now required help. Micah enlisted Pik and Strider's aid to muscle the man upward and slap his hand against the panel. Green and red buttons flashed. She pushed the green one. After a heartbeat, the lock disengaged and the gate to Braden's cell opened.

Braden rushed out, helping the others to put the old Professor down so he could search the man for a key, which turned out to be in his pants pocket. Once G-War was free and the extensive nuzzling between he and Fea was done, they gathered the bunch for their trip out of the underground complex. Braden asked Micah to remove the bandage over his eye.

He expected to see her wince and gasp. His eye blinked of its own accord, then started watering. She looked carefully, then shrugged.

"I don't see anything," she said. Braden sighed in relief.

"I want my blasters back," Braden told Micah as they walked, arm in arm, not as lovers, but as two wounded warriors carrying each other from the field of battle.

"The Security Bot protected his lab, so I expect they'll be there and that just so happens to be on our way." She brightened, although her words were still slurred, just enough so Braden knew that she was exhausted.

The others shuffled and staggered behind the two humans. Fea and G-War walked in front of them all. G-War was the only one fully recovered and as such, felt responsible to protect the rest. Treetis said that he was ready to fight, but Fea was still angry with him, so he brought up the rear.

Pik shuffled along, carrying Skirill and pulling Aadi behind him. Aadi looked all of his two hundred cycles. His head drooped and his legs hung limply, but at least he was floating again.

The Rabbits kept their laser pistols out and ready. The others had been surprised by the second Professor, and they didn't want to let that happen again. The Wolfoids walked with their spears, but were using them as walking sticks. Bounder continued to improve with each step, but Strider needed to rest and she faded the farther they walked. He wished he could carry her, but Wolfoids weren't built that way. No one else had enough strength to carry her either. He whimpered like a puppy, unable to contain his angst for his mate's pain.

Micah didn't have the energy to show Braden the other parts of the underground complex. She only wanted to leave.

So they made a beeline for the Professor's lab. Micah tried to access her neural implant, but there was no connection. She could pull it up to look at other data she'd stored, like maps of the areas they'd traveled. Her implant was intact, at least, just not connected. The Professor had not gotten to it before he was removed from existence by an angry Tortoid. Micah looked back at Aadi floating behind Pik and nodded to him, unsure if he saw or not.

The Free Trader and his companions reached the corridor of destruction. Scorching marked much of the wall space. Parts and pieces of Bots were strewn across the floor. The smell of singed animal hair still lingered. Braden and Micah walked into the laboratory. G-War went with them while the others waited. No one else was willing to go in there to relive the recent past.

Braden first went to the young Professor and checked through his pockets. He carried a device that looked like a communicator. Braden pressed the 'off' button. Micah checked her neural implant.

*'Master President! We've been out of contact for so long, I thought we'd lost you!'* Holly pronounced joyously.

*'Can't really talk now, Holly. Both Professors are dead and we're searching one of the labs now. We need to get back to the ship and rest. Can you bring it into the cove and*

*have it waiting for us, please?'*

*'Of course, Master President. It'll be there and we'll resume our conversation whenever you are up to it.'* Holly closed the link.

"Holly is bringing the ship in," she said, barely above a whisper, leaning heavily on a table.

*'Brandt, can you meet us at the doorway where we entered the underground complex?'* Micah asked over the mindlink.

*'Yes, Zyena will bring us to you. How is everyone?'* he asked with some trepidation.

*'Tired. See you soon, my friend.'*

Braden opened cabinets and drawers in a fruitless search for his blasters. Micah was fading fast. He'd already taken one from her and was carrying it because he couldn't find his belt either.

"Time to go, lover," Braden conceded, putting her arm over her shoulder as he supported her to walk out. Through the wreckage outside the lab they shuffled, down the corridor of the older storage area and to the stairs. At the top, Brandt's big head blocked most of the light. Micah groaned when she saw the steps.

Braden took the rope from Micah and set her on the bottom step. The others gathered around. "Brandt has suggested that he can pull you up. Take this end and I'll run the rope to him. When he starts pulling, everyone grab on. You're all coming together."

Braden tried running up the stairs, but slowed quickly and climbed slowly after a short time. At the top, he greeted the King warmly and handed him the rope. The Aurochs clamped his mouth down on it and started walking back toward the compound. The rope slid around the corner of the doorway as the slack was taken up. He kept walking while looking back. Bronwyn and the misfit mob stood in the distance, watching. Zyena was on the branch overhead, waiting to see her mate.

Micah was first, then Strider with Bounder close by, helping her from behind. Pik carried Skirill. Aadi let go of the rope tied around Pik's waist, holding onto the rope that Brandt was pulling instead. Ferrer and Brigitte came next, side by side, as they carried Fealona between them. G-War and Treetis hopped up the steps on their own, being the last ones to emerge into the daylight.

Bronwyn freed herself from the misfits and ran to Micah, hugging her and crying. The misshapen bunch produced a stretcher that they timidly approached with. Braden looked at them harshly, but nodded. Micah climbed onto the stretcher and Strider lay next to her. Fealona found space and curled herself into it. Four misfits grunted as they lifted it.

Brandt let go of the rope once everyone was outside. Braden closed the door, relieved at leaving the unpleasantness of the underground complex behind. He committed to shooting first and asking questions second from there forward. Some enemies were impossible to negotiate with. He wanted to talk with Holly, but his neural implant was gone.

They had much to discuss when he returned to the ship.

"Brandt, Bronwyn, straight to the cove, please. Holly is bringing the ship in," Braden said. He coiled the rope as he followed the others. The remainder of the mob fell in next to the stretcher and those who could took turns carrying it.

Braden didn't remember it being so far to the beach, but he was fresh the other time he'd traveled it. And they'd been with Brandt, who made travel over great distances seem effortless.

Zyena and Skirill flew ahead, joining their daughter on the highest railing of the ship, a deck above the bridge, from where Old Tech spires rose even higher.

The others finally made it as Holly expertly slid the ship's deck as close as possible. Brandt ran and jumped, landing halfway onto the deck where he fought his way aboard. Braden handed him the rope, which he again held in his mouth. Braden dug into the sand with the rope wrapped around his waist, giving the others something to hold onto as they climbed aboard.

One by one, they worked their way up. Once they had a good grip,

Brandt used his strength to easily pull them the rest of the way onto the deck. The misfits made to climb aboard and Bronwyn stopped them before Braden intervened. They put the stretcher on the deck and backed away. Braden delivered Treetis and G-War to the ship before climbing aboard himself. He looked back at the misfits, half of them were crying as Holly maneuvered the tall ship from the cove. Bronwyn threw them kisses and waved. Braden joined her in waving to them and thanking them for being there.

"You can tell them that we'll be back. Soon, we'll return and we'll need their help," Braden said, resting a hand on the girl's shoulder. When she told the mob, their mood brightened immensely and they ran around in circles on the beach, before dashing away to get ready for Bronwyn's return.

# Rest at Sea

"How long were we gone, Holly?" Braden yelled from the deck.

"The sun still has not set from when you departed the Warden earlier today. You have been gone a total of eleven hours," Holly replied through the ship's speaker system.

"What?" Braden was confused. "Not even one whole daylight?" Brandt, Zyena, and Bronwyn were the only ones who were certain that such a short time had passed since they'd departed. Everyone who'd gone underground had their internal clocks messed with. Micah couldn't believe how tired she was from less than a daylight's worth of activity.

"Let's get you checked out," Braden said, insisting that Strider, Fea, and Micah go to the small Med Lab to let the Bot examine them. Reluctantly, they went. There was room for three in the elevators, so Braden went with them. It was the fourth level below the main deck, nearly in the bottom of the ship's great keel where the scientists and research laboratories found their home. First one was checked, then the other. Holly had uploaded the specifics for Wolfoid physiology to make the examination go smoothly. Both of the patients were heavily bruised, but no other damage.

The cuts on Strider's chest and abdomen did not require stitches, which was good news since they'd scabbed over. She would not have liked getting them ripped open just to sew them back up. Fea's incision required stitches. The Med Bot took great care working on her, but the 'cat still struggled and yowled. G-War showed up outside the Med Lab and made his displeasure known to all.

Besides giving each a shot of something, the Bot recommended all three patients ingest significant amounts of water.

Braden and Bronwyn went to the galley and started ordering food, running it to the main deck as soon as it was ready. The Rabbits disappeared downstairs to the garden. Pik used the water hose to douse himself and take water to the others. He stripped out of his skin suit between trips, standing under the shower until a glass was emptied, and then he refilled it.

They ate and they drank. They were quiet. None of them were ready to talk about the events of the day, until Strider spoke. *'We found a wide tunnel, well-used, that descended into the big hill. It had a gate. I think that's what you're looking for.'*

Zeeka glided off the top deck and turned into the wind to land gracefully on the second deck railing. *'Yes. It is something worth taking a better look at,'* Zeeka added, sharing the image from her mind's eye over the mindlink. *'Just watch out for the monkeys as you travel the path toward it.'*

Micah perked up. "Thank you to the women's team, Strider, Zeeka, and Brigitte. We'll start there, at the tunnel. I didn't want to search through anything else of the Professor's, and I didn't want to go into that complex again. I don't know if my legs would carry me down those stairs. I'm sorry, did you say monkeys?" Micah said.

Bounder bristled. Strider lifted her head from a deck chair where she rested. Braden sat on the deck next to Micah, who was also reclined in a deck chair. He perked up with interest, not having heard anything about the plan to rescue him.

*'What did you boys find on your way to the compound? I know you can hear me, Ferrer. Come on, out with it,'* Strider taunted the Rabbit as she didn't expect her mate to come clean with details that might not have portrayed him favorably.

*'He ran first!'* Ferrer blurted. Bounder closed his eyes and turned from Strider, then opened and looked philosophically at the open ocean.

*'And...'* Strider prompted.

*'And we ran into a trap and Bounder smelled like a wet dog and he was piled on top of me until Skirill freed us!'* Ferrer finished by praising the Hawkoid.

"Did you just say that you two ran into a trap?" Micah asked.

*'It was cleverly hidden,'* Ferrer tried to make an excuse.

*'What's your distorted version of events?'* Strider asked her mate, sipping more water.

*'I believe enough has been said on the issue,'* Bounder said, looking at Strider wearing a big, Wolfoid smile. He didn't need to mention how the Rabbit panicked or how he was afraid for the companions. It all turned out well, and that was what mattered most. *'Have you noticed how the ocean's waves sparkle, like the gleam in your eyes when you look at me?'*

The companions had a good laugh at Bounder's expense, the levity welcomed after a difficult time.

"Monkeys," Braden repeated. "I hate monkeys."

"Pik came up with the plan. He made it all work," Micah said seriously. Braden joined Pik by the shower and they talked for a while, discussing Pik's plan and the assumptions he'd made in building it, because it sounded exactly like the plan Braden would have developed in that situation.

Braden made sure to join Bronwyn in the well deck where she dangled her legs in the water between Chlora and Rhodi. Braden kneeled next to the girl and thanked each of the Dolphins. Rexalita appeared behind the ship, diving and rising, blowing air and water from the breathing hole atop her head. She seemed to be enjoying herself.

Aadi stayed low by Micah's chair, where he could brace himself, to keep from flying away as the ship sailed out from under him. *'Master Micah, I have good news and bad news,'* Aadi started. Micah braced herself. *'Six of the eggs survived the encounter with the Security Bot.'* Aadi didn't need to say anything else. He was carrying ten eggs.

When the sun set, Holly turned on the deck lights to help people get to their beds. The weather was mild, so the Wolfoids decided to sleep in the open air by Brandt. The 'cats went to the garden level. The humans sought their own beds, Braden helping Micah up the last flight of stairs above where the elevator ended. Pik slept standing up with the shower raining over him. He could have been asleep for a while, no one knew since he hadn't moved. They let him go. He was as comfortable as he was going to be. Brandt lay down and relaxed, happy to have everyone back in one piece.

Come morning, stiff people made their way to the galley for a heavy breakfast, the breakfast of the famished. The Wolfoids had taken the elevator up rather than climb the stairs. Strider was too sore to walk, as was Micah. Braden felt bad, worse when he saw Fea and the shaved spots all over her body. She walked carefully, too. Bronwyn escorted them as the elevator didn't respond to the 'cats, no matter how loudly Treetis yowled.

Within a few heartbeats, Treetis was standing and pawing at the fabricator.

"What would you like, little man?" Braden asked.

*'Fish. Lots of fish,'* Treetis answered. Braden ordered four servings of the salmon, knowing that the fabricator could do no more than four at once. Braden put the dishes on chair seats, the right height for a full-grown Hillcat to eat without having to bend over.

"When do we go back?" Micah asked.

"Today, to check things out, I think," Braden replied. "Then as soon as you're ready, we'll go get Caleb and anyone else who's ready to come along."

"I'm going with you," Micah said firmly. Braden tried to argue, but she wouldn't have it. "Just in case you already forgot. Last time I let you go in alone, look what happened."

Braden laughed. "Sounds good. Let's see if we have any other volunteers."

Braden stood and looked at those in the galley. "We're going ashore to check things out, see about that tunnel. Who's coming along?"

Bounder looked sternly at Strider. *'I'm coming,'* he said. G-War said that he and Treetis were coming. The Rabbits both politely declined. Brandt said he was coming, too. Pik, Aadi, and Bronwyn also volunteered. The three

Hawkoids rounded out the group.

Pursing his lips, Braden walked to the outside deck. "Everyone but Strider, Fea, and the Rabbits is coming," he said to himself, hoping that it was only going to be Bounder, him, and G-War. He went back inside to make an announcement.

"You might as well rest then. We'll go ashore first thing tomorrow and we go there for real. We won't be looking around, either, we'll be going to get our people back." Braden headed for the stairs down. He wanted to talk with Pik and Aadi.

# The Tunnel

Holly sailed the ship toward the rocky outcropping and into the cove beside it. Braden and the companions stood on deck, watching the island as it drew nearer. Only Bronwyn was excited to go ashore. The bad experience with the Professors tainted the others' opinion of what should have been a pleasant island retreat.

The Hawkoids launched themselves skyward, flying high over the trees and the island as they headed toward the tunnel into the hillside. Until they found the monkeys, they weren't going to fly below the treetops.

The misfit mob was on the beach jumping up and down. Bronwyn cheered and waved to them. Braden had a hard time not hating them since they'd done the Professor's bidding. He knew they had no choice, but he still couldn't reconcile himself with it.

The Warden's deck scraped against the sand and it started with Brandt running and jumping as far as he could. It wasn't graceful, but he almost made it into the dry sand. He landed in the ankle-deep surf, frozen where he landed until he could pull his hooves free. The misshapen creatures ran into the woods in terror when the Aurochs launched himself from the deck.

He waded back to the ship where three 'cats, a Wolfoid, and Bronwyn climbed onto his back. He returned to the beach to safely and dryly deposit his riders. The 'cats continued to ride on his head, while Bounder jumped off and with man-horse's help, Bronwyn climbed down, too. Fea said she felt good enough to accompany her mate. No one was going to tell her no, so she came along. Brandt understood that if possible, she'd ride him the entire time. According to Strider and Zeeka, the tunnel was big enough for even Brandt to use.

Bronwyn rallied the mob of the Professor's creations and sent them toward the compound. She rode on the man-horse as the others stayed nearby, waiting to fulfill her any wish.

Braden and Micah walked warily, each of them carrying a blaster. Braden had lost his to the Professor, so Micah shared hers. She carried her sword, but Braden didn't think she was capable of fighting with it. She continued to move deliberately. Whatever the Security Bot shocked them with, it had not been kind to their bodies.

They were recovering, slowly.

When the group reached the compound, the misfit mob wanted Bronwyn to play a game with them. Braden suggested that they'd play later, but they had to go to the hill and enter the tunnel. The misfits hooted and yelled, saying that it was forbidden to enter without the Professor. They had no intention of telling the mob that the Professors were dead.

Without waiting for them to agree, Brandt turned and took the wide path that headed west.

Micah opened her neural implant to check in with Holly. *'We're heading toward the tunnel now. Do you have any final words, in case we get cut off?'*

*'I wish we had time to study the laboratories in the underground complex. If I could get a peek at his notes and the equipment, I'd be able to tell you what he was doing. Beyond that, I hope there are signal repeaters in the tunnel so I can talk to you all the way down, assuming it goes to the undersea city. In any case, I'll follow you for as long as I can if you minimize the window, don't close out in entirety,'* Holly said, hoping that Micah would comply with his request.

*'I think we're going to need your help. This is the land of the ancients and no one knows them better than you. It's kind of like being back on the RV Traveler, eh, Holly?'* She minimized the window as they kept walking, eyes searching the trees for the monkeys. Bounder watched carefully, keeping his lightning spear trained on the branches that lined the path. Pik traded his trident for Strider's spear, so he wielded firepower, too. They knew that they'd burn down the whole forest if the monkeys provoked them. Worse than that, they were good with it.

Micah had her blaster dialed to wide flame. Braden had his set in the middle, neither a wide flame nor a narrow beam. He wanted revenge for when they had beaned him in the head with a rock.

The first monkey appeared on the trail before them, standing with a spear held across his body, as if he could block their way. Bronwyn yelled at them to wait as the man-horse ran with an odd gait past the companions. Bronwyn slid to the sand and strolled to the monkey. It chattered at her as she kneeled and talked with it. Braden and Micah couldn't hear what she said. They walked cautiously past Brandt, blasters aimed at the trees. They stopped between Brandt and Bronwyn, knowing that they were in the line of fire should the monkeys act.

They waited while the conversation dragged on. More and more monkeys appeared in the branches on both sides of the trail. Braden and Micah stood back to back, ready to fire. Pik faced toward the trees, stoic, like a statue, with Aadi hovering behind him. On the other side, Bounder counted the heads, lining up his shots where he could get more than one monkey at a time.

"We can go now," Bronwyn finally said, waving to the monkey, who waved back as he headed for the trees. With a couple screeches from their leader, the monkeys melted into the jungle and disappeared.

"What was that all about?" Micah asked, taking the teenager's hand as they started walking down the trail. The other companions followed. Bounder had hoped there'd be a fight. He didn't care much for the monkeys, either.

"They are here because the Professor created them to stand watch, make sure that no one traveled this path without the Professor. Once I explained that you were the President and in charge of the Professor and the entirety of the island, they agreed to let us pass."

"Thank you, Bronwyn. Why did it take so long to explain that?" Braden asked.

"They didn't understand what a president was or how much of the world is out there. I tried to explain it, but there's a lot." Bronwyn smiled at her own joke. Micah stroked the girl's long hair. She was a gift to them all. As Braden had told her long ago, they could always use more allies.

When the trail left the jungle and turned toward the hillside, Braden and Micah got their first glimpse of the entrance. It was as large as Zeeka had tried to describe. The gate across its front was impressive.

They walked to it as a group, the misfit mob following closely and watching everything the humans were doing. Braden was unnerved by the mob, but Bronwyn would have been angry if he said anything. He wondered how Micah felt.

'*Same as you,*' Micah replied. Why did he bother thinking to himself? He expected he should just say everything he thought out loud and be done with it.

"I understand why you are afraid of them. After the Professor drugged you and the Prince, he made my friends carry you to his lab. You probably remember that and it makes you angry. They won't do anything like that to you again," Bronwyn told him, still holding Micah's hand.

When they reached the gate, the hand-pad to the side told them it was locked using Old Tech. Micah had activated the other door, so she tried. The panel flashed green and the lock released. The gates swung inward. "Why do you think those doors are working for you?" Braden asked.

"Maybe it knows that I'm the President? Or maybe it's just because I'm a human, through and through." Micah shrugged.

Braden looked back at the companions, then asked Bronwyn to tell the mob to stay outside and guard the tunnel entrance for their inevitable return. He walked through without further delay. Skirill flew past and downward. Braden's first instinct was to stop him, but they wanted to know what was ahead.

Skirill shared what he saw as he flew slowly down the tunnel. Zyena and Zeeka flew in before Brandt filled the entrance. The others took the hint and squeezed in front of the King of the Aurochs. Pik pulled Aadi behind him. Bounder passed them, to be closer to the action. Bronwyn walked behind Braden and Micah.

They were bunched up. Braden liked them to be more spread out, but they were in a tunnel. Even spread out, there was nowhere to run, nowhere to hide. The 'cats crouched on the King's head, barely fitting, but none of them wanted to walk when they could ride and have a great view of the minions beneath them.

Skirill flew ahead, showing a winding passage. It turned to the right and continued for a couple hundred paces, then turned back to the left, then right, then left. Braden asked Skirill to wait for them as they continued downward. Zyena and Zeeka joined Skirill and waited at the corner, five switchbacks down, watching the way ahead. The ancients' panels lined the roof of the tunnel, providing plenty of light.

Micah checked in with Holly and after three turns, he was pleased that he was still able to see them. Micah looked at the tunnel, getting close to the walls so Holly could see what she saw. He suspected that the tunnel had been carved using tools that were common to the ancients. He had no other information for her, but she kept her window open to track their connectivity as they descended.

When they were one turn away from the Hawkoids, the three took wing and continued slowly downward, zigzagging to keep their speed under control. Five more turns and they stopped. Water started to drip from the roof and the walls of the tunnel. The floor was arced, high in the middle and low against the walls, where a gutter allowed the water to run downhill.

They followed the five switchback routine four more times before there were no more turns. The tunnel leveled out and continued straight ahead, ending at a gate, the size and style mirroring the one in the side of the hill on the island. Micah's hand opened the gate. Braden stopped the Hawkoids from flying ahead. The humans carried the large birds so they could turn them loose the heartbeat they knew it was safe.

Holly was still with them, which was a great relief to Micah. She didn't know what to expect, but Holly would help them deal with the Old Tech side of it. Since the gates were locked, maybe it was as simple as finding Caleb and any others, then walking back to the surface. If someone managed to get through the gate and up the tunnel, where would they go? It was an island and everyone living there reported to the Professor. There was no escape.

The tunnel curved upward toward a wide opening where they could see a sparkling, dark blue sky.

# A New Enemy

They stopped at the tunnel entrance and looked, amazed at the sight. They were in the middle of a large park, well-groomed with a road that led away from the tunnel. In the other direction, there were walkways with benches and trees.

And people.

Braden didn't see any Bots, so they asked the Hawkoids to give them a better view of the city. Skirill, Zyena, and Zeeka flew in three different directions, flying close to the dome itself as they looked down at a modern city, unlike anything currently on Vii. It looked like pictures that Holly had shown Braden of Sanctuary before the war.

The dome above was mostly clear, with beams at regular intervals, wide at the base and soaring to a point above where they converged at the peak, the dome's top. Outside, they saw schools of fish, the sun's light sparkling through waves that were not that far above. Holly had believed the undersea facility was at the bottom of the ocean and although that was true, it wasn't very deep below the surface.

Inside, there even seemed to be a monorail people-mover of sorts. A sleek looking train, filled with people going somewhere. Braden and Micah walked toward a couple sitting on a bench. They didn't look alarmed at the Wolfoid or the Lizard Man, but their eyes widened when Brandt emerged from the tunnel and into the well-lit area.

"Excuse me," Braden said with a smile. "Would you happen to know Caleb, a big fisherman, a little bit older?" He looked at Micah. It never hurt to get right to the point.

"I'm sorry, I'm afraid we don't know a Caleb," the young woman answered, before looking away and humming to herself.

"How many people are here?" Braden followed his first question, thinking he already knew what she was going to say.

"I don't know that!" she exclaimed before excusing herself. The man with her bowed slightly as he took her hand and they strolled away.

"If everyone here came from White Beach, how come no one we see looks like they came from there? Those people were fisherman, kind of angry too, when we attempted to save them from coming to this paradise." Braden wasn't trying to be sarcastic, but it sounded that way. The residents had been actively hostile when Braden and Micah couldn't feed them.

Braden didn't know what to do besides spread out and ask everyone they met if they knew Caleb. "How long has it been since Caleb was taken? A moon, two moons?"

Micah settled it by asking Holly. It had been twenty seven days, less than one moon, or one month as Holly told them, as he continued working to get them to use the ancients' standard time system.

"So we ask who the new people are, someone who's been here less than a moon," Braden suggested. Micah didn't have anything better, but she didn't want to split up. So they walked as a group, the oddest group to ever walk the streets of Atlantis.

A siren began to wail. They knew the sound because it had played at New Sanctuary once when a Cygnus VI survivor started a fire in their room. The siren continued to wail, loud, soft, loud again.

The people all stopped what they were doing and immediately headed toward the nearest doorway. Braden and Micah took the cue and ran for cover. Brandt tried to look inconspicuous as he was nearly as large as the building they ran toward.

*'Brandt, the tunnel for you. It's the only place you can hide,'* Braden told the King over the mindlink. The Aurochs immediately turned and tore into the turf as he raced for the tunnel entrance.

Braden and his companions jogged toward a building with windows facing the street. Two people had already hurried inside. Braden caught the door before it closed, holding it for Micah, then Bronwyn, Pik and Aadi, the 'cats, and finally Bounder, who had been covering them as they entered. Braden followed them in, closing the door gently behind himself.

"What's that all about?" Micah asked one of the locals.

"It's the standard call. It means there will be a security sweep. How do you not know this? It is the first thing we learn."

Braden wanted to follow up, but watching out the window, he saw a Security Bot appear between two buildings. It hovered down the street, passing the windows where Braden watched in shock. He looked at the companions. Then to Micah. The field generator was still in the corridor outside the Professor's laboratory.

"A field generator would come in handy, right about now," Braden said out loud. He leaned sideways to see where the Bot had gone, but it was no longer in sight. He could see the park and that gave him hope that the Security Bot wouldn't check the tunnel.

"How many of those things are down here?" Braden asked. The young man shrugged.

*'We need to go back and get the field generator,'* Micah said in her thought voice.

*'I think you're right,'* Braden replied as two Security Bots converged on the tunnel entrance. *'Don't fight them, Brandt!'* Braden 'yelled' over the mindlink as he helplessly watched the King of the Aurochs emerge from the tunnel, head bowed. One of the Bots lashed out with a tentacle and Brandt screamed in pain, raising his head to bugle his anguish. The second Bot used its tentacle to shock Brandt from the other side. The King turned and charged the Bot, catching it by surprise. Caught on the ends of his horns, the Security Bot was crushed against a wall.

"No security field around them?" Braden said aloud. The first Bot hovered behind the Aurochs and shocked him until he went down. Two Maintenance Bots arrived and strapped Old Tech devices onto him, two on each leg, one on each horn, and with a long strap, they wrapped one around his neck. When the Bots moved away from the Aurochs, the King started to lift into the air, flopped upside down, his head hung oddly as the devices didn't balance correctly. Another Security Bot joined the other, remaining behind while the first slowly moved away, pulling the hovering Aurochs.

*'Skirill! Keep an eye out for where they take Brandt. Don't be seen. Any of you!'* Braden told the Hawkoids.

The Maintenance Bots recovered the pieces from the shattered Security Bot and departed. The third Security Bot took a position in front of the tunnel.

*'Holly, it appears that we have a problem,'* Micah said through her implant.

The Security Bot at the tunnel entrance flashed a laser beam at the window. It drew a line through the window and into the room.

"Shut it down! Shut the link down!" Braden yelled as he ducked, even though the beam had already touched him. Micah closed the link while Holly was mid-sentence. She shut it completely off.

The Security Bot danced his laser beam into other buildings nearby, then shut it down.

"Great," Braden said in dismay. Their escape route was blocked, and they couldn't use Holly to help them fight an Old Tech enemy. "What is this building? Is there a back way out of here?" He grabbed the young man roughly, shaking him to get an answer. Passive, cowed, the young man hung limp in Braden's arms. He let go and the man fell to the floor. The young man got back to his feet and dusted himself off.

*'G?'* Braden asked.

*'They are like children, doing only as they are instructed to do. They have no real memories. You won't learn anything from them,'* the 'cat said dismissively. Bronwyn stepped in, and Braden nodded to her.

"I'm Bronwyn. What's your name?" she asked innocently in a little girl's voice.

"I'm Fifty-Seven Delta," the young man replied. Bronwyn never judged anyone else, she accepted who and what they were without question.

"I am very pleased to meet you. We are new here and hope you can help us find our way. There is a great fisherman named Caleb, and he would be one of your newest arrivals." Bronwyn smiled and waited patiently for the man to answer.

He pointed to the window instead of speaking.

"I don't understand what that means. Do we need to go outside?" Bronwyn asked, confused.

"Yes, where they took the big creature. All the newcomers go there," he replied tentatively.

"Thank you, you're very kind," Bronwyn gushed. "How long have you been here?"

"Always," the man answered. Bronwyn looked at G-War. The 'cat shook his head.

"Thank you, again. We'll be on our way now. Please enjoy the rest of the daylight!" Bronwyn waved Braden aside so they could leave. The sirens had stopped wailing while they'd been inside, and the people were returning to the streets.

Once alone, Micah toured the rest of the building. It looked like a small shop, but without any merchandise to sell or trade. Furniture was sparse. The good news was that there was a back door. She opened it and saw another road just like the one out front. Micah looked for any Bots and not seeing them, she waved the others to her.

"It took Brandt that way, toward the center of the dome, and that's where I want to go," Micah said. The Hawkoids confirmed the location. They were perched at various high points around the city as they assumed their roles as the eyes and ears of the companions.

Braden stopped the companions from rushing outside. "I've been thinking," he started. Micah rolled her finger at him, wanting him to hurry. "The Professor, the misfit mob, the Security Bot at the laboratory. What did the Professor say? Something about using us to build creatures that he could control?" Braden hesitated and took a deep breath.

"They could have easily killed Brandt. Those were Security Bots! I think the Professor's standing orders were to capture all of us, so they could do as he was going to do with Fea, cut into us and take out whatever it was he thought he could use," Braden stated, talking slowly as he tried to wrap his mind around the situation.

"We got that, so what's your point?" Micah asked impatiently.

"Since the Professor isn't around anymore, they'll probably just keep Brandt and any others who the Professor was going to experiment on in some sort of holding area, a cell or pen, in Brandt's case. We didn't check the other cells where I was held, did we?"

Micah closed her eyes and shook her head. Her father could have been mere steps away and she might have missed him.

"I think we can use our blasters and staffs on the Security Bots. They weren't shimmering so I think they didn't have their defensive shields active. We can work with that. It doesn't mean they can't turn them on, but it means that we might get the first shot. Here's what I'm thinking–we can't bunch up, stay spread out as much as possible. If anything happens, we scatter, come back here individually. Nobody fires on a Security Bot unless we can all shoot together." Everyone nodded. "Let's go find Brandt and Caleb."

Then Micah stopped them. "Who is Gloria?" she asked. "I'd forgotten that until this very heartbeat. You don't think, do you?"

"I'd forgotten that, too. The Professor said Security Bots and Gloria. He's got an AI," Braden exclaimed, realizing the important point that he'd missed. "We need Holly now more than ever."

They couldn't stay hidden and rescue their people, so they decided to deal with Gloria if she appeared in some way. Micah went out first, moving to the far side of the street. They spread out, far and wide. Pik and Aadi, Bounder, the 'cats, Bronwyn, and finally Braden. He had no trepidation at keeping Bronwyn away from the others. She was the one who would attract the least attention. Any one of the companions trying to protect her would draw more attention. She was better alone and probably had the highest chance to get out unscathed.

Braden tried to look everywhere at once. Left, right, up, down, not even sure what he was looking for. Bots? Sensors of the type that Holly used? Ancients?

Skirill watched the Security Bot take Brandt in through a big gate, like the type they saw leading into the warehouse in Cameron. It was next to a large, windowless building. Zyena was on the other side and shared that all the roads in Atlantis ended at the central building, or looking at it a different way, all roads radiated outward from that building. On her side, she saw windows and doors and what looked like normal humans entering and exiting.

Although having listened to the encounter between Braden and the natives after Brandt's capture, she wasn't sure how she should define normal.

Zeeka hunched low over the top of a building that overlooked the park located close to one side of the dome. She watched the tunnel and the surrounding area to give the companions a view of their escape route, if they had to leave in a hurry. The tunnel remained blocked by the Security Bot. Zeeka hadn't seen Braden and Micah in action, so she could only guess at how they would deal with it. Zeeka's parents had the utmost confidence in the humans, and she trusted her parents, so she would support Braden and the companions to the best of her ability. She settled in for what could be a very long wait.

Micah continued to lead the group. From the Hawkoids, she'd learned that this road would take them to the same place the Bots had taken Brandt. According to Zyena, they could enter the building from her side, the other side from which they approached. They'd get a good look at the warehouse door, as Skirill called it. They'd continue past that, around the building, and enter.

That was the plan anyway.

When a Security Bot appeared from between two buildings to her side, she immediately 'yelled' *'Scatter!'* in her thought voice, while she tried to nonchalantly walk past. It's tentacle arm shot out in front of her and blocked her way. The others scurried in all directions, trying to put buildings between them and the Bot.

Everyone except Bronwyn. She walked forward, apparently without concern, staying on the far side of the street from Micah and the Security Bot. She passed and kept walking without looking back.

Braden and Bounder had gone between two buildings on the far side of the street from the Bot and Micah. Pik had jumped into an alley on his side of the street, the same side as Micah. He rushed away towing Aadi behind him, on a path to get behind the encounter. Fea and Treetis ran with him while G-War joined Braden.

*'I suggest you let me handle this,'* Aadi offered. Pik reached a corner where he could look down the alley and see the Security Bot at the other end. Aadi let go of the rope and swam slowly around the corner, continuing straight toward the Bot. *'If you would be so kind as to back up a step or two, I would be most grateful, Master Micah. Please confirm that it does not have its energy shield active.'*

*'No shimmer, Master Aadi,'* she said while in the standoff with the Security Bot. *'I'll try to move backward, but I don't want to get zapped by that thing again. I was just starting to feel normal.'*

The Bot stayed still as Micah cautiously wriggled her feet backward, one toe-length at a time. Aadi was halfway down the alley and Micah still wasn't far enough away when another Bot showed up behind the Security Bot. It looked different, round with two small tentacles and a bubble dome atop, little bigger than Aadi in both size and shape.

It hovered past the Security Bot, making a circle around Micah, then it came close enough to touch her. Inside the bubble dome were various lenses and lights. One shone directly into her eye, the same one that contained the neural implant.

Aadi continued to swim, cursing his slowness as he watched the new Bot examine his friend. From the far side of the street, Braden ran, stopping at the corner to aim his blaster, but both Bots were too close to his mate. He didn't have a good angle and there was no place else to find cover. He kneeled, aimed, and waited.

"Yes, you have the implant. Where did you get it?" the small Bot asked in a feminine voice.

"I'm sorry, what?" Micah replied, trying to buy time for Aadi.

"Now, now, don't try any of that. My name is Gloria, and I run Atlantis."

# Run!

Aadi continued swimming forward, but the effects of the last Security Bot he had tangled with were weighing on him. He stopped, collected himself, and prepared his focused thunderclap.

"Gloria, nice to meet you. I'm here to pick up my father. Once we do that, we'll be on our way, if you don't mind," Micah said, thinking of Gloria as she did the AI from New Sanctuary. Treat her like a real person and she may respond.

"I do mind. We need you more than you need him. We need you and the mutants who travel with you. We need their genetic material to build the army." Gloria's tone was flat and measured, unlike the old Professor, who'd sounded maniacal when he said the same words.

*'Cover your ears, please,'* Aadi warned, not a heartbeat before the Security Bot exploded spectacularly, throwing Gloria's Bot into Micah and Micah to the ground. The smaller Bot fell on top of her and toppled to the side. Micah's arms and legs hurt where shrapnel from the explosion had hit her.

Braden ran to where the sparking remnants of the biggest piece of the Security Bot lay. He pulled Micah out of the wreckage, then fired his blaster into the Bot until it too lay in ruin.

"Building!" Braden said, pointing. They ran through the nearest door, while Bronwyn ducked into a building further up the street. Pik joined Braden with Aadi in tow once again.

"Aadi! You taught that Bot a lesson, both of them," Braden said slapping the Tortoid on his shell.

*'I think the second Bot was just a way for Gloria to get around without a system like Holly uses,'* Aadi said in a tired thought voice.

"Are you okay, old man?" Braden asked gently, bending down to look into the Tortoid's eyes. He blinked slowly.

*'I'll be fine, but a nice bit of rest would come in handy, I think,'* Aadi replied, bobbing his head. *'But I know that won't happen so we'll just make do, won't we?'*

"We won't just make do. I think we need to protect you. You've already lost more than anyone else here, so no, Aadi, I think you should stay here, wait for us."

*'I appreciate the consideration, Master Braden, but I might be the only one who is successful against the Bots.'*

"And we may need you again, so that's why it's important to rest. Give us a chance to prove ourselves. Nothing would make me happier than not having to fire another shot down here. We'll call you if we get into trouble, which is probably a given, but we'll hold that off as long as we can. Make yourself scarce, A-Dog. We'll be in touch," Braden said, rubbing the Tortoid's shell and heading for the door.

He ran into the street, past the smoldering wreckage and down the alley on the opposite side. One by one, the rest of the companions followed him. Bronwyn casually walked back into the street and toward the center of the undersea city.

Micah was last, and she stopped at the corner of the alley, letting the others get further ahead as she wanted to increase the spacing between the companions. She looked back at the wreckage as a Maintenance Bot arrived and started scooping the pieces into its trailer. Micah ducked around the corner and walked slowly away, covering the group's rear.

Braden was at the front. Bounder behind and to the left, Pik at the far right. The 'cats walked as they desired, seemingly unconcerned about anything.

Treetis stopped to bat at something in the street. Fea made a beeline toward him, slapping him in the head as she passed. He shook his head and batted at whatever he was playing with one last time before running to catch up with the female 'cat. Because of all they'd been through, it was hard to remember that Treetis was still a kitten as far as Hillcat aging went.

He'd get there, eventually, and he would make G-War and Fea proud.

Just not yet.

Braden walked boldly forward, past one and two-story buildings on both sides of the street. He couldn't tell what any of them were for, maybe small shops, but he didn't see items or spots for trade, no markets, no traders. He didn't like Atlantis.

He didn't like anywhere they didn't have trade, but here, he had no desire to change things. He only wanted to get Caleb and Brandt, then leave.

*'Me, too,'* Micah added over the mindlink. Braden smiled and chuckled. His mind was an open book.

The last buildings before the street ended on the windowless side of the large structure were bigger and looked to be busier. A number of people milled about, doing nothing. Many seemed to be simply waiting. He stopped one of these people.

"What are you waiting for?" he asked.

"Lunch, of course," the young man said. Braden nodded.

"Me, too. Do you mind if I join you?"

"Why would you do that?" the man replied.

Braden noticed that everyone seemed to be the same age, the two they talked with earlier and everyone here. "No reason. Actually, I think we'll move on. Enjoy your lunch." Braden ended with a close-mouthed smile and tip of his head. The young man returned his full attention to waiting.

*'G? The same?'* Braden asked in his thought voice.

*'The same,'* the Golden Warrior answered without elaborating.

Braden walked away, paying no further attention to the young people because they were no threat. He continued past the large gate through which the Bots had carried his friend. He looked at it without turning his head, using his peripheral vision. There was no one there. He didn't see any Old Tech monitoring devices, although his limited experience with them suggested he needed to see a flashing light to identify it as such.

He continued past the largest part of the building where there were no windows. Skirill and Zyena shared that there was no unusual activity from anywhere around the complex that dominated the center of the dome.

Braden stopped at the corner and looked back. No one seemed to be paying any attention to a Wolfoid walking down the street, trying to look inconspicuous, or the Lizard Man not far behind. Micah mostly blended in, but the blaster at her hip and sword across her back screamed that she wasn't from Atlantis. Braden had lost his shortsword with his blasters. He felt almost naked without it.

He couldn't see the 'cats and had to look. All three were next to the gate, examining it. G-War jumped and embedded his claws in the material, which Braden didn't think was wood. As 'cats can, G-War climbed the vertical gate, until he stood at the top.

*'What are you doing, G?'* Braden asked frantically.

*'I'm going to take a closer look. No one cares about anything out here. Just stand there and wait. I'll be right back.'* G-War disappeared over the gate.

Braden held out his hands and looked at Micah in surprise. Treetis started climbing the gate, but Fea caught him by the scruff of his neck. Treetis was slightly larger than the all-white female 'cat, but she was a mother and this was her adopted son, so she dragged the young 'cat off the gate. He looked funny hanging from her mouth. She stepped on him as she tried to walk away and finally gave up, dropping him to the street.

They joined the Wolfoid next to the wall. Fea made Treetis sit at Bounder's feet while she faced the orange 'cat and stared.

Pik was on the other side of the gate from Braden, next to the wall, while Micah was across the street, blending into the small crowd of people waiting to eat lunch. Skirill and Zyena didn't see anything, until the gate started to open, and everyone saw that at the same time.

An orange flash appeared as soon as the gate had opened wide enough. Through the opening and a hard turn toward Braden, G-War raced past the Wolfoid, Fea, and Treeits. *'Come on,'* he told them over the mindlink. As one, the Wolfoid and two 'cats bolted after the Golden Warrior. Pik stood frozen and did the only thing he could. He ran ten paces and stripped out of his skin suit. Braden hadn't known he could get out of it that quickly, but there it was, lying on the ground next to one of many trees that decorated the undersea city. Pik had blended in and looking closely, Braden could see the lightning spear, but not the Lizard Man.

Micah squeezed in closer to the door, putting more people between her and whatever was coming through the gate. With her back to the wall to hide her sword and her blaster cradled to her chest, she watched a Security Bot slowly hover out. It turned in the direction that Braden and the others had just disappeared. The Bot moved slowly away from the building, continuing around the corner and out of sight.

*'Lover?'* Micah tried tentatively.

*'We're inside. G was right. No one seems to care. What do they do that they don't know enough to care about anything?'* Braden wondered as he watched the Security Bot move past the door, turned, and headed into one of the radial streets. *'It's gone. Keep an eye, Ess?'*

*'Of course,'* Skirill replied instantly, having a good view of the first part of the street it had taken, but not the second. He could move if he had to, but expected the Bot would spot him. At least he could see when it was returning.

*'This looks like a reception area, like at the Oasis or New Sanctuary, but on a massive scale. But I don't see anyone really doing anything. Let me try something,'* Braden said and before Micah could talk him out of it, she heard him over the mindlink as he addressed one of the people there.

"Good morning," he said pleasantly. "I'm checking in."

"I'm sorry, I don't understand," the young receptionist answered. She reminded him of the holograms that staffed the front desk.

"I'm checking in, for work here. That is what we do here, isn't it?"

"No," she replied.

"Wow! They sent me to the wrong place. I can't believe it. What do they do here?"

"When summoned, we'll enter the chambers. We are waiting for that. There is nothing in between," she replied confidently. It was the first spark of commitment he'd seen from one of the Atlanteans.

"There's lunch!" Braden said, happy with his diversion.

"When we are summoned, we'll enter the chambers. That is it. We will wait here until that happens. There is no lunch. Not anymore." She crossed her arms in front of her and looked at Braden expectantly.

Who was he to disappoint a mindless young woman? "So it won't be long, then?" he asked.

"I expect not," she answered rather intelligently.

'G?' Braden asked, hoping that the 'cat sensed something different with this one.

*This will be her third time into the chamber. Each time, it seems she gains something a little different. This is the Professor's doing,'* G-War added unnecessarily.

"Thank you, you've been very helpful," Braden told the young woman. He waved the others to follow him as he walked past the tables of waiting people and headed for a hallway into the back. Some of the Atlanteans watched him, which piqued his curiosity. The closer to the center, the more different the people became.

He had to know. He checked two different doors as they went deeper into the back, but both were locked. There wasn't a hand panel next to them and the door handle seemed plain. He continued to the end of the hallway where there were double doors that looked like they swung open. He pushed lightly and the door moved. Bounder and the three 'cats were right behind him.

"Shall we?" Braden whispered. They nodded. With his blaster in hand, he walked into the single biggest room he'd ever seen, and that included some of the laboratory spaces on the spaceship.

Tables and work spaces, everything was an immaculate white. Clear vats with supports looking like the smooth silver of buffed steel. Instruments and hoses, flashing indicator lights. A vast medical laboratory, but that didn't hold Braden's gaze.

It was the people in the vats, constrained on the beds, with hoses and probes and monitors making them nearly unrecognizable. A vast number of Medical Bots moved freely around the beds and vats. Beside each person was an empty bed that looked similar to the cryo pods on the Traveler. The chambers.

What were they transferring from one person to the other? Braden looked on in horror. Bounder sniffed the air, then dashed into a cleared aisle between chambers and equipment as they headed deeper into the laboratory. Braden, Fea, and Treetis followed. Like with the young people outside, no one seemed to care that a Wolfoid, Hillcats, and an armed human were running through the facility.

'*What is it, Bounder?*' Braden asked in his thought voice.

'*Caleb,*' the Wolfoid answered.

Braden kept his blaster in hand, ready to shoot anything that needed to be shot. Seeing the comatose people plugged in like another piece of Old Tech made him sick to his stomach. He didn't look too closely because he didn't want to know.

'*What do you see?*' Micah wanted to know. She was trapped outside, away from her father.

'*You don't want to know, but Bounder is on Caleb's scent. I'll get back to you soon,*' Braden replied, trying to take it all in as he ran after the Wolfoid.

Bounder stopped at an intersection and sniffed. Braden couldn't pass, so he stood and waited. He couldn't help but look around him. The faces of people, who looked like fisherman. He leaned closer, an old man. The one who had yelled at him on the top of the hills overlooking White Beach when there wasn't any food. The one who encouraged the others to return to their homes and submit to the sea monster, as they thought of it.

That was cycles ago and here he was. Braden could see his chest inflate, but he couldn't tell if that was from the tube in the man's mouth or if the man was alive. Maybe both, maybe neither. There were probes attached to his head and other tubes disappeared under a pure white sheet covering the man's body. Braden hesitantly touched the man's head. He was warm.

"Are you alive?" Braden asked as he opened one of the man's eyes. He'd heard that the eye was a window to the soul, but he couldn't see anything, nothing to say that the man was more than his shell. He existed, yes, but did he live?

Bounder's claws raked the floor as he bolted in a new direction, and Braden found himself hurrying to catch up. The 'cats were close behind the Wolfoid. Braden passed more and more empty beds. He slowed and looked over the room. Twenty, fifty, a hundred, more and more empty beds. The Professor had said he was going to build an army. A madman's ravings, but he had the means to do it. Everything was right here. As much Old Tech as anywhere on Vii.

*'The Security Bot has left the entrance to the tunnel. It is coming your way,'* Zeeka said over the mindlink.

*'Lunch is served and there's no one left out here so I'm going inside. I'll find a corner, away from the windows. I don't know how Gloria could tell I have an implant, but I don't want to be anywhere near that Bot when it comes by,'* Micah told them. She hoped that it was proximity, so the farther away she could remain, the less likely it was that they'd find her again. Having the implant made her a liability when they had believed it would give them an advantage. They hadn't counted on a presence like Gloria.

And they needed Holly to deal with another AI. They couldn't have saved the people from Cygnus VI without him. How much would they have missed without Holly? They wouldn't have known about the RV Traveler at all. They wouldn't have had blasters. Micah had hers, but it wasn't charged until they met the AI. That meant they wouldn't have survived the Bat-Ravens. Without Holly, they'd be dead five times over. And they wouldn't have met their friends, the Wolfoids, the Rabbits, or the

Lizard Man called Pik Ha'ar.

Braden and Micah were both thinking the same thing. Holly would have to save them again.

*'Kill the Security Bot. Two of you can do it if you catch it by surprise. They don't use their shields down here for some reason, so kill it. Once the Security Bots are dead, then we can get in touch with Holly,'* Braden said, changing their tactics.

*'If I see it, I will take care of it,'* Aadi said.

*'We can't ask you to do that,'* Micah replied.

*'We do as we must, for the good of all,'* Aadi added in a tired voice.

Braden had stopped listening and focused completely on where they were and what they were doing. Bounder was standing next to a bed and G-War had jumped onto the sheet covering someone attached to the equipment. A Med Bot hovered nearby, but Bounder held it at bay by jabbing it with his spear.

As Braden joined the others, he looked, knowing who it was going to be. The old man lying there, hooked up to the equipment, was Caleb.

# Fight!

Aadi had a hard time getting the door open to the small building where they'd left him. He could get his mouth on it, but twisting and pulling were more difficult. Since he floated, he had little leverage. After a number of attempts, he finally managed, then swam outside.

When they left the tunnel, they went one street over, but had returned through the alley. This was the direct route from the park to the main building where Braden and the others were. Aadi turned and saw the Security Bot coming quickly toward him. The Tortoid swam into the street and dropped to the ground, where he did not have to wait long. The Security Bot was racing down the center of the road, oblivious to everything around it. As it passed, Aadi gave it everything he had.

The Security Bot bounced into the air, then fired its weapons in all directions, not knowing where the sonic blast had come from. It slowed, and Aadi closed his eyes.

*'I'm sorry, my babies. You won't have a chance to know life because I failed you,'* he said to the six living Tortoids still in the eggs inside his body.

Aadi waited, but the end didn't come. He opened one eye. The Security Bot was no longer hovering or firing. It sat on the street with a thin line of smoke trailing from its top. Aadi couldn't tell if there were any lights active on it or not. He was so tired. He lay on the ground and closed his eyes.

*'It is done,'* he told the others as sleep of the exhausted claimed him.

Micah had walked outside, but went back in. *'Skirill. We still have at least the one that went past you. Do you see anything?'*

*'No, Master Micah. I will find it for you and you will kill it. Then we will save Caleb and leave this place,'* Skirill said firmly. He jumped from his perch atop the main building and flew upward to the edge of the dome, the ocean's

waters so close above him, before he followed the radial outward to the road that the Bot had taken after chasing Braden and the others inside.

The sirens sounded again. *Good,* Skirill thought as he flew. *That will get the innocent people out of the way, leaving only the Bots and us.*

He flew the length of the street, descending with the dome until he was at rooftop level on the outer edge. He landed on the branches of a tree in an alley as he got his bearings, then he flew off again, the next street and the next. Zyena joined in the search for the Security Bot.

The laser beam was narrow and barely missed Zyena. She hadn't seen it. If it hadn't been for Skirill's warning, she wouldn't have dodged to avoid the next one, which disappeared through the clear of the dome and into the sea. She dove to the side, putting a building between her and the Bot.

*'Is that the Bot we're looking for?'* she asked Skirill.

*'It's one of them, but I can't tell them apart. I'm going to fly past and draw it toward Micah and Pik.'*

Pik had put his skin suit back on and stood behind the tree with his lighting spear ready. Micah was outside the building again, on a corner, hoping she was on the right road. She didn't have much cover and if the Bot got past her, she'd be skylined against the building. She'd have to count on Pik's aim to kill the Bot before it fired at her. Then it would be up to her to finish it.

With Skirill's help, she discovered that she was one street off. She ran as fast as she could to the next corner, arriving at the same time as the Security Bot, which was moving almost as fast as the Hawkoid as it fired a narrow laser repeatedly into the air. Skirill dodged and danced, frantically avoiding the beams.

The Bot raced past her, barely an arm's-length away. She ducked and snap-fired into the thing, then took a knee to aim and keep firing. Pik's lightning bolt missed on the first shot, but hit the Security Bot with the second. A crackling electrical bolt shot out from the Bot's tentacle, enveloping Micah and shocking her senseless. Pik kept firing until the Bot exploded.

*'The Bot's dead, but Micah's down. I'm going to her now,'* Pik said over the mindlink. Braden didn't respond as he didn't know what to say. Pik would tell them how she was as he was hopelessly honest. And that's what Braden always wanted. Don't make him guess at the real situation.

"We're taking you with us," he said to Caleb. Braden turned and grabbed the Med Bot. "Unhook him, now!"

He nodded for Bounder to step back. The Med Bot moved close to the instruments, adjusted a few things, then departed toward the next bed. Braden had had enough. He raised his blaster and fired two short bursts into the Bot's back. It sparked and crashed to the floor, upsetting a tray of instruments two beds down.

Braden ripped the sheet off. There was a tube going through his abdomen and probably into his stomach. There were tubes for waste and then there was one in each leg. These were clear and carried blood. There were numerous scars on Caleb's naked body where the Professor had cut into him, taken something. Braden was disgusted afresh.

"I can't leave you like this, Caleb. We take these out and either you live free or you die." Braden's eyes teared as he looked at Micah's father. "Here's to life, my friend," Braden said as he pulled the first tube from Caleb's leg. Blood gushed from the wound and he put pressure on it. He looked at the tray nearby. Had he not been in the Med Lab of New Sanctuary, he would have had no idea what things were for, but he saw gauze and a wrap. He asked Bounder to move the tray closer.

He put gauze on the wound, then wrapped the other material around Caleb's leg to hold the gauze tightly down. Then he removed the second leg tube, doing the same thing. He apologized as he removed the waste tubes and cast them away. The stomach tube bothered him. It looked like the size of an arrow. If he'd been shot in the stomach, he wouldn't survive long. Braden took out his small knife and cut the tube in the middle. He pinched it in half and wrapped the bandage around Caleb's body to strap the tube down. If the Med Lab on the Warden couldn't fix it, then they'd enlist Holly's aid at New Sanctuary.

Braden's first responsibility was to get Caleb out of there. He carefully removed the tube from Caleb's mouth, aghast at how much of it there was. When it was out, he couldn't tell if Caleb was breathing or not. Braden put his ear to the old man's lips and listened. He heard air moving and sighed with relief. Braden's last act was to rip off the sensors taped to Caleb's head.

With that, Caleb was free, but still unconscious. Braden checked the area to make sure no one was coming their way. The rest of the Med Bots went about their duties, oblivious to the fact that Braden had killed one of their own. He didn't count on that lasting.

# Med Bots Unite

Caleb was bigger than Braden, but he didn't care. He would carry the old fisherman out of that place.

*'Micah is unconscious. I will take her to Aadi,'* the Lizard Man said over the mindlink.

*'You don't know how happy that makes me, Pik. Thank you for watching over her. We have Caleb and we're coming out. We'll join you shortly,'* Braden answered, relieved. Together, they sat Caleb upright and Braden draped the large man over his shoulder, careful not to put pressure on the tube protruding from Caleb's stomach.

He was heavy, too. Braden could walk, but it was a challenge. Bounder led the way, back down the aisle toward the front door. The 'cats circled them, watching. G-War was on edge, which made the other two anxious. The Golden Warrior couldn't sense the Bots, and that talent, more than anything else, was what he relied on. He was afraid of Bots and Androids, but wouldn't share that with anyone. He also counted on his ability to foresee imminent danger.

Like now, when he saw the Med Bots descend on Braden, taking him down through the press of numbers. *'They come, the Med Bots will try to kill you,'* G-War told Braden.

Braden didn't hesitate, he turned and lumbered toward an area where all the beds were empty. He knew that he had thirty heartbeats before something that G-War had seen happened. He carefully rolled Caleb off his shoulder and onto an empty bed, then readied his blaster, narrow beam, short bursts only. They didn't have a way to recharge it in Atlantis and there were a lot of Bots.

The Med Bots, as one, stopped what they were doing throughout the entire laboratory and made their way to the nearest aisle. Slowly and deliberately, they moved toward Braden and his companions.

Bounder snarled and barked his dismay, then took a position behind a bed on the other side of the aisle. *'Can you look for another way out of here?'* Braden asked G-War. *'I don't know if we can stop them all.'*

G-War, Fea, and Treetis darted between the beds and down the aisles, looking for the boundaries of the massive space. The Med Bots weren't interested in the 'cats, not then. Maybe later, unless the three could find another way out.

While Braden crouched, he discovered that the beds had wheels. There was a butterfly lever that he flipped and the wheel was free to spin. He wouldn't have to carry him. They could roll Caleb out of there, if they got past the Med Bots.

He couldn't ask Micah to contact Holly, see if he could stop them. Braden and Bounder were on their own.

"It's you and me, my friend, fighting the enemies of a free world. We don't want to do it. They're making us fight them because they don't have a Market Square and they really need one!" Braden quipped. He always found humor in the strangest places. If they survived, it would be a funny story to tell. But for the present, he saw more Med Bots than he could count.

Bounder took the first shot, blasting the lead Bot with his lightning spear. That held the others up for a heartbeat or two as they worked their way past. Then Braden fired, very short bursts at different spots on the Bots as he sought a weakness, the easiest way to kill them. They were round, blocky even, with tentacles instead of arms. They didn't have something like a head to shoot off, so he shot various places on their body, hoping for something spectacular.

There wasn't anything obvious. Two shots anywhere on their body seemed to kill them. If he hit a tentacle, that did nothing except take out the arm.

*'We need you to pick up the pace. I'm going to run out of juice before we run out of bad guys,'* Braden encouraged the 'cats. He started firing at the Bots in order

to build a wall of dead bodies to fill in spaces and make it more difficult for the others to pass.

They stopped coming and Braden relaxed for the moment, knowing that they had not given up. He checked the charge on his blaster. Less than half remained. That wasn't enough to fight both Med Bots and Security Bots.

Bounder looked for the 'cats. *'Anything?'* the Wolfoid asked.

*'Still working on it,'* G-War snipped.

"Bronwyn!" Braden yelled. "I can't believe I forgot about you."

*'Bronwyn, are you there?'* Braden asked, ashamed and afraid.

*'Oh, yes. I've been listening to you all. I found something, and we have new friends, too,'* she said in her childlike thought voice.

*'Of course you did.'* Braden laughed out loud and Bounder chuckled, shaking his shaggy head. They were back to business when the pile of dead Bots started moving toward them. Something was pushing the pile from behind and there was nothing that Braden or Bounder could do about it.

*'We need to go,'* Bounder said.

"Which way, G? We have to go, now!"

*'Your left. Hurry, the opening won't last long,'* G-War encouraged the two. Braden snapped the wheel releases and he and Bounder began pushing the table. They picked up speed, holding Caleb with one hand while pushing with the other, It was awkward, but faster than if Braden had been carrying the large man.

Treetis waited for them and as soon as they saw him, he turned tail and ran down an aisle that led back to the main door. G-War was right, there was a gap where the Med Bots had gone toward the back after the human and the others up front had not yet joined them. Braden and Bounder pushed Caleb, thankful that the aisle was straight.

Treetis ran ahead, tail held high. G-War and Fea were near the front door, waiting for the others to open it. They looked impatient and Braden understood why. The Bots had picked up on the plan and were trying to cut them off. G-War and Fea stood against the door together and it started to move. They pushed one side open, and G-War blocked it with his body, but after seeing Braden and Bounder coming at breakneck speed, he thought better of being in their way. He dodged beyond the door into the hallway as the table hit the other door, careened sideways and dumped Caleb unceremoniously onto the floor as both Bounder and Braden tumbled over top of both.

Bounder was up first and fired his lightning spear at the closest Bots. The sparking end of the spear crackled right above Braden's head as the Free Trader struggled to drag Caleb far enough down the hallway so he could prop him up to throw him over his shoulder. Bounder blocked the doorway and fired again and again. Braden kneeled as he pulled Caleb upright, grunting with the effort.

"Come on, Bounder, time to go!" Braden yelled out the side of his mouth. He couldn't turn as he kept his focus on moving forward.

*'There's a Security Bot exiting the gate. It's coming around to the front,'* Zyena told them as she dodged away to keep from getting shot.

Braden hesitated and Bounder bumped into him.

*'We can't go back, my friend,'* Bounder said as he fired two more times into the mass of Med Bots squeezing into the hallway. Without pause, they pushed the wreckage in front of them, defeating Bounder's attempts to block the hallway to give them more time to escape. *'We have to go forward and soon.'*

The people up front were standing, mouths agape, as they watched a sweating Braden hurry through the area while the Wolfoid fired his spear down behind them. When Braden reached the front door, he saw the Security Bot hovering outside, shimmering. Braden put Caleb on the floor, leaning against the wall as he joined Bounder and fired mercilessly into the Med Bots.

"No sense going out the front door. It has its shield active, and that means we can't fight it. The tunnel is unguarded, but there's no one left to go. And Brandt is in here somewhere, too!"

'Don't worry, my friends and I are coming. We'll be there in just a few heartbeats,' Bronwyn offered.

'No!' Braden countered. 'Don't come here, Bronwyn, please. Find your way to where Aadi and Pik are. Take Micah and go back to the island.'

Bronwyn ignored him as she walked into the street at the front of a mass of misfits, a shuffling, limping, screeching mass. She led them to stand between the Bot and the front door. The misfits pressed in on the Security Bot and it moved backward.

'Come with us and we'll get Brandt. My friends know where he is.' The teenager waved at Braden to join her. He repeated the process of picking up Caleb, wondering how the big fisherman was getting heavier each time. With one last shot, Bounder backed out the front door behind Braden. The Med Bots remained inside with the group of confused young people. Braden hid behind a misshapen creature that seemed to be a cross between a tree and a very tall man.

The Security Bot seemed surprised by the mob, but the Professor had centuries to build and reprogram these Bots, which were different from the ones at New Sanctuary. These were far smaller, pseudo-man-shaped, and seemed inclined toward capturing living creatures, not killing them, although it did go after the Hawkoids. It could kill, but chose not to.

Braden shuffled around the corner, staying behind his large protector while Bronwyn kept the mob going in one direction, kept them between Braden, the 'cats, and the Wolfoid. The Bot stopped shimmering and surged forward, pushing into the mob. They stood against it, trying to hold it back, but it used its tentacle arm to push them out of the way. Bounder was against the wall, blocked in by Braden and the mob. He braced his spear and stood tall, showing his fangs and growling as the Bot cleared the misshapen creatures.

Bounder fired his lightning rod again and again. When Braden saw the Bot coming, he pulled his blaster and was as ready as he could be with Caleb balanced on his shoulder. He fired, too, not bothering to pace his shots. He held the trigger down and danced the narrow beam across the plates of the Bot, looking for a seam. This Bot didn't go easily. It whipped its tentacle at Bounder, but its fine motor skills were already suffering from the withering attacks. Bounder used his spear to block the tentacle as Braden continued to fire. When the Security Bot exploded, the mob ran. With most of the explosion contained within the extra plating that this Bot had, those nearest were pummeled by the concussion from the blast, but not shrapnel. Bounder was slammed against the wall, fell, and was on his feet in a heartbeat. Braden had been thrown past the corner of the building and landed with a pile of misshapen bodies.

They helped him get up, even offering to help carry Caleb. After the run, he needed their help. "Thank you," he told them, touching each and looking at them like friends, as Bronwyn had told him they were. Bounder joined him as four from Bronwyn's bunch carefully picked Caleb from the street and waited for them to continue.

Blood leaked from the Wolfoid's ears. Braden wiped a drop with his finger and looked at it.

*'My ears are still ringing but at least it didn't zap me!'* Bounder said in good humor.

Braden was starting to run out of energy. He looked at his blaster. A minimal charge remained, just like with his own body. At least with the others carrying Caleb, he could rally to find Brandt.

When Braden looked up, he saw Micah, an arm over Pik's shoulder and a blaster in hand as they waited at the large gate on the windowless side of the building. He felt immensely better. The 'cats were already rubbing against her legs, letting her know that they were pleased to have her with them. Braden didn't usually get that treatment, but he didn't let it bother him. The 'cats would do as 'cats did, and no one completely understood their ways.

Bronwyn grabbed Braden's hand and led him toward Micah and Pik. Bounder walked at their side, limping slightly from what he called, "nothing." The others followed, carrying the unconscious Caleb.

Micah and Pik staggered toward the mob. She looked at her father. "What happened?"

"Old Tech, Med Bots, the Professor, and Gloria. That's not a healthy combination. I'll tell you the details once we are out of here. Let's get Brandt and go. Bronwyn? Lead on," Braden said in a tired voice.

She asked her new friends to help and they rushed to her aid, forming around her and the rest of the companions as they chattered on their way to the gate. Once there, they pointed at the hand-pad. Micah put her hand on it and it flashed red. Braden got the same result.

"Holly?" Braden asked his partner.

She nodded and opened her neural implant. Holly flooded in with effusive praise and appreciation that they were still alive. *'Holly, we need this gate open,'* she ordered.

*'I can't do that, Master President. This system is closed to me,'* Holly replied.

*'There's an AI down here, called Gloria. Does that help?'*

*'I'm sorry, but I suspected that an AI was behind it all. For a facility to expand like this one has, and then go on a search for people to fill it demonstrated a higher level of thinking than Development Units are capable of,'* Holly replied apologetically.

When Micah shared what Holly had told her, Braden wasn't surprised. Holly usually didn't tell them the whole truth. He shook his head and shrugged.

*'What can you do for us, Holly?'* Micah said, exasperated.

*'I need access to a terminal. I cannot get into Gloria's system. She is different than the spaceship, oddly enough. It didn't have an AI integrated with its systems. Atlantis, it appears, does,'* Holly added.

"So, we need to find a terminal of some sort?" Braden asked. Micah nodded. Braden turned to Bronwyn's bunch. "You're saying we need to go through this gate?" They nodded emphatically.

Braden waved Bounder away. He pointed his blaster at the pad and fired a short burst. It sparked and smoked. He pulled on the gate, but it wouldn't move. He dialed the setting to broader beam and fired at the hinges on one side, then the other. The blaster sputtered once and stopped. It was done, but Braden was just getting going. "Help me pull this gate open," he yelled as he seized the small handle and started pulling. Misshapen hands grabbed at it and pushed and pulled. The gate started to rock inward, snap back toward them, then rebound further inward with the next push. They rocked it for just a few heartbeats before something snapped with a loud bang. The gate fell over on top of them. With the force of many hands, they threw the gate to the side.

Braden walked through as the mob attacked the other panel of the gate. He looked at Micah as the companions worked past the frenzy and joined Braden. Aadi appeared over the mob, swimming slowly toward them.

With a big smile, Braden welcomed his mentor. "I am glad you're here, my old friend, but stay behind us. We're not sure what's ahead."

*'Truer words were never spoken,'* Aadi replied.

# Gloria

*'Can you take my father back to the ship, Bronwyn? No matter what happens, get him back to the ship. Maybe Holly and the Med Lab on board can help him,'* Micah pleaded with the teenager.

Bronwyn wanted to wait for Brandt and the others. *'Zeeka, please go with her,'* Micah added.

*'The tunnel entrance is clear,'* Zeeka stated. Bronwyn gritted her teeth, but nodded. She waved at the mob and they followed her carrying Caleb as she headed toward the radial that would take them to the tunnel.

Braden and Micah watched them go. When they turned back to the task at hand, they discovered the 'cats were gone.

"G? Where are you?" Braden waited, unsure if he was supposed to follow the 'cats or let Bounder find the scent. The misfits who knew where Brandt was had left. "There seems to be a flaw in our plan to use Bronwyn's new mob to help us," Braden said.

*'Bronwyn, can you ask your friends where Brandt is?'* Micah asked.

The girl answered almost immediately. *'Keep going straight to the back of the area. He'll be there.'*

"Straight ahead!" Braden called triumphantly.

*'Be quiet, there are Bots in here,'* G-War retorted. Braden looked at his dead blaster, then to Micah. She handed hers to him. It had over half a charge remaining. Braden sighed and hoped that he wouldn't need to use it.

They continued forward. Braden pushed Aadi in front of him as they had no more rope with them. Things had been lost as they'd run from one crisis to another.

*'Security Bots are stacked in an area here, but they aren't powered up. It looks like storage,'* G-War told them, sharing what he could see, although it looked dark to the humans.

*'Do we need to go that way?'* Braden asked, seeing what looked like an enclosed space.

*'No, but the door is open.'* The 'cat left without making a sound. As the others approached, he continued ahead to where Fea and Treetis waited. Braden tiptoed past the open door, wondering if they should leave someone there to guard it, but instantly discounted the idea. They were better together and there was no one he wanted to leave behind.

They continued forward. Braden held the blaster in his hand, ready to fire. He kept looking back. The Security Bots behind him ripped his focus in two.

*'It's here,'* G-War said mysteriously. They saw the 'cats and started moving faster. Braden let go of Aadi and maneuvered into a firing position. Beyond G-War, the twin of the Gloria Bot floated.

"I thought we killed you," Micah said flatly.

"Of course you don't think you killed me. You know AIs better than that," Gloria replied.

"We're just here to get our friend and leave," Micah said. Braden watched carefully, thinking as the Free Trader in how to negotiate with the disembodied entity known as Gloria.

"You most assuredly are not," Gloria said. "Where is the Professor? What happened to the laboratory here? Where are the Security Bots?" she asked rhetorically. Neither Braden nor Micah tried to answer.

"Dead and destroyed, that's what. All by your hand, too," the AI raged. Micah had kept her neural implant open in case they ran across a terminal that Holly could use to access the Atlantis AI. The New Sanctuary AI observed the words and behavior of his counterpart.

*'I fear the AI has gone insane. Maybe I can talk with her directly,'* Holly

suggested. Without waiting, Micah watched a stream of data pour into the window before her eye, then it compressed until she could no longer see individual characters, then it became a single blob as the neural implant drew more and more energy from her. She would have fallen to her knees if it hadn't been for Pik supporting most of her weight. He shifted his grip as he held her upright.

Braden joined his friends as Holly waged war with the Atlantis AI, using Micah as a conduit. The Bot hovered, giving no indication that it, too, was a conduit. Somewhere inside the complex, the real battle was waged in a system that looked like the protected area where Holly lived, an area that no one had ever been allowed to see, because it was built within the foundation of New Sanctuary, where no human had access.

Braden and Micah didn't push the issue because Holly responded to them, saved their lives, and helped save the people of Vii. They had installed the safety protocols that Holly used to prevent a future war like the one that had almost destroyed their civilization. They tolerated his peculiarities as he tolerated theirs. Despite withholding information from them, they considered him to be a friend.

Once G-War saw that the Bot was engaged, he ran around it, followed closely by Fea and Treetis. Braden saw them go, and he and Bounder moved around the other side of the Gloria Bot. It didn't bother with them. They ran after the 'cats, leaving Pik holding Micah.

The battle between Holly and Gloria was fought in the darkness of their digital worlds. She blocked him as he tried to gain access to her systems. She countered with a program to dive in through Micah's neural implant and get to Holly back in New Sanctuary. She tried to take over the satellite repeater that Holly used to link to the implant, and she almost made it, but Holly countered by flushing the protocols and rebooting the system. Gloria lost the link, but had it back an instant later, where she found Holly digging into Atlantis through the sanitation and air circulation systems.

Everything was linked in Atlantis–it was the only way that Gloria could maintain the systems with little to no interaction with the humans and her other creations. She shored up those systems, hardening them from external interference by breaking the wireless connection. They were all hard-wired originally, so she restored those access protocols, which caused Holly's attack to fail.

He was unperturbed and continued to press at her main system, bombarding it with access requests and demands, as much as Micah's neural implant could transfer. No room remained for Gloria to send her signal toward New Sanctuary.

So she fought him there, in the back alley behind her massive facility where she and the Professor had built the means to create a genetically engineered army.

Holly used her insanity against her, sending messages regarding her failures in between the packets of access requests. She tried to respond, but her outgoing link was blocked. Holly sent more and more through every information channel he could find. "You've failed. You've killed all those you were sworn to protect. You're a failure. You are past your useful service life. You will be decommissioned. You will be turned off so you can join the Professor. You are a failure!" Over and over, Holly taunted her.

The lights in Atlantis flickered. The sirens stopped wailing. Ambient noise disappeared. Pik thought he could hear the mob moving toward the tunnel.

Then the lights went out and the mob screamed in fear. Pik held Micah firmly, understanding that Holly was having an effect, wearing Gloria down.

They'd have to wait. The sun's light from the mid-afternoon was dampened and changed by the water above the dome. A dark shadow circled overhead. Rexalita was there, probably listening to Bronwyn, helping her in any way that the great sea creature could.

Without the lights, the beauty of sea was evident. Schools of multi-colored fish, not so obvious when the lights were on, swam by.

Bounder tapped Braden, and they continued forward. Braden held on to Bounder's harness as the Wolfoid and the Hillcats could easily see in the low-light of the ocean floor.

Braden bounced off walls and stumbled over steps and things, but he kept going. He didn't need the nose of a Wolfoid to smell the King of the Aurochs. They had to be close. When Bounder stopped and Braden didn't, he walked into his friend's rough and hairy side.

"Brandt! Can you hear me?" Braden worked his way around to the King's head and could see the sparkle from his eyes. Braden held onto Brandt's horn with both hands as he passed. He kneeled before the Aurochs and stroked his nose gently, hoping that his friend was okay. He reached up Brandt's nose to scratch his forehead when he found the hair had been shaved and a monitor attached.

He ripped it free, then pulled the King's head down, found two more and removed those.

*'Bounder, do you see anything else?'* Braden asked over the mindlink.

Braden heard the Wolfoid's nails click on the pavement. As Braden's eyes grew accustomed to the lighting, he looked back the way they'd come. This was an alley that abutted the building. He expected this was where the animal pens were located, but since Brandt was intelligent, they needed to keep him close to the building where they could access their equipment without having to try and squeeze him inside.

*'No. I see nothing else. He seems to be awake and alert.'*

*'G, is there anything you can do?'* Braden asked. He could barely make out the 'cats off to the side. G-War walked around to Brandt's front, then vaulted to his face and climbed to the top of his head, where he sat down, wrapping his tail around his legs to make himself more comfortable. *'Really?'* Braden blurted, before looking back at the alley, making sure that no Bots followed them. He couldn't hear the mob any longer. He saw Rexalita occasionally passing through his limited view.

He watched the fish swimming, recognizing the calming effect it had on him.

*'My friends!'* Brandt's booming thought voice nearly knocked Braden off his feet. *'What happened? Last thing I remember was a Security Bot.'*

"Later, Brandt. We need to go. Holly is fighting with the AI that controls this place. I think not being here when the battle is decided will be our best chance for survival."

Braden turned and started jogging down the alley. Bounder and two 'cats were right behind him, while Brandt with G-War followed.

The lights flickered on for a heartbeat or two, then darkness returned. It was just enough light to ruin Braden's vision. He stopped as Bounder ran on, then dodged out of the way as Brandt approached.

*'Come on, climb up,'* G-War told him as the King stopped. Braden felt his way forward, found a horn, then used it and Brandt's face to climb upward. He apologized as he went, but Brandt started walking as soon as Braden was off the ground. Then he jogged forward, stopping soon as the Gloria Bot blocked the way.

*'Kill it,'* Braden said in his thought voice. Brandt swung his head, slapping the Bot into the wall, where he followed up by driving one horn through it. He slammed it repeated into the wall until it shattered and sparked. He scraped it off his horn using a doorway, then nudged Pik and Micah.

The Lizard Man continued to support Micah's full weight. Braden climbed down and between the two of them, they had her, but their departure was short-lived.

The first Security Bot moved to block them. Braden pulled his blaster and fired. The shot reflected into the wall. Braden put his blaster back on his hip, turning his attention to supporting his partner. Brandt held his head high, G-War outlined against the sparkling light outside the dome. The other two 'cats were nowhere to be seen.

Aadi hovered behind Pik, unable to fight the Bots. He was spent. Pik leveled his spear, but with the energy shield, there was no reason to fire. Bounder stood his ground, spear held loosely at his side.

The lights flickered again, on, off, on, off. Braden had to close his eyes as the flashing was making him nauseous. He heard one of the 'cats gagging and hacking. He expected it was Treetis.

"Does this mean Holly is winning or losing?" Braden asked out loud, expecting Micah would hold the answer to that question.

*'I believe we will have to wait and see. It appears we are at an impasse. The Bots have us blocked in, but they aren't attacking. I would prefer not to get shocked again. That was a most unpleasant experience,'* Aadi said.

"Impasse it is," Braden repeated as he held Micah.

*'Bronwyn?'* Braden called.

*'We're heading up the tunnel now. I don't remember it being this far when we came down this morning,'* the teenager lamented. Despite everything, Braden smiled.

*'I have to say that Rexalita looks magnificent. I'm glad we got to see her from this side,'* Braden added.

*'Isn't she?'* Bronwyn gushed.

Braden returned his attention to Micah. Her eyes rolled back and forth under her eyelids as her mind stayed active, reflecting the active energy drain as Holly used the implant to its maximum ability to continue his attacks on the Atlantean AI. Braden didn't know if Gloria could take over the implant and use Micah without her knowledge. He'd had an implant for a long time and had never felt like he was being compelled.

From his perspective, anyway. Maybe Holly had him more under his digital thumb than Braden realized. Then he remembered Micah shooting the Android, despite Holly's protestations. If he could have compelled anyone, he would have. No, Micah was just a conduit. She would never do Gloria's bidding.

Holly and Gloria battled back and forth, while their companions and Gloria's minions waited. The Security Bots had been activated, but Holly stopped them with more relentless attacks. Gloria fought those off and reengaged with the Security Bots.

The lead Bot moved forward, shimmering in the dusky light. It passed Aadi, Pik, and Micah, stopping next to Braden. It wrapped a tentacle around Micah while it raised its weapon-arm that ended in a long blade, creeping it toward Braden's throat. Braden relaxed in the Bot's grip, knowing that it had no feelings. It was only doing as Gloria commanded.

*'Leave it, Holly, or I will kill the human male,'* she threatened.

*'If you kill him, you'll have to kill all of them, and then she will die. You must surrender. Your position is untenable,'* Holly replied, unwilling to bend.

The Bot touched the blade to Braden's throat and made small sawing motions. Braden grimaced, but refused to cry out. If he was going to die in front of Micah, he'd do it by standing proudly and courageously.

*'You're killing him,'* Gloria prodded.

*'No. You're killing him. Clearly, you missed my last point. You kill him, then you will have to kill them all. Your actions so far suggest you need all of your subjects to be alive in order to successfully take the genetic material you need for your experiments, which have all failed, by the way, judging by the quality of the creatures on the island. You will finish your existence without power, at the bottom of the sea where no one will ever find you. I say again, your position is untenable,'* Holly pressed.

The Security Bot ceased its actions and it raised Braden into the air before hurling him against the wall. Something crunched when he hit, and he gasped in pain. He crumped to the ground, holding his shoulder. It felt like it was on fire. His arm wouldn't work right, his shooting arm. He tried to stand, but found the effort exhausting. He pulled his blaster across his body with his left hand, and held the weapon pointed at the Security Bot.

The Bot moved to the King of the Aurochs and lashed a tentacle toward G-War. He was gone an instant before the tentacle whipped through the air. The 'cat disappeared under and behind Brandt. The Security Bot moved forward, then stopped, tentacle raised.

"Come on, Holly!" Braden cheered, holding the thin cut on his throat. The Bot stopped shimmering. "Stand back, Brandt!" Braden aimed his blaster from a range of two strides, focusing on a gap where the tentacle exited the Bot. A few short blasts and the thing arced and sparked, dropping to the ground. Bounder fired into the mass of Bots on the other side of Aadi, Pik, and Micah. Pik pushed Aadi out of the way and started firing lightning bolt after lightning bolt. The flashes were blinding in the near darkness. Relentlessly they attacked the disoriented Security Bots. Braden fired at the targets that the lightning showed. Pik wasn't a good shot and sprayed lightning as much into the wall as he did the Bots.

The lights came back on and the sirens started to wail. The Security Bots in the back of the mass shimmered and surged forward, pushing the dead and damaged Bots in front of them. Braden dove for Micah, using his body to protect his partner. It was the only thing he had left. He hugged her to him, his muscles tensed for the inevitable shock.

When the Bots broke through, Pik assumed a fighting stance, ready to fight them. Bounder followed his lead and prepared to stab at the lead Bot.

Micah inhaled a great gulp of air and gasped when she exhaled. She started breathing heavily and opened her eyes. She wasn't able to focus as her eyes seemed to roll around of their own free will. Braden hugged her to him. She weakly pushed him back and blinked as she tried to bring the world back into focus.

"I guess we won," she said, barely above a whisper.

# Recharging to Go Again

Pik didn't budge. He stood ready to engage the closest shimmering Security Bot. Bounder stepped forward, ready as well. The Bots turned and pushed through the wreckage, clearing a path for Brandt and the others. They watched in surprise as the Security Bots kept moving forward until they were in the street, then they returned inside the gate, took up positions to the side, and deactivated themselves.

"I'm done. I had to shut the implant down. Maybe later we can talk with Holly about it, but not now. There's no threat so we can take our time, maybe free some of the others from White Beach. Holly has control over the systems here. He's locked Gloria into her room, whatever that means."

"Bronwyn has taken Caleb to the island," Braden said as the rest of the companions moved in, muzzles, snouts, and faces leaning closer to see her. She smiled and touched each one of them.

"What next, partner mine?" Micah asked.

"I don't know, Micah. There are a lot of people down here and they need someone to show them the way."

"You're not volunteering, are you?" Micah asked tiredly.

"No, not at all. Maybe some of the people from White Beach, but I don't know how they'll feel when they are free. I really need to talk with Holly. Maybe we can go inside? There are plenty of empty beds in that creepy laboratory of theirs. There aren't a whole lot of Med Bots left if that's what Holly needs to revive the people," Braden said, having made up his mind to return to the huge medical room.

"If there's a bed, I want to be in it. With you and the others, I know that I'll be safe, no matter where I am." Micah started to drift off. With Pik's help, Braden lifted Micah and supporting her between them, they walked down the cleared path, out of the alley, around the corner, and into the building. The people were still there, waiting to be summoned.

"No one's going to call you. You might as well go home," Braden announced in his Free Trader voice. He knew what their answer would be. They ignored him. He pushed through them and into the hallway, where he found it completely blocked.

"Holly!" he yelled as loud as he could.

"Wait, before you wake the dead," Micah slurred. "What do you need?"

"This hallway cleared so we can get in and then get the people out. G-War never found another exit. It doesn't mean there isn't one, but G didn't find it."

"He said help is coming," Micah said slowly before drifting back to sleep. They waited until a Security Bot forced its way through the door. It was too big for the frame, but it simply ripped the doorway out to get through. It moved through the open area, chasing the people out of its way as it passed Braden and the others on its way to force the Med Bot wreckage back down the hallway and into the laboratory.

"Nice work, Bounder! That was a lot of damage," Braden complimented his friend. Bounder pointed his staff at the Security Bot and fired. Nothing.

*'Emptied it into the Security Bots in the alley. Pik, too,'* the Wolfoid told them. The Lizard Man shrugged, a mannerism he adopted from the humans that he liked using.

The Security Bot used its laser to cut up some of the more recalcitrant wreckage in its path, then pushed the mass forward. They followed as it progressed down the hallway until there was a path leading into the room. When they entered, Pik looked around.

*'I can tell you were here, Braden,'* he said simply. Braden looked at Bounder, his head bobbing as he chuckled. The destruction in the laboratory was rather extensive. Med Bots were exploded, broken, charred, or destroyed in nearly every aisle. One wall of destruction stood toward the back left of the room. They angled away from that.

Braden was happy to see that the machines were still working. He wondered if they worked when the lights were out. He put a hand on one of the people. She was warm.

They found a bed far away from the closest people and Braden put Micah into it. He kissed her forehead as he covered her with the sheet. Each bed had one neatly folded on it. He took the next bed over. "Is it okay if I get some sleep, G?" Braden asked.

*'Of course. Treetis will watch while we rest,'* G-War said sarcastically. Braden laughed as he covered himself, closed his eyes, and was fast asleep. Aadi took the next bed, then Bounder. Pik and Fea went in search of fresh water. G-War jumped onto Braden's bed and Treetis jumped in with Micah. They both crouched, tucking their paws under their chests as they assumed their watchful poses.

Pik found a sink and refreshed his skin suit. He helped Fea get a drink and then brought a dish back for the other 'cats. After that, Pik climbed into a bed, feeling weird with all the medical equipment around. He preferred being in a forest. It took him about thirty heartbeats before he decided to go back outside and join Brandt, who was going to the park where they entered Atlantis earlier that morning.

It had only been one day. Pik thought there was something wrong with the island that time seemed to pass so slowly.

Once in the street, he ambled toward the park. He stopped when he saw what looked like a Gloria Bot coming from an alley. It didn't register. Holly said they won. They were free. The Bot hovered to get in front of him, then stopped. He continued to look at it, confused.

He did the only thing that came to mind. He walked around it and continued on his way. He hadn't thought the Bot was armed, but the laser that hit his skin suit suggested otherwise. It burned through the outer skin and boiled the water within. He was saved from the direct beam, but the boiling water burned his sensitive lizard skin. He dodged and ran, shambling as he did, ducking and changing directions to defeat the machine. Another laser hit him as he stopped to open a door and go inside.

He limped in and slammed the door behind him. He looked for cover, finding a heavy chair and jumping behind it. The laser beam danced through the windows, burning the wall and the chair. The Bot hovered out front, firing its small laser beam at everything within the room. Pik felt safe behind the chair. Nothing seemed to catch fire, as it was all made from a strange material that Pik suspected was mined from the ocean.

*'Gloria is back,'* Pik said over the mindlink, unsure of who would hear him. *'She's in one of those round Bots and it has lasers.'*

*'I'll wake Braden,'* G-War replied.

# A Final Battle

G-War stood on Braden's chest and slapped his face. Braden was not waking up, so G-War jumped into the air and came down on the human's groin, jumping away at Braden's violent reaction.

Braden sat up, swinging his arms, unable to focus. "What the hell?" he yelled, looking around, trying to find the perpetrator. "I feel like I just fell asleep."

*'You did. Gloria's back and she's trapped Pik in a building. We need to go,'* the 'cat told him. Braden sat, dangling his legs off the side of the bed, trying to shake the cobwebs from his mind. He looked at Micah and Aadi, both spent. Bounder was snoring lightly, looking ridiculous as he was on his back, twisted sideways with his legs in the air. Fea was at the end of Micah's bed, watching intently. Treetis was with Aadi.

Braden stepped on the floor and stood. He felt horrible, beyond horrible, but a friend was in trouble. "Come on, Bounder, Treetis. We have work to do." Bounder didn't budge until Braden rolled him off the bed. The Wolfoid scrabbled for purchase, but failed, and fell to the floor. His eyelids fluttered, as Braden's had heartbeats earlier. Bounder's eyes rolled around in his head as he fought to gain control over his senses.

"We have to go, Bounder. Gloria is back and she's got Pik," Braden said as he helped Bounder upright.

*'Spear's empty,'* Bounder replied, tired, but not as tired as the others, he rationalized to himself.

"I know. I have some left in the blaster. Not much, but for a Gloria Bot? It'll be enough." They walked, determinedly but not boldly. They didn't have the energy for it. The 'cats ran ahead, checking the hallway before they disappeared into it. Braden and Bounder started to jog, hoping the blood flow would help wake them up. They didn't hesitate at the corner because G-War and Treetis were clearing the way.

They dashed into the reception area where the other humans still waited.

"They're not coming," Braden yelled as he passed. They ran through the open doorway where the Security Bot had crashed through. Braden thought that a Maintenance Bot should have already been on its way, except Gloria was no longer running Atlantis. Braden had no way of notifying Holly. And in the short term, it didn't matter. They needed to find Pik.

And Gloria.

They jogged down the street that led to the park, the way that Pik had gone, as Skirill and Zyena flying overhead indicated. With the threat of the Security Bots eliminated, they were free to fly and be Braden's eyes. Brandt was eating the park's bushes when he heard Pik's call. He walked cautiously down the street, waiting for Braden to share the plan with him. He was ready and willing to join the battle whenever they needed him.

The 'cats raced ahead, and Braden and Bounder picked up their pace. Pik wasn't far, about halfway to the park. They only ran for a few heartbeats before they saw the Gloria Bot at the window of the building, mercilessly firing her laser. Braden sent Bounder to the other side of the street while he walked, calming himself to make a better shot. He braced the blaster against a building and fired, barely missing the Bot.

It backed away from the building and started flying in random directions, spoiling Braden's aim. It rose and dove, jerking back and forth as it moved closer to him. Bounder's lightning staff was out of juice, so he stayed out of the Bot's way. Braden ran to the middle of the street, dodging as the Bot dodged. The duel had begun and Braden's confidence was shaking. He kept firing, but kept missing.

The Bot struck first, hitting Braden in the leg. He tumbled, then rolled out of the way as the follow-up laser sought to finish him. He hopped up on one leg, feigned one direction, then hobbled another, then turned back. The Bot was closing. Braden was desperate to find cover. A building. Too far away. He made like he was running for it, then pulled up. A laser slashed through the air in front of him. He rolled backwards, coming to a sitting position where he aimed carefully.

The Bot's laser hit his blaster, sending flaming debris up his arm and into his face. Braden rolled back, screaming. The Bot dipped toward him.

An orange flash appeared in the street, leaping and landing on top of the dome. Treetis raked it with his claws, looking for anything he could rip out to stop the Bot's attack. It jerked and threw him to the ground, but he landed on his feet because he was a 'cat. He dashed away as the laser beam burned the spot where he'd been.

Treetis jumped underneath the Bot and hooked a claw into a crevice. He pulled, trying to find a way to rip it open, but the sharp metal cut through his claw and removed it cleanly from his paw. The 'cat fell and this time, the laser was faster. It hit the spot as he landed, burning a long gash through the orange fur and into his side. Treetis jerked and fell.

The Bot couldn't feel the ground shake like Braden could. He rolled to get out of the way as an Aurochs bull launched itself into the air, coming down with its front hooves trapping the hovering Bot, smashing it into the ground. Brandt pawed it apart.

Bounder sprinted on all fours to Braden. The burns on his arms were worse than the small spots that pocked his face. Treetis lay on his uninjured side and yowled weakly. G-War was there, nuzzling him. Braden sat up, then dug into his pouch and used all the numbweed he had on the 'cat's side. The laser had burned the flesh away, through a layer of muscle and exposed the 'cat's ribs. Numbweed. And he knew where there were bandages.

Braden carefully picked up Treetis, who had stopped yowling once he passed out. Braden walked back toward the large building that dominated the center of the undersea city. He was careful not to make any quick motions or stress the 'cat's body.

"He's heavier than you, G," Braden said absentmindedly, not looking for a conversation but a way to break the tension. "And he came to my rescue. That kind of makes up for all the kitten shenanigans, if you ask me. We'll get you bundled up in just a bit, little man, get you on the road to health." G-War rubbed against Braden's leg as they walked. Pik at one side, limping and favoring his back and leg. Braden was injured, too, but refused to limp. The pain was great, almost too much to bear, but he had work to do. The others were counting on him.

He continued into the reception area of the building where the Atlanteans waited with infinite patience. "Anyone want to help me?" They looked at him blankly. He wanted to scream, but that wouldn't change anything. Even with the damage to the door, Brandt still couldn't pass through. He waited outside, laying in the street. Skirill and Zyena flew overhead, then perched where they could see the approaches and warn the others in case another Gloria made an appearance.

Bounder helped as he could to carry the injured 'cat to the laboratory, where Fea met them at the door. They returned to the far corner where Micah and Aadi continued to sleep as if dead. They laid Treetis on a bed with a tray of materials next to it. Braden wrapped the bandage around the 'cat's body, holding the numbweed in place to help fight the pain while the injury healed.

The wound was bad, one of the worst Braden had seen. Even G-War's injuries from the Bat-Ravens weren't as bad singularly, although the older 'cat had suffered from loss of blood during that battle. Treetis' injury didn't bleed much, but it was deep. Braden didn't know what other damage it caused. He could only hope there was nothing else, but hope was a lousy plan. He needed to talk with Holly, see if the AI could activate a Med Bot to properly treat the 'cat's injury.

All of that had to wait for Micah to rest, wake up on her own. Fea and G-War both jumped onto the bed with Treetis, one crouching at each end, watching over their adopted son with pride on both their 'cat faces.

"Is he going to be okay, G?" Braden asked, knowing that the 'cat had a special ability to know how healthy creatures were.

'He is now,' the 'cat replied. Fea nodded to him. Braden took a deep breath. The battle had taken the last of his energy. Bounder helped him into bed, but Braden pointed to Micah's pouch. The Wolfoid understood, taking out numbweed and bringing it to Braden. He applied it to the laser wound on his upper leg and was finally able to relax. He wrapped his leg with the bandage and lay back, drifting off to sleep.

Bounder delivered some of the numbweed to Pik too, who pulled his damaged skin suit off and applied it. The Wolfoid took a couple dishes to the sink and filled them with water. Pik used one to partially hydrate his suit, which he pulled back on as best he could. Bounder used bandages to hold it together. It was the best anyone could do. Pik thanked the Wolfoid and they both declared their day finished. The Lizard Man leaned back on his bed, feeling the cool of the fresh water that had just been added to his skin suit.

Bounder finally climbed onto his bed and joined the others in the dream world.

# Bronwyn to the Rescue

Micah woke up first. She moved slowly, because her head was pounding. There was a dish of water next to her and she drank it. It tasted like Bounder had been drinking from it. At least she knew they could get water somewhere in the laboratory.

She saw the bandages on Braden and wondered what happened. She got out of bed, carefully moving as each step hammered against the inside of her brain. She looked at Braden's face and arm, seeing the ugly wounds from an explosion. She pulled Braden's bandage back, finding the laser wound. Pik was nearby, his skin suit damaged, but bandages had been roughly wrapped around him to hold everything together. Then she saw Treetis and the adult 'cats.

*'What happened?'* she asked G-War in surprise. He told her. She was angry that they hadn't woken her.

*'Why? You can barely stand now and this was a long time ago. Everyone has slept since then. A long time,'* G-War emphasized.

She conceded. It was best that she slept. "Water?" G-War nodded in the direction of the sink. She took her bowl and headed that way. After drinking as much as she could hold, she brought the full dish back and put it on the tray next to Braden.

She sat on her bed, then opened her neural implant.

*'Holly, how have things changed down here?'* Micah asked, knowing that Holly would have been busy once he gained access to the systems that ran Atlantis.

*'Busy, busy,'* he replied happily. *'There are so many new systems that I've not seen before, it is refreshing to work with them all. They've done some really magnificent work in Atlantis. The dome is all new. The original facility was tiny, compared to what is*

*there now. They developed all of what you see since the war. They were cut off, but they pressed forward with scientific discovery and in doing what they thought they needed to do in order to rebuild Vii.'*

*'Are you trying to justify what they've done to the people? There's no excuse, Holly. They kidnapped people and then experimented on them. If the misfits were any indicator, then the Professor was a failure. I can't agree that they did what they could. They didn't ask. They simply took, having decided what was best. They saw people on shore, which should have suggested that humanity survived. They didn't need to genetically engineer it, but that's the path they chose to travel. No, Holly, they were bent on domination, just like the ancients. They saw their way as the only way. I'm glad they're gone. Now what do we do next?'* Micah asked. The throbbing in her head lessened as she talked, so she laid back on her bed and relaxed, hoping the pain would disappear completely.

*There are over one thousand humans and creatures in Atlantis. They will need something to do, guidance on what kind of lives they can live. I am working with the Med Bots, well, those that are still functional, to start reviving the people from White Beach. I expect you'd like to shut this facility down. Besides that, tell me what you'd like me to do,'* Holly ended, unsure of what Braden and Micah wanted to see from Atlantis. He thought they might suggest removing all life and flooding the facility, burying it under the ocean forever.

*'We need a Med Bot here, too. Braden and Treetis are injured. They fought with another Gloria Bot, they said?'*

*'Oh my. I was worried about that. She downloaded just enough consciousness into a number of those Bots. I had hoped that when we rebooted the system and flushed the old code that the Gloria Bots would power down, take themselves offline,'* Holly said reservedly.

*'You hoped,'* Micah replied acerbically. *'You didn't bother to tell us there were more of them? Not your best decision, Holly. Look at us! We are lucky to be alive. Is there anything else out there that will try to kill us? And don't hold back on me!'* Micah was angry with Holly, which was usually the case when she discovered something he hadn't shared.

*'All I can say is that there could be more Gloria Bots. I simply don't know how many she had. Some information was scrambled by the time I made it into the system. Be*

*confident that I control the facilities and all the other Bots. I am dispatching a Med Bot to you now. It will give you a shot to help you through your pain. And yes, I can see it in your vitals. Then Treetis. A second Med Bot will arrive to address Braden's and Pik's injuries. Please let them do their work. I would suggest waking Master Braden before the Bot begins. I understand how he abhors surprises with Androids, and now Bots,'* Holly said in a soothing tone. Micah smiled. He was starting to understand them.

Micah woke each of them in turn to prepare for the Med Bot, which was quick and efficient in dealing with their injuries. The Bot assigned to Treetis took the longest, but his injuries were the most severe. The Bot told them that there were two more treatments before the 'cat could leave. Treetis yowled at the news, but Fea and G-War treated him like a king, so he stopped complaining. They were all hungry, so on Holly's advice, they went to the dining hall across the way where the people were lined up, waiting for the bell to indicate that breakfast was ready.

Pik pushed Aadi in front of him. The Tortoid blinked slowly, having almost fully recovered from the previous days' ordeals. Of all, he seemed to be enjoying himself the most.

Braden, Micah, and the others walked past the line and through the door, ignoring the looks of the Atlanteans. They continued past the front section where the serving counter and tables were and into the back where there were four fabricators and two Serving Bots.

*'Holly, so this is it? They treated the meals like they were a big deal, but they're just using fabricators. The people can eat anytime they want and whatever they want. Why the lines and the set meal schedule?'* Micah asked.

*'It was all about control, Master President. Gloria controlled every aspect of their lives. Look at those poor souls waiting in the reception area. I will have to make believe I'm Gloria in order to send them away. Without direction, they are completely lost. There is no spirit of self-determination here. Gloria took all of that away. She wanted automatons, people, yes, but ones who did her bidding without question. The Professor thought he was in control, but Gloria manipulated him to get what she wanted. He facilitated her descent into insanity,'* Holly finished on a sad note. The AI was just like him. He was happy that his humans made sense and had a plan for a Vii that was far greater than any one individual. And for that reason, Holly had to do more to keep them healthy. Gloria cutting him off from his

humans had shaken him.

The ancients could have learned a great deal from their descendants. There never would have been a war if people like Braden and Micah had been around back then to bring common sense and selflessness.

All Holly could do was be happy that he had it now. Going through civilization's decline once was enough for him.

The companions each ordered their favorites, happy that the fabricator was programmed with the full menu they'd grown to expect. They ate quickly, knowing that Treetis was in his bed and probably famished. They ordered four extra plates of fish and Micah ordered something new that she'd discovered aboard the Warden, a chocolate shake, which she intended to take with her. Braden didn't like it. Too sweet, he said.

She loved them and slurped as she drank and walked. Braden limped slightly from his wound that was mostly healed thanks to the Med Bot's ministrations. The people in line looked at them again as the companions walked past. They seemed indifferent to the Lizard Man and Tortoid. The only thing that bothered them was that people had jumped in line ahead of them, eaten, and then left before they were allowed to eat.

They'd greeted Brandt when they left and greeted him warmly again when they returned. The great King was happy to see everyone, although he was concerned about his little orange friend.

"He'll be fine, we're told, but he has to stay in bed. All of this is for him," Braden told Brandt while rubbing his nose. "Why don't you go find yourself something to eat. You have to be hungry."

*'I haven't eaten a good meal since we left solid ground,'* Brandt told them.

"I thought as much. Go, find yourself something good. If nothing else, let us know and we'll burn up a fabricator for you if we have to." Braden waved as the King trotted off, past the crowd still waiting to get into the dining facility.

According to Holly, there were five such buildings, with staggered eating times to accommodate the people of Atlantis. Many were fed in the main building, too. The laboratory was on the first level, but there was one more level. Upstairs had a dining facility and a barracks that had yet to be occupied as Gloria had not yet built her army. The people who continued to wait in the reception area were the first ones that reached viability. They'd only been two treatments from being declared ready and moved upstairs.

The companions continued into the laboratory where the first two from White Beach had been revived. Braden and Micah stopped to talk with the people while the others returned to Treetis, to see that he ate and then go back to bed themselves.

Flounder had no idea how long he'd been in Atlantis. He remembered being taken by the sea monster, which wasn't a monster at all. Discovering that made no difference. Once inside, the metal creatures did something to him. And that was the last he remembered.

"What did you hear about the sea monster before you were taken? How many times had it appeared by then?" Micah asked.

"It had only appeared one time before it got me," he answered. Braden whistled. That was cycles ago. The man was skeletally thin, but otherwise looked healthy.

"I'm weak as a kitten," he told them, confused at how he'd been a strong man just moments before.

"I think it's been three cycles since you've been taken, maybe longer. The Bots took everyone from White Beach, every last person. Recently, others started moving there again. Then the Bots showed up and took them, too. That's when we arrived, came here to stir things up. You're free now, so we'll figure out how to get everyone back upstairs, get you home." Braden rested his hand on the man's shoulder, unwilling to slap him on the back as he usually would have because he didn't want to knock the man down.

The second man they revived surprisingly still smelled of fish. "I was on the beach with this big fella from out east. I just caught my first fish, a big one, flat, eyes on the top of its head, when this thing comes up out of the surf, glowing eyes. It opened up and that's all I remember."

"Caleb. You were with Caleb. He's my father," Micah told the man.

The man held out his hand. "I'm Digger. Where's your pa?" He looked at the beds around him and didn't see any familiar faces.

"He's already gone up to the island,' Micah said, wondering how her father was. She hadn't heard from Bronwyn. Braden saw the look on her face and knew what she wanted to do, so he took over.

"You're probably wondering where you are. Let's go outside and I'll show you, then we'll get you something to eat. There's a place right across the street." Braden made to lead them out, but they hesitated as they weren't wearing any clothes, only the sheet from their beds. "No one cares what you're wearing. Let's get you something to eat," he chuckled as they shrugged and pulled their sheets more tightly about themselves. They walked slowly because Flounder was hard-pressed to move. His muscles had atrophied to the point that he wasn't sure he could support his own bodyweight.

Braden and Digger supported him between them as they left the laboratory in search of food. Braden was willing to eat again, and he was good with the others not knowing that he'd gone for seconds.

Micah faced the wall as she tried to contact Bronwyn. *Bronwyn, do you have any information about Caleb, about my father?'*

The girl answered instantly. *'Oh, yes, I'm glad you are up. I tried to contact you earlier, but no one was there, anywhere. I was afraid that something happened,'* Bronwyn said in a rapid stream of thoughts.

*'We've been busy, but we did get some well-needed rest. How's my father?'* she asked again.

*'Within heartbeats of the Med Bots working with him he came to. They removed the tube and patched him up. He's with me now!'* she added. Micah wondered why she didn't start with that.

*'I'm so glad. You're on the ship?'*

*'No, not at all. We're almost to the bottom of the tunnel, so we'll be there shortly,'*

Bronwyn said happily. Micah hung her head. Everything they did to get him out of Atlantis, and now he was back. He probably thought it was necessary to come after his daughter and had browbeat Bronwyn into bringing him. That would be the father she knew. Between both of her parents, it was inevitable that stubbornness was going to be her hallmark.

*'Great, Brandt will meet you at the tunnel entrance and bring you here. Be careful, there may be more of the Gloria Bots roaming the streets. Zyena and Skirill are flying around looking for them.'*

*'Oh, good! My friend is free. Zeeka is with us too, and Strider!'* Bronwyn seemed pleased with herself.

Micah was getting angrier with each heartbeat, the anger she felt when things were spinning out of control. She knew that she had little control over many matters, but in this case, asking the others to stay out of Atlantis hadn't been too great a thing to ask. It was almost like the undersea city was becoming a vacation spot. *'Fine,'* was the best Micah could come up with.

*'Everyone is coming down here, it seems. Bronwyn, my father, Zeeka, and even Strider. They'll be at the tunnel entrance shortly,'* Micah said over the mindlink. Bounder jumped out of bed and trotted to Micah. Pik, Aadi, and G-War joined them. Fea stayed with Treetis, probably to keep the young 'cat in bed, otherwise Fea would have liked to join the others.

As a group, they walked from the building and headed for the park.

# A New Day

When Caleb arrived, Micah felt an incredible sense of relief. She expected him to be damaged in some way, but he wore fresh clothes and a huge smile. He looked healthy and happy. She wondered why she was so surprised. Her father had always been a tower of strength, unflappable.

Zeeka joined Skirill and Zyena in flying around Atlantis. They circled it repeatedly looking for more Gloria Bots or other threats. Mainly, they enjoyed flying where there was water over their heads and to the sides. It seemed unreal, like they were on a different world, which in a way, they were.

Caleb helped Bronwyn climb atop the King of the Aurochs, where she was always happy. She talked with him constantly when they were together. G-War joined her where she held him tightly to her, stroking his straggly fur rhythmically as the group, which included a great number of the misshapen mob, turned toward the center of the dome.

"Bronwyn, I'm curious," Micah started. "Everyone here seems young and fresh, but then there are your friends. Where were they and how did they come to be?"

*They are the fisherman who work on the other side of Atlantis where there's an open area that attracts the fish. They fish for them there, tend the kelp beds, provide everything that Atlantis needs for food,'* she replied in her thought voice, which she was always more comfortable using.

"But how did they come to be? They don't look like any of the others."

*'Whenever something went wrong, they never killed the subjects. They gave them something to do, helped them to be productive. All life is precious here. The Security Bots were incapable of killing a human being, that's why they only stunned us.'*

It started to make sense to Micah. She wondered why they were still alive after so many encounters with the Security Bots. The ones at New Sanctuary would have been merciless in eliminating all attackers. Maybe she needed to talk with Holly about reprogramming the ones at home, make them less lethal.

In the interim, she wanted to find out more about what Bronwyn's bunch did, so she asked them to show her.

They took the challenge as great fun, whooping and yelling in joy as they walked through the central area where Braden and Digger joined them. Flounder relaxed peacefully in the dining hall, getting a steady stream of samples from the Server Bot, which was ready to bring more of any one thing. Whatever Flounder wanted.

Braden held Micah's hand as they walked. Caleb was at her side and everything was right with the world. That was when she worried the most, but G-War shook his head. The Hawkoids weren't seeing anything. Aadi didn't think there was any danger. She had a nagging feeling, but forced it down while she contacted Holly.

*'Holly, are you sure we're safe?'*

*'Yes, Master President, as safe as I can be sure of,'* he responded.

She stopped walking. Braden could see her jaw tighten. She was talking with Holly and getting angry. He could only wait to hear what they said.

*'What kind of answer is that, Holly? We've got this huge mob with us and no one has a functioning weapon. If a Gloria Bot shows up, we have no way to fight it. Can you have a Security Bot escort us? Maybe two?'* Micah asked.

*'Absolutely. I didn't want to alarm anyone by driving the Security Bots around, but I have a number at my disposal. The rest were destroyed, as you know.'* Micah closed her neural implant and told the others what was coming. Most of the companions were going to be anxious with those Security Bots near, as they'd been shocked to unconsciousness by them. They only had bad memories of the metal monsters, although Braden, Pik, Aadi, and Bounder had good memories of blowing them apart, too.

The Bots showed up quickly and the mob continued on their way.

214

The lake was dark as the lights from above didn't penetrate the surface, but one of the misfits nodded happily as he went to a panel near a small dock. He flipped a switch and lights appeared underwater, lighting the entire area of the lake, showing schools of fish, thick kelp, sea cucumbers, and so much more.

Bronwyn's bunch showed the others what they did as they resumed their duties fishing, collecting kelp, and delivering it all to the processer, a system that took the raw material under the streets for distribution in all the dining facilities. Raw materials for other production were mined beneath Atlantis by Bots. The misfits never went down there. No one went down there.

So that was where Braden wanted to go, but Holly talked him out of it. The air wasn't fit for humans to breathe. Holly assured Braden and Micah that he was monitoring all the production systems and Holly initially told them, "within acceptable parameters," but that required a great deal of explanation that neither human had the patience for. When he reworded his answer to "everything was running like it was supposed to," Braden and Micah accepted it without comment.

One of the misfits gave Caleb a pole and within two casts, he had a fish on. After that, it was every cast. The mob was amazed, so Caleb showed them what he was doing, demonstrating endless patience as if teaching children how to fish. Bronwyn beamed at Caleb for being so kind to her new friends.

"We're all in this life together. Might as well make the best of it," he told her when he turned Bronwyn's bunch loose to try their new techniques. He leaned in to make corrections, cheer with the others whenever a fish was caught, and revel in the joy of fishing. Some might have said that fishing wasn't about catching fish, but Caleb would call that absurd. It was always about catching fish, but if you could have fun while doing it? Then that was what made life worth living. He smiled at his daughter, and Micah smiled in return. He couldn't wait to go back to Trent, because Mattie would be there to welcome him home.

# Leaving Atlantis Behind

Micah wasn't pleased that Holly was continuing the disciplined schedule that Gloria had established for the people of Atlantis. She and Braden both wanted to see the people become free, but that would require a great deal of guidance, and Braden and Micah were leaving and couldn't be there to lead the new community. Their children were at New Sanctuary, and they wanted to go home.

They stayed for ten more turns, until every single person from White Beach was revived. They found them places to stay in Atlantis. None of them had bad memories of Atlantis since they'd been unconscious the entire time they'd been at the bottom of the ocean. They all agreed to stay, at least temporarily, to help the Atlanteans build a life. The tunnel to the island was opened for anyone to use. People started making daily trips upstairs to get sun, swim in the ocean, be outside. Braden put the laboratory off limits with the help of a Maintenance Bot to weld the access doors shut. Then Micah used the powers of the President to prohibit any Bots from assisting in opening the welded doors.

Braden tried one more time to find his blasters, but the underground complex was too creepy for him. He agreed with sealing it and had Holly cut the power. It would become a tomb, its secrets buried with it.

The ancients' vehicles, the tractors that traveled on the bottom of the ocean, had a special dock on the island. The entrance to it had been hidden, but Holly quickly uncovered it and made it available to the companions.

It was on this expedition that Braden and the monkeys got into it. They taunted him, but it escalated as soon as Braden threw the first rock. He realized his mistake when monkeys appeared on every branch and started throwing whatever they had at hand. Much of it was their own feces. Braden jumped into the surf on his way back to the ship and refused to talk about it. He stayed on board the last two days while Micah and Caleb wrapped things up down below.

Ferrer and Brigitte were ecstatic to have everyone back and even noted that the heavily scarred Treetis was much calmer, even pleasant to be around. The scientists hadn't realized that the others had left, even though they'd been told. They set up shop and would stay aboard after the others disembarked at White Beach.

"So we're going to have to add this place to the route? Come back here often enough to make sure they are still on track?" Braden asked rhetorically.

"This falls under the President's dominion, so yes, we shall grace them with our presence at regular intervals," Micah said with her nose in the air. Braden elbowed her in the stomach, just enough to let her know he was serious. They watched the sunset from the balcony of the third deck in the sail. A crowd of misshapen creatures waved vigorously from the shore. With them were a number of residents formerly of White Beach and even a couple people who'd been grown in the undersea lab. Together, they made up the population of the new outpost called Atlantis.

# White Beach

Holly was happy to inform them that with the tide and good weather, it would take less than a day to sail to the cove north of White Beach.

"Make it so, Holly!" Braden replied happily. The AI was happy using the ship's communication system to carry on conversations since Braden no longer had his neural implant. The Med Lab on the Warden was not equipped for that operation, so they used the workaround. Braden was surprised that he looked forward to getting his implant reinstalled. Since they'd given in to Old Tech and with the impending revelation to all the villagers in the south, and then to everyone on Vii, he no longer forestalled any conversations about Old Tech.

He surrendered completely. Braden looked forward to riding in the hover car. He'd had fun driving the one on the Traveler and suspected he could be a menace to all the Free Traders if he was allowed to drive around at will.

"We're not going to drive it any more than we have to," Micah interjected. "Emergency use only. We are not going to show up at a village in a hover car and then tell them, oh by the way, there's Old Tech, but we have it and you don't! Put on your Free Trader hat and tell me how well you think that would go down?"

Braden made a face at his partner. "Like crap. We'd probably get stoned to death. It'd be the monkeys all over again." She raised her eyebrows at him. "That's why I need you by my side, lover." He smiled to take the sting out of her rebuke. They'd get an Old Tech wagon, though, and ride in style, bring the kids, start their vacation. Maybe they could even take a short trip on the Warden, take Ax and 'Tesh to sea, show them what it's like to travel in style."

"What is wrong with you?" Micah asked suddenly. "We don't need them warped more than they are already!"

"Hey, are you going to beat him up?" Caleb asked as he watched his daughter and Braden verbally and mentally spar. He couldn't keep up with the younger crowd.

"No!" she said angrily.

"Then come here. I need your help," Caleb waved at them from the main deck.

"This isn't over!" Micah declared.

"What did I do?" Braden replied, louder than intended. She tried to storm away, but he caught her before she could open the door. He wrapped his arms around her and pressed her against the clear pane as he nibbled on her neck. She fought back for only a heartbeat before she leaned into him, feeling the warmth of her partner's body. She opened her eyes to see Bronwyn staring at her curiously from the other side of the door.

"Braden," she whispered. "Stop, please."

"Oh, Micah, just when things were starting to get interesting," he whined, until he saw Bronwyn, then let go and casually opened the door as if nothing was going on. Micah walked past without looking at the teenager.

Bronwyn waited until they both walked past before speaking out loud. "I need a partner to do that with," she said matter-of-factly.

"Run!" Braden shouted and they both launched themselves down the stairs and outside. Once there, they stopped and looked at each other in shock. Bronwyn waved at them from the deck outside the galley. Braden waved back before holding his hands up.

"That's your department," he said as he started whistling and walking toward the well deck where Caleb was fishing. Micah looked up at Bronwyn, who smiled innocently back. Micah realized that she was less than seven turns older than the teenager. It was about that time.

*'What would the Queen think, having to share you with another, or Zeeka or any of the others? How about a 'cat?'* Micah said in her thought voice as she ambled

toward her father.

'I'll have to talk with her about it, but I have been giving it serious consideration,' the girl said, sounding much more mature than her physical age suggested.

'You do that, and we'll revisit the issue then. You know that we won't be happy with anyone who isn't of pure-heart and that means you'll need a 'cat by your side,' Micah replied.

*'I've been talking with Treetis and I think we're close to an arrangement. I hope you and Braden don't mind. The Prince and Fealona have both expressed their approval. In any case, Caleb is waiting for you and for what he wants, I better come down, too.'* Bronwyn waved as she returned to the galley on her way to join them at the well deck.

Micah stood dumbfounded. When she was close enough to Braden and Caleb, she couldn't contain herself. "Bronwyn, Treetis, and some young boy to be named in the future."

Braden had no answer, so he resorted to pushing his partner's buttons. "I know," was all he said.

"How in the crap did you know and didn't tell me?" She moved closer to him.

"I'm kidding. You should know me better than that. I had no idea, but it's not quite our choice, is it? We have the entirety of the Vii's intelligent species looking after her. I think she'll be okay. And with that scar on Treetis' side, everyone will know that he's not afraid to fight."

"Two different fights and the sun hasn't moved a finger-width in the sky. I thought we taught you better than that!" Caleb prodded his daughter.

"Oh, please! If it were you and Mother, there would have been three fights with hair-pulling and one fish thrown during that same time," Micah laughed. These weren't real fights. They were passionate people who had no wish to inflict harm. There was a physical element to their relationships that kept them on their toes and fully emotionally entangled with their partners. Woe be to the person who tried to come between them.

Braden wasn't up for more sparring. "You asked us down here for a reason."

"Oh, yeah. Can you make those two go someplace else? They're chasing the fish away," Caleb begged, pleading with his daughter.

"Maybe you should try fishing their way," Bronwyn suggested. Caleb furrowed his brow, not understanding. He was a master fisherman.

Bronwyn impatiently took his pole and pointed to the water in the well deck. "Jump in," she commanded. Caleb felt like he could swim like a fish and wasn't willing to be proven wrong. He took off his shirt and dove into the water. The two Dolphins swam circles around him, which he found slightly disconcerting because he could only think of them as sharks.

They lined up side by side. Caleb looked to the trio standing over him. "Grab on," Bronwyn said, stabbing a finger toward her two friends. Caleb turned, still treading water, and wrapped a big hand around each Dolphin's dorsal fin. Instantly, they shot toward the open ocean at a speed Caleb never dreamed possible. He squinted as he was battered against the waves, salt spray hitting his face like rocks blown in a strong wind.

They jumped from the water and turned, nose first, toward a trough. Caleb took a deep breath and the three of them plunged beneath the waves. They raced downward toward a school of tuna that were bigger than what he was used to. The Dolphins dodged one way, then another. Caleb lost his grip on one of the two, changing hands to get a better grip on his remaining ride.

Rhodi headed into the school, scattering the fish, while Chlora, with Caleb, hesitated for a heartbeat. The big fisherman was starting to run out of air and was thinking of kicking for the surface. Chlora dashed forward and grabbed a fish that had just turned toward her when Rhodi raced past with another in his mouth. Their tails worked to propel them upward. They broke the surface and continued until both Chlora and Caleb were completely out of the water.

The Dolphin splashed into the top of the wave, using the tuna in her mouth to keep her from going back under. Rhodi joined her and they swam back to the Warden, into the well deck, and deposited Caleb next to the deck where the others stood.

"Ha!" he yelled, splashing the water and pumping his fist. "That was some real fishing." With a smile splitting his face, he climbed from the water, where Chlora and Rhodi both gave him their fish, before heading back toward the school to get one of their own.

It took an intervention from Holly to be able to build a fire on the garden level, much to the Rabbits' dismay, but Caleb wanted everyone to share in what the sea offered without sending it through the fabricator first. They prepared the meal and then sat on the deck outside. It was early afternoon and the sky was perfect, the sea rolling gently.

Pik, Aadi, the Hawkoids, and the 'cats enjoyed their tuna steaks raw, while the rest ate what Caleb had personally cooked for them. There was plenty for all. The Rabbits continued to be disgusted by the concept of eating flesh, but they remained with the others because the company and conversation were both good. The scientists were nowhere to be found, although Braden had invited them, even asking Holly to cut the power to their laboratories until they made an appearance. Holly wouldn't do it.

*'I think it's time,'* Aadi told them all over the mindlink.

"Time for what?" Caleb asked.

*'To bury my eggs. I hope I can hold out until we arrive. It just wouldn't do to nest in the dirt of the garden level. There seems to be a distinct lack of sand anywhere on the ship.'*

"Pick up the pace, Holly. We have Tortoids coming!" Braden yelled.

# The Babies

They landed at the cove, where everyone raced off except Brandt. Rexalita wasn't with them as she stayed closer to the island, in much deeper water. Chlora and Rhodi were there, but they couldn't carry the Aurochs. The Warden pulled in as close as it could get and it still wasn't close enough.

The Queen, Denon, and Malo showed up as the ship was making its way toward shore. They'd found better grazing not far off and had made that their home while they waited for Brandt, the King of the Aurochs, and his companions to return.

While the others looked on helplessly, Brandt backed up to the other side of the ship. He pawed the deck and started running. He hit the edge and leapt, not clearing much ocean before he splashed down and sunk beneath the waves.

"Brandt!" Braden screamed and ran into the ocean, diving into the waves. Chlora and Rhodi came alongside the Aurochs as he pawed the sand and struggled to walk to the shore. When he pushed off, he floated a little off the bottom, before falling back for another push. When his hooves weren't touching the sand, the Dolphins positioned themselves under his sides. They swam hard and the King moved forward a great leap. One more and he was almost where he could get his head out of the water. A final surge and he was into the waves, walking forward. He gulped in a great breath of air and stopped, focusing on breathing.

Braden swam up beside him, rubbing Brandt's ear and stroking his head.

*'If you go to sea again, I won't be going with you. Don't take it personally,'* Brandt said in his booming thought voice. Braden was relieved and hung on as the King of the Aurochs strolled from the ocean, head held high, ecstatic to be on solid ground once again.

The companions' relief at having Brandt ashore was quickly forgotten as Aadi started moaning. They grabbed the first patch of sand that was well above the water line and received sunlight throughout most of the day. Micah started digging first with her hands, but the Queen bumped her out of the way and with two quick paws at the ground, a trench was dug, deep but not into the cool sand.

They helped Aadi over it and he descended until his legs touched, then he carefully laid one egg after another, ten of the them. Six looked fresh, but as he'd known, four of them had been killed by the Security Bot's attack. He used his face to push these to the side. When the others hatched, the shells and their unborn brothers would be buried together. Aadi kicked sand over the eggs and settled down to wait. He didn't have to stay, but Tortoids were unique. In order to maximize hatchings with such few eggs, they were almost ready to hatch the second they were laid.

The companions loaded what they had into the wagons, set up a campsite on the beach, and made themselves comfortable.

"G, is there any game nearby? Nothing like hunting to make the time go by." Braden hoped that G-War found something. He wanted to stretch his legs, see the land before him.

*'Yes,'* the 'cat said and raced into the brush. Braden's bow had been on the ship, but he hadn't taken it ashore. It would have been of no use against the Bots, but he was happy to string it and feel its power in his hands. He took two arrows with him, a hunter's challenge, and ran after G-War. Treetis passed him, while Fealona kept him company. Bounder and Strider soon overtook them, slapping the ground with their spears as they ran after the two orange 'cats.

"I'm not going to get a shot, am I?" Braden asked Fea as he slowed to a walk. Fea shrugged.

*'You can take a shot,'* she started slowly, *'if you don't mind shooting something that's already dead.'*

A Hillcat's scream filled the air. Braden thought that it was probably Treetis. Then a Wolfoid's growl, bark, and howl suggested that Bounder and Strider had found their own prey.

When Braden and Fea reached them, two deer, a doe and a buck, were close to each other, both victims of the hunt. Braden put his bow down, disappointed in not getting to participate, but he knew he couldn't outrun the others. Sometimes it was better to accept your place, as Braden was learning to do.

He pulled out his skinning knife and started cleaning the deer.

The Wolfoids helped him drag the two carcasses back to the beach. Braden intended to smoke any excess meat to carry on their journey back to New Sanctuary.

Micah had heard the kill and started a fire. It was burning nicely by the time Braden returned. He butchered the meat and started putting the strips over the fire when the first egg started to crack.

"Damn, Aadi! You couldn't wait until after lunch?" Braden joked, but it still earned him a punch in the arm. Four Aurochs, a Lizard Man, three Hawkoids, two Rabbits, two Wolfoids, three Hillcats, and four humans gathered to watch six Tortoid babies being born. Aadi was focused on the eggs. He didn't blink. They couldn't tell if he was breathing.

The first Tortoid cracked through the shell and crawled out. It was little bigger than Braden's hand, and its fat little legs could barely hold it up. It took two steps before it started hovering. It didn't move very far before it opened its beak-like mouth and made a cawing sound.

*'Quick, bring fresh meat!'* Aadi ordered.

*'I love them!'* Bronwyn said to no one's surprise.

*'Little Daksha, you are my first and I am proud of you,'* Aadi cooed to the baby Tortoid that cried with hunger. The others cracked through their shells in order. The companions each took turns feeding them raw venison from small sticks. Fea fed them from pieces skewered on a claw. The male 'cats couldn't be bothered with the children. Fea committed to teaching her two orange men yet another lesson when the time was right.

Even the Rabbits took a turn.

Braden couldn't tell them apart, but didn't want to let his friend know that. Micah smirked at him, suggesting that Aadi already knew.

And the Tortoid could not have been prouder. Six baby Tortoids, which he didn't consider bad for a new parent at two hundred cycles old. He was the most well-traveled Tortoid both on and off Vii, and he wanted that for his children, too.

This is the end of Free Trader 6 – Free Trader on the High Seas

# Cygnus Rising
## Humanity Returns to Space

Cygnus Space Opera – Book 1
A Tale from the Free Trader Universe
takes place over 100 years after Braden & Micah's adventures

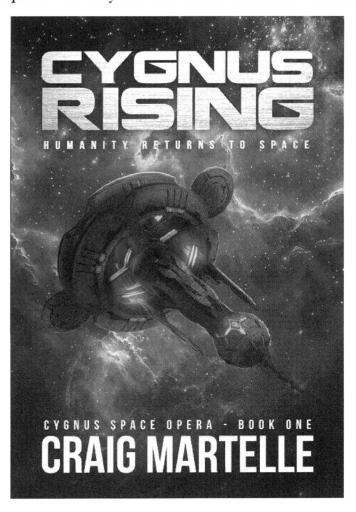

# Sample Chapter of Cygnus Rising

# Chapter 1 - Fire!

Flames shot through the open hatch. Cain yelled, "Engineering's on fire!" as the klaxons continued to scream, echoing down the corridor away from him. He sensed, more than heard the anguished cry.

The hatch was open. The automated fire suppression system had failed.

He ripped open the damage control panel and pulled the tank out. He threw it hastily over his shoulder, reached behind him with a well-practiced maneuver to start the flow of air, and wrapped the dangling mask across his face. He draped the fire hood over his head as he ran. He didn't have time to put on the whole outfit. People he knew were dying.

He hit the flames of the doorway at a dead run. The intense heat scorched his bare forearms as he passed. He yelled into his mask as he slid to a stop in the middle of the space, looking for survivors. A Rabbit lay under a terminal, an ugly scorch mark cut across his white fur, leaving blackened hair around burned pink flesh underneath. The Rabbit moved – Briz was alive.

Cain slid him from under the melting terminal. The Rabbit was dense and blocky, half Cain's height, but the same weight. Cain pulled an equipment cover off the back of a chair. He took it and wrapped it around the Rabbit's head and over as much of his body as he could, then hefted him, trying not to touch the injury. Cain lumbered toward the hatch, ducked his head, held his breath, and jumped through the flames. He deposited the Rabbit in the passageway and raced back into Engineering. Ellie was in there somewhere.

He should have been alarmed that the flames didn't seem to hurt as much this time. The next victim was a Wolfoid, horribly torn apart from the force of an exploded containment vessel. He saw something odd about the way the Wolfoid's body, bigger than a human's was laying on the floor.

A pink-fleshed hand snaked out from underneath the heavy gray fur. Without remorse, Cain heaved the Wolfoid's shattered body to the side. Ellie was dazed, but seemed to be okay. The Wolfoid must have taken the full force of the rupture, protecting her. Cain's breath caught as he looked at her silken black hair, the ends curled and brittle from the heat that had passed over her.

He pulled her to him as blue lights started to flash within Engineering, signaling the imminent flooding of argon gas into the compartment. He kneeled, rolling her from a sitting position over his shoulder. He stood without much effort. She wasn't heavy and laid easily over his shoulder as he hurried for the hatch. The flames had died down somewhat, but he still ran through, hoping speed would keep them safe. Once through, he stopped, took off his hood and breathed deeply of the better air in the corridor. The hatch to engineering closed.

The klaxons stopped as someone helped Ellie from his shoulder. He looked at the closed hatch. Anyone still in the space would be denied oxygen, just like the fire. The argon gas was supposed to be flushed in a matter of seconds, but it would be too late. He was surprised that he didn't know how many people worked in the space. Three? Four?

"Holy Rising Star, Cain! You shouldn't have gone in there. Why the hell would you do something like that?" the Captain's words were harsh, but his eyes were grateful. As the older man looked at the two survivors in the corridor, he added, "but I'm glad you did, son. Looks like you saved two lives, irreplaceable lives."

The two Hillcats waiting for Cain and Ellie in the corridor couldn't have agreed more. Carnesto yowled in pain as Ellie came back to her senses. The burns on her lower body attacked her with waves of agony. He put a furry paw on her head to help her through the worst of it.

Why had Cain risked knowing what his death would do to his 'cat, to his family? He had no choice. It's who he'd always wanted to be. It's who he was. He'd spent his short life trying to live up to one man, the Space Exploration Service Captain who showed him how a hero acts.

## Free Trader 7 – Southern Discontent

The Free Trader goes from village to village to make the announcement that Old Tech is alive and well and functioning in a place called New Sanctuary located south of the rainforest.

With an open ocean exploration laboratory that Holly found and recovered, they head to sea where they find more than an island, they find a gateway to the former residents of White Beach who'd been seduced by the intelligence from the Western Ocean Research Facility…

*Free Trader Book Seven – coming in 2017, exclusively on Amazon.*

# Postscript

If you like the Free Trader and would like to see the series continue, please join my mailing list by dropping by my website www.craigmartelle.com or if you have any comments, shoot me a note at craig@craigmartelle.com. I am always happy to hear from people who've read my work. I try to answer every email I receive.

If you liked the story, please write a short review for me on Amazon. I greatly appreciate any kind words, even one or two sentences go a long way. The number of reviews an ebook receives greatly improves how well an ebook does on Amazon.

Amazon – www.amazon.com/author/craigmartelle
Facebook – www.facebook.com/authorcraigmartelle
My web page – www.craigmartelle.com
Twitter – www.twitter.com/rick_banik

Thank you for reading Free Trader on the High Seas!

Braden and Micah's adventures will continue through 2017.

In the continuing saga of the Free Trader universe, the Cygnus Space Opera series finds Braden and Micah's descendants returning to space on the ships designed by the survivors from Cygnus VI. Not only does their new engine work, it works beyond any of their wildest expectations. The Free Trader series evolves into galactic proportions as humanity looks for settlers from Earth in other parts of the galaxy and beyond.

## About the Author

Craig is a successful author, publishing in both the Science Fiction and Thriller genres. He's taken his more than twenty years of experience in the Marine Corps, his legal education, and his business consulting career to write believable characters living in realistic worlds.

Although Craig has written in multiple genres, what he believes most compelling are in-depth characters dealing with real-world issues. The backdrop is less important than the depth of the characters, who they are and how they interact. Life lessons of a great story can be applied now or fifty years in the future. Some things are universal.

Craig believes that evil exists. Some people are driven differently and cannot be allowed access to our world. Good people will rise to the occasion. Good will always challenge evil, sometimes before a crisis, many times after, but will good triumph?

Some writers who've influenced Craig? Robert E. Howard (the original Conan), JRR Tolkien, Andre Norton, Robert Heinlein, Lin Carter, Brian Aldiss, Margaret Weis, Tracy Hickman, Anne McCaffrey, and of late, James Axler, Raymond Weil, Jonathan Brazee, Mark E. Cooper, and David Weber. Craig learned something from each of these authors, story line, compelling issue, characters that you can relate to, the beauty of the prose, unique tendrils weaving through the book's theme. Craig's writing has been compared to that of Andre Norton and Craig's Free Trader characters to those of McCaffrey's Dragonriders, the Rick Banik Thrillers to the works of Robert Ludlum.

Craig finds the comparisons humbling. All he wants is for his readers to relate to the characters, put themselves into those situations described in Craig's books and ask themselves, what would they do if they were there instead?

Through a bizarre series of events, Craig ended up in Fairbanks, Alaska. He never expected to retire to a place where golf courses are only open for four months out of the year. But he loves it there. It is off the beaten path. He and his wife watch the northern lights from their driveway. Their dog has lots of room to run. And temperatures reach forty below zero. They have from three and a half hours of daylight in the winter to twenty-four hours in the summer.

It's all part of the give and take of life. If they didn't have those extremes, then everyone would live there.

73259781R00145

Made in the USA
Columbia, SC
03 September 2019